Roux
Morgue

Books by Claire M. Johnson

Beat Until Stiff
Roux Morgue

Roux Morgue

Claire M. Johnson

Poisoned Pen Press

First Trade Paperback Edition 2011

10 9 8 7 6 5 4 3 2 1

Library of Congress Catalog Card Number: 2007935733

ISBN: 978-1-59058-910-6   Trade Paperback

Poisoned Pen Press
6962 E. First Ave., Ste. 103
Scottsdale, AZ 85251
www.poisonedpenpress.com
info@poisonedpenpress.com

Printed in the United States of America

To my husband, Mark

Acknowledgments

First of all, I would to thank my publisher, Poisoned Pen Press, and my agent, Linda Allen, for not forgetting about me when I temporarily dropped off the face of the earth. My critique group, once again, played a pivotal role in helping me write this book: Ann, Carole, Colleen, Gordon, Janet, Margaret, Mike, and Rena. When I say I couldn't have done it without you, I REALLY couldn't have done it without you. I'd also like to thank my pals on LiveJournal for their pats on the back: Avi, Cordelia, Dana, Emma, Jan, Kara, Lin, Lizzie, Lyric, Sandra, Rispa, Ver, and Zelda. Dr. Leslie Russell helped me during a particularly bad patch when I just couldn't write; I thank her for that. I would also like to thank my family, especially my husband, Mark, and my children, Emma and Paul, for their unqualified support. I would also like to thank my dear friend Tanya Wodinsky for letting me steal her husband's last name one more time, and my dear friend Micheal O'Connor for letting me steal his last name one last time. Drs. K. O'Neal and G. Chiaravino deserve a loud round of my applause. I might be missing a few organs, but who needed them anyway. And finally I would like to thank Mary Ryan. A character who will not leave me alone.

Preface

This story is about fathers and children. My father died in the middle of writing this book. I suppose on a subconscious level I knew he wouldn't be around to see this book published, and as there is always a heavy voodoo factor when writing, it wasn't until I was nearly done with it that I realized it was about fathers. I'd like to say that whatever you bring away from this book regarding fathers and daughters or fathers and sons, there really is a restaurant out on Hegenberger Road in Oakland, California, where decorative stone donkeys are chained in the iceplant. For many years, they've been painted the colors of the Italian flag. But when I was a child they weren't painted, and on a rainy winter's day, to a man with rather bad eyesight, they looked like real donkeys.

Chapter One

If he didn't shut up and stop attacking that plate, I was going to hurl myself across the table, grab his fork, and stab him with it.

I coughed to sneak a glance at my watch. I'd been smiling non-stop for exactly one hour and forty-three minutes. The longer I maintained this false bonhomie, the crankier I got. By this point, it didn't feel like a smile so much as a bad case of lockjaw. Benson kept scraping his fork across his plate in a precise effort to capture every milligram of his dessert. He'd been prattling non-stop for the last fifteen minutes, only pausing to make determined grooves on a plate that couldn't have been cleaner than if it had been through an autoclave. With every pass, my ballistic meter rose a few notches. We were now at level "irritable" and heading into "dangerous." He'd been dangling this job in front of me for nearly two hours, keeping the taste of financial solvency just out of reach.

"We now have a total of ten schools," scrape, "in six states," chafe, "each one with four hundred students, and," grind, "plans to open in five more states by the end of next year."

December 12th. I'd been without a job since mid-October. Bob Benson and I were negotiating my hire for after the New Year. If I was lucky, on January 4th I'd begin teaching students how to bake. In fancy terms: pastry. That's what I do, I'm a pastry chef. And when Bob isn't beating up china, he's dean of École d'Epicure in San Francisco, one of the first and best professional cooking schools in the country.

If I was unlucky, I'd be making Christmas presents for my family out of those plastic baskets that strawberries come in.

The dining room had been done for the holidays. Elaborate swags of candy pink and white-striped satin festooned the walls, culminating in big, cheery bows every fifteen feet. In my ten-year old black linen suit and a cashmere sweater sporting a gigantic moth hole in the cuff—which I discovered halfway through lunch—I felt like a ninety-nine-cent present wrapped in an elaborately beribboned box.

We were the only diners left.

With another scrape of Benson's fork, my smile slipped. The cranky meter shot passed "dangerous" and was hovering frighteningly close to "fury." Even though I possess the business savvy of a kumquat, no hint of impatience or garden-variety ennui could cross my face. I'd be fired before I'd been hired.

Memo to self: mortgage payment, Mary Ryan, mortgage payment.

Grabbing my coffee cup, I swilled down the entire contents, ignoring the little rivulets of pain as the scalding coffee scorched my throat. By the time the cup was back in its saucer, the smile was back in place. I needed this job, and if it required parking my self-respect at the door, I'd do it.

"Well, Mary, I've explained my concerns. Your qualifications are, of course, impeccable. It's the other…" Benson's voice trailed off. To really turn the screws, he pulled a fountain pen the size of a Cuban cigar out of his jacket pocket, gestured to the unsigned contract lying on the tabletop, and placed the pen maddeningly beyond my reach. "I must admit the other teachers would be thrilled to have you on the faculty. You really were an exceptional student, and your subsequent career…With Christmas only two weeks away, we must make sure the position is filled by the New Year. Whether you are the right candidate…." There were those annoying trail offs again. "What do you think of our current batch of students? Pretty impressive handiwork, eh?" Benson gestured a plump, well-manicured hand toward the showpieces in the corners of the dining room.

I turned up the wattage on my smile even more. A muscle on the left side of my face I never knew existed started a minute spastic tic in protest.

Not one but three gingerbread houses, big enough to stable miniature ponies, were grouped in one corner of the room. Picture if you will a student piping out twenty feet of melted chocolate for the "fencing," although she only needed five, because most of it would break from the heat of her hands. My back ached in sympathy.

"Very impressive," I chirped enthusiastically. Having constructed more than my fair share of confectionary extravaganzas, I'd come to the sad conclusion that these are a form of culinary masturbation. Most of them aren't even edible.

"Although it's been a number of years since you were a student, I'm sure you'd have no problem getting in the swing of things. When I heard, I mean when you…" Benson's voice trailed off yet again, clearly at a loss on how to finish his sentence. Funny, how visions of me stepping on a dead body stuffed into a laundry bag, or discovering a body shot in the head at point blank range, effectively kill most conversations.

In brighter financial times, I'd have relished his discomfort. But right now Mary's financial larder was looking mighty thin. If I didn't get this job, I'd be forced to break an IRA to pay next month's bills. I continued to smile, not giving in to my overwhelming desire to rip a swath of that fabric on the wall, strangle Benson so that he would finally shut up, and then stalk to the nearest bar for a very cold martini. No Vermouth. Six olives.

Memo to self: keep smiling, no matter how much it hurts, keep smiling.

Only last September I'd been at the peak of my professional career. In addition to being the pastry chef at San Francisco's top restaurant, American Fare, I'd been on the cover of all of the national food mags. If my career had gotten any hotter I'd have had to start wearing asbestos underwear.

Yes, it sounds insufferable; yes, it sounds incredibly arrogant. Guilty.

It's amazing how the sweet aroma of smug can turn to the sharp tang of desperation.

A mere three months ago, I was one of the top pastry chefs in the country. Two months ago I'd stepped on the dead body of one of my employees at the restaurant where I worked and found the owner/chef of the restaurant shot dead in my bed. In my house. Overnight I became virtually unemployable. Not that I'd known that just yet. After all, for six years running, American Fare had been voted one of the top ten restaurants in the United States by all the top food organizations, and, I say without false modesty, the desserts always got more than their fair share of notice.

The restaurant closed for a facelift and, with a naïveté that in hindsight seems unbelievably dumb, I'd assumed job offers would be pouring in once word got out I was willing and able. Funny how a couple of dead bodies can kill your career. Who knew food people were so superstitious? And stupid. Like being involved in a murder meant they were the next in line for a ten-inch chef's knife in the gut. I mean, it wasn't as if I'd killed them!

Be that as it may, my job prospects evaporated like beads of water on a hot griddle. People who'd been begging me to work for them for years wouldn't return my calls. Even old classmates refused to consider hiring me. I'd become the Typhoid Mary of pastry chefs. The day after Thanksgiving, I sat at my dining room table, the bill for my property taxes in one hand and my mortgage notice in the other, a mere three minutes from a full-blown anxiety-induced stroke, when Antonella de Luca, an old teacher of mine, phoned to tell me that there was a teaching position open at École d'Epicure. Was I interested?

I called Benson immediately, and by his manner on the phone, I'd assumed it was a slam dunk. The snarky side of my personality rose to the fore, and *in absentia* I thumbed my nose at all those people who wouldn't hire me; I'd be returning in glory to my alma mater, numerous awards and accolades under inbelt. He'd mailed me the standard boilerplate about the school, we played telephone tag for weeks, and still the warning bells didn't go off until I'd actually sat down for this lunch, still flush and sassy, thinking that this job was mine. In. The. Bag.

Five minutes into lunch I knew it wasn't in the bag. It was beginning to look like Down. The. Toilet. Every sentence he uttered began with qualifiers: "If I was sure you were the person for the job…" "Your qualifications are exceptional, but…" and the one that caused me to mentally review every bank statement I'd received in the last three months, "There's a little problem with hiring you…."

Hence, the smiling and groveling. Play to the man's weaknesses I told myself. The school. His Achilles heel.

"Reading over the material you mailed me, the curriculum seems to have really changed. So much more academic," I clucked in approval. The fact that the students were actually cooking for what looked like a mere twenty hours total out of a sixteen-month course was not something I should be concerned with.

"Oh yes, we've really revamped things since your time. How many years has it been?" Benson peered at me from across the dining table, his eyes scrunched inward in that tortured way of people who need glasses but refuse to wear them.

"Thirteen," I said, trying not to sound wistful. My thirty-fifth birthday was next week. My physical self was pretty much intact: tall, skinny, with green eyes and reddish hair cut just this short of a crew cut. The green eyes were courtesy of my Irish grandmother and the rangy frame my father. The red was now courtesy of what bottle of Clairol magic my Safeway had in stock. Lately, I'd been using Radiant Ruby.

Thirteen years had turned Benson from a painfully skinny, thirty-year old man with a striking resemblance to a young Frank Sinatra into a solid, older man who moved with the ease of someone who liked the guy he saw in the mirror every morning. The extra pounds had softened his strong Italian features: a Roman nose with a pronounced hook, deep set brown eyes nestling under smooth heavy black brows, and a too full, too red upper lip. He now resembled a prosperous Mafia don, much as

Old Blue Eyes did in his later years. Whatever he paid his Hong Kong tailor, it was worth it.

"Well, it certainly doesn't seem that long, Mary." The tone of his voice suggested that Neanderthals were still eating raw meat, the advent of cooking fires still two million years away.

I hated being the last resort. I hated being humble. But most of all, I hated not knowing where my next dime was going to come from.

"I'll take ten thousand dollars less a year than your initial offer," I said flatly. And, since I'd already parked my pride at the door, I groveled. "It's a great school. You should be proud."

Benson eyed me, eyed the pen, eyed me. Thinking I hadn't gone far enough, I was considering yet another two thousand less when I heard the scratch of the fountain pen across the paper as he amended the amount of annual salary, initialed the change, signed it on the bottom, and then pushed the pen and contract to my side of the table for signature. Somehow I managed not to sigh audibly in relief.

With fingers sticky from nerves, I uncapped the pen, initialed the change, and signed the contract. It was probably way too tacky to ask when I'd receive my first paycheck.

Benson gathered up his pen and the contract, and tucked them away in his jacket pocket. Then he smiled; a tight, satisfied smile. I realized he'd gotten what he'd wanted all along—a top-notch chef for a lot less money than she was worth. He stood up and pushed away from the table to signal lunch was over.

"We'll see you on January 4th. Go to the office and see my secretary. She'll have you fill out the necessary forms. And give Allison Warner a call. The two of you can catch up while coordinating the curriculum. She's in charge of the evening group. She's an old friend of yours, yes?"

I nodded.

Benson moved to pull away and then remembered his manners. "Merry Christmas." He held out his hand for one final handshake. Wiping my sweaty hands on the back of my skirt,

I shook his hand and smiled what I hoped was my final smile until after the New Year.

"Merry Christmas to you, too." I tried to churn out yet another chirpy, happy reply, but it sounded more like a growl, a tribute to the strain of the past two hours and the fact that Benson had played me like a violin. I'd underestimated him; I wouldn't make that mistake again.

Fortunately for me, Benson either didn't care or didn't hear the sullen note in my voice because I heard his, "And Happy New Year" behind me as I rose and crossed the dining room. I trilled the fingers of one hand in acknowledgment, not trusting myself to say another word. I was all niced out.

Financial stability and personal livelihood taken care of, it was time to deal with the real question of the day. Should I hoof it downtown for those martinis or, to hell with it, hit the bar across the street. Vodka or gin? Absolut? Stoli? Bombay? A little Christmas cheer? Ho. Ho. Ho. I was nearly at the entrance to the dining room when Benson's voice stopped me.

"Oh, Mary. There's one thing I've forgotten. The morning pastry chef is in charge of the desserts for the buffet. I'm sure that won't be a problem, will it? You know what a tradition the buffet is here at École," he chuckled and clapped me on the back.

Problem? Oh, yeah, a big problem.

I loathe buffets.

But I smiled.

Chapter Two

My first day was a nightmare.

At 6:30 a.m., on a rainy Monday morning in early January, I entered the dining room of École. Despite the new location, I noticed that some of the old traditions hadn't changed; the chefs still drank coffee together in the dining room before classes began.

When I'd been a student, the school had occupied the top floor of a tired 1940s office building in the Mission. Despite the school's grandiose claims to "European dining this side of the Atlantic," the dining room had sported the sort of plastic chairs favored by industrial cafeterias, cheap fluorescent light fixtures, and carpet just one step above astro-turf. Restaurant patrons routinely stepped over the sprawled legs of passed-out drunks lined up on Folsom Street, and the local bars opened at 6:00 a.m. to standing-room only alcoholics.

Shortly after I'd graduated, Benson's colossal ineptitude with money—think about it, students paid for the privilege of working for free and he still nearly went bankrupt—necessitated a corporate bailout. Overnight, École transformed from a funky hole in the wall school where you actually learned how to cook to, well, a business. Enrollment shot up from one hundred students to four hundred, churning out a hundred graduates every four months. Advertisements began appearing in every major magazine in the country, pictures of the requisite young man and woman, paper chef's hats perched on their heads at a jaunty angle, positively beaming at the thought that they were going to cook *your* meal.

I'd often thought there should be a disclaimer in miniscule fine print on the bottom of these ads, like the three-point type on packs of cigarettes warning you about cancer: "Graduates will work like dogs for not much money." The corporation doubled tuition, opened up branches in other cities, and still had a waiting list. The aroma of greenbacks induced other corporations to open their own schools. Parents with no hope in hell of getting their unruly, barely one-step above juvenile delinquent into college jumped at the idea that their kids would be earning $80,000 per year after a sixteen-month course. Anyone with half a brain would question the math on this, but the era of the celebrity chef, like Wolfgang Puck, Emeril, or Jamie Oliver, seduced parents into thinking that the $40,000 dollars in tuition was a bargain.

A part of me wondered where all these graduates were getting work, with young chefs flooding the market every four months, but that wasn't my problem.

I was going to teach my first real love: pastry—perhaps a slight clue as to why my marriage didn't work out.

Teaching pastry had always been the part of cooking that floated my meringue. Trying to impart to my employees my love of creaming butter and sugar to just the right consistency, knowing when to add the eggs so the batter won't curdle, tempering chocolate back and forth on a marble slab and the enormous satisfaction gained when the chocolate hits the right temperature and assumes that sensual gloss, so rich in contrast to the matte of the marble, just begging to glaze a cake or blanket a truffle.

And now I'd have a whole room full of people to ooh and ahh with. I hadn't been this excited in years.

I spent most of the month of December poring over cookbooks, generating handout after handout about the history of pastry, the chemistry of baking, and the cultural traditions behind the art of patisserie. Benson had smelled my desperation and capitalized on it, the turd. Considering how clueless he was with money, it must have been nothing more than a power play.

Cutting the puffed-up pastry chef who's too big for her checked pants down to size. But so what? I wanted this job. I wanted to teach. I'd worked with assholes before. He wouldn't be the first or the last.

Loaded down with handouts and flush with anticipation, I eagerly wove my way through tables and chairs to where the chefs were congregated. When I reached them, I stopped short.

It was the culinary version of the Sharks versus the Jets. The older, Escoffier-trained chefs occupied one table, stiff and starched in traditional white jackets and drab, checkered pants, white kerchiefs tied smartly around their necks. White paper chef hats stood at attention next to their coffee cups. At the other table, the new, cool, younger generation of chefs lounged. Their outfits ranged from chef's jackets lined with wild fabric and matching balloon pants to checked overalls. The hats were equally eclectic ranging from floppy colorful toques to baseball caps.

One seat beckoned at each table. All eyes were on me. The atmosphere was so thick you could hack through it with a meat cleaver. Obviously, I was expected to choose between my original mentors and my contemporaries.

I raised my eyebrows at my former teacher Antonello de Luca, who was sitting with the older guard, as if to say, "What in the hell's going on here?" He shrugged imperceptibly in the Italian manner that conveys both humor and resignation.

"Sit here, Mary," said Étienne Broussard, one of the original teachers with the school, and pulled out the chair next to him.

"Yo, Mary," hailed Tessa Dunn, an old acquaintance. She jerked her head toward the seat next to her. "This seat's more comfortable."

I had no intention of choosing sides. Dumping my paperwork on an unoccupied table, I bounced back and forth between each table, shaking hands, hugging old friends, and introducing myself to people I didn't know.

I refused to sit down, stalling for time until 7:00 a.m. when classes began. I'd forestalled the inevitable.

Before Antonello made his escape, I pulled him aside.

"Why didn't you tell me it was like *West Side Story* here?" I hissed.

He threw up his hands in Italian-speak. "What is this *West Side Story*?"

"For God's sake, you've lived in this country for twenty years and you've never seen *West Side Story*? The two camps: the old guard at one table, the new guard at the other, both obviously hating each other's guts."

He laughed. "It started last semester. I didn't tell you because I was hoping all this," his hands rotated in large circles, "would have blown over during the Christmas holidays. Good luck on your first day." He cupped my chin, gave it an affectionate shake. "I need to go, Cara." The dining room was empty, everyone now in their respective classrooms.

I watched him walk off to the *garde manger* kitchen, the white toque artfully concealing the shiny bald spot at the back of his head, the old-fashioned chef's jacket hanging smartly on his broad shoulders. I sighed. Still sexy, still smart, he's one of the few men I've met in my life who really likes women.

Time is so unfair to women. The thirteen years since I'd been a student had not whittled away one ounce of his physical appeal. I, on the other hand, had recently started dyeing my hair and routinely spent a small fortune on face creams with ludicrous anti-aging claims. Even though I was still in the financial shits, I'd gone to Saks yesterday and plunked down $150.00 for a matchbox-size container of *La Mer*. And let's not even mention my recent devotion to support hose. Professional kitchen floors are murder on your legs.

Back to the task at hand. I squared my shoulders and headed off to the pastry kitchen. I wasn't going to let some culinary turf war ruin my first day.

My students were assembled by the time I made it to the pastry classroom. I hate being late and tripped slightly in my haste to get into the room. Not an auspicious beginning. I greeted everyone with a smile, expecting to see twelve eager, happy students excited by their first day at school.

Nine sullen faces, slack with exhaustion, stared at me. The tenth guy stood out like a strawberry in a flat of green beans. He was much older, I'd guess in his early forties, and in contrast to all the other students, who could have auditioned for extras in some zombie flick, this guy's vibes were shrieking "ON!" Traditional chef's jackets have little or no tailoring. Basically they are boxes with arms. He filled his out, both the arms and the chest, suggesting that a lot of his spare time was spent pumping iron. Time would tell if he had any kitchen smarts, but given all that muscle, I couldn't help but think him more suited to forging horseshoes, not decorating petit fours.

The rest of the students were in their late teens or very early twenties, with that total lack of posture endemic to youth. Their spanking new chef's jackets hung on them like shrouds, industrial strength creases down the middle of each flap, a sure sign that they'd been taken out of the package that morning. My smile began to slip. I tried again. Bigger smile this time. No one smiled back.

"Did the storeroom run out of coffee this morning?" I joked, trying to get some sort of response.

Nothing. I've seen more animated cantaloupes.

I tried again.

"My name is Mary Ryan. I'm a graduate of École d'Epicure. I've cooked at a number of restaurants in San Francisco. At my last job I was the pastry chef at the restaurant American Fare."

That perked them up in a hurry. When in doubt, pull out the I-was-involved-in-a-notorious-murder-investigation gambit. Eyes bulged and necks craned forward, even though we were only a table's width from each other. I'd have done the same in their shoes.

"If you guys show a tad more enthusiasm for being here, like you actually decide to breathe, I'll give you the gory details of the murders at the end of the day. This is a freshman class, right?" Now that everyone was awake, a few had the courtesy to nod their heads. "How about introductions? If you were alive last October, no doubt you know all about me"—that got a few giggles—"so let's start with you. Tell everyone your name, why you're here, if you have a special interest, *garde manger*, pastry, whatever." I pointed to the blacksmith-type. "You get to be first because you're the only student whose vital signs appear to be working. You interested in pastry or just here because your schedule dumped you here?"

While the class went through their introductions, I kept an ear open for the last two students. As everyone went through their spiels and still no one else appeared, I began to get irritated. I had a lot of material to present this morning, and I didn't want to repeat myself.

The whoosh of the door signaled at least one arrival. I turned, narrowing my eyes in what I hoped was a teacher-is-not-amused glower. A waif of a girl glided into the room, so slender I wanted to relieve her of her knife-roll before she tore a rotator cuff. Hair no longer than three-quarters of an inch, cut to a peak in a sweet little vee at the center of her forehead, her dark brown eyes swallowed the rest of her delicate features. One of those elfin, petite women that brings out the maternal instinct in women and the protect-the-wimmin-folk impulse in men.

"Oh, I'm so sorry, Chef," a breathless and apologetic voice begged forgiveness. "Cab driver didn't speak English, French, or Italian. He took me to some college out near the beach. And then he was so sweet. He wouldn't let me pay."

Apparently this charm worked on cab drivers as well.

"You must ask for the trilingual cab driver next time," I commented dryly. "All the others here have introduced themselves. Your turn."

She turned to everyone and, with an easy, sweet charm reminiscent of Audrey Hepburn with a tongue ring, introduced herself as Coolie. She'd just graduated from Brown, was twenty-one years old, Daddy wanted her to go to law school, but she wanted a profession that was creative, trend-setting, and wasn't devoted to the almighty dollar. Didn't everyone feel that way? The other students nodded eagerly, her innate helplessness demanding agreement.

Freedom from the mighty dollar? I didn't think it'd be a problem accommodating everyone on that score. The average wage upon graduation probably is around twelve dollars an hour. I didn't have the heart to tell her that the Dean would order her creative and trend-setting tongue ring gone by the end of the day.

"Thank you, Coolie, and tomorrow you will be on time." Time to get moving, the remaining student would just have to get notes from everyone else. "Okay, people, listen up. We have a lot to cover this morning, and I hate repeating myself. I want to say right off the bat: ask questions. No question is too stupid. I'd rather you clarify something with me than throw out thirty dollars worth of butter because you weren't sure how to use the scale and added three pounds of baking soda instead of three ounces. First, I'll give a quick tour of the kitchen...."

From behind me I heard the final student enter the room. Finally, I said to myself in exasperation. I turned to greet him/her. My vocal chords shriveled to the size of a raisin. This will teach me to read the student roster before I begin teaching.

O'Connor nonchalantly eased by me to take his place among his fellow students.

For a delicious millisecond, shivers went down both my legs. A hot, hot blush blanketed my face and chest and then vanished, leaving me as lifeless as if a vampire had been feasting on me for breakfast. The only thing alive in my entire body, the spot between my shoulder blades that throbs only in times of extreme exhaustion or stress, began pounding so hard it was difficult to breathe.

"Mr. O'Connor, introduce yourself to the others," I squeaked out in between shallow breaths. "I think I need some coffee myself. Here." The blacksmith stepped forward; his name, he said, was Brad. "Why don't you hand these out. I'll be right back."

I managed a weak smile before I exited the room, the voices of the students buzzing behind me as I ran down the hall to the bathroom. Locking myself in a stall, my sweaty hands fumbling with the catch, I perched on the toilet as mortifying visions of me and O'Connor behaving like sex-crazed teenagers in the front seat of his car last October filled my head. We'd been oblivious to everything: his wife, his kids, my ex-husband (who happens to be his best friend), not to mention the police cruiser parked not twenty feet away. Only the shrill ring of a cell phone had stopped us from committing several felonies in broad daylight.

After five minutes of squirming on the seat of the john, I realized if I didn't get back to that classroom and face him it wouldn't just be my peace of mind that was shattered; I'd be fired on my first day with equal trauma to my bank account. The job for which I'd swallowed pretty much every ounce of self-respect I possessed.

Splashing cold water on my face for a full minute until the pounding between my shoulders subsided into a dull ache, I checked myself in the mirror. Naturally pale, the shock of seeing O'Connor had drained every ounce of color from my face. My eyes, spooked and tired, looked like two slices of kiwis marooned on the top of a cheesecake. In my bathroom mirror at home, my hair, recently dyed to stop people from calling me "Ma'am," looked fun. In this light it looked garish and pathetic, a too-obvious attempt to fool the march of time.

The repeated chill of water on my face brought me back to reality. We were both sensible people, we'd work this out.

I straightened up to my full five feet, eight inches and pinched my cheeks to restore some color. At some point during the day, I'd nail that sorry Irish hide of his to the wall and demand what in the hell was going on.

Filling a cup of coffee for show, I made my way back to the classroom to begin. My impending mental breakdown aside, the freshman pastry class is responsible for providing the *mise en place* for the more experienced students.

There's an immediacy about cooking that is impossible to convey to people not in the profession. If you make a mistake in a recipe, you can't shove thirty ruined Sacher tortes in a drawer and deal with it the next morning like unfinished paperwork. You remix and re-bake those thirty cakes right then and there because you have a luncheon for two hundred and forty Rotarians who have paid for and expect Sacher tortes for dessert. Which meant that while the pit of my stomach never let me forget O'Connor was somewhere in the room, I didn't have time for a wing ding, a nervous collapse, or a quick trip across the street for a double whatever.

At 10:30 a.m., we broke for lunch and I had my chance. As everyone filed out into the dining room, I grabbed the sleeve of O'Connor's chef's jacket and roughly pulled him into the alcove where the ovens were located, giving us a modicum of privacy.

"What in the hell are you doing here, O'Connor?" I demanded.

Chapter Three

Ignoring my question, O'Connor stared at the top of my head.

"What'd you do to your hair? It's horrible; like someone painted your head with redwood stain."

All my intentions of being a paragon of poise evaporated.

"My hair is not the issue here, O'Connor," I bristled. "What are you doing here? I thought we had an understanding of sorts."

He picked up an oven mitt, turned it over a couple of times, and threw it back on top of the oven.

"I don't know what you're talking about, Mary." O'Connor's voice was just short of belligerent. All the camaraderie and respect that we'd developed toward each other during the course of solving last fall's murders disappeared in the three seconds it took to utter that sentence.

"I told you I was going to be teaching here. Ever hear of the telephone?" Tears of frustration smarted my eyes. "Couldn't you have given me a head's up, instead of sneaking up on me and just appearing like the Ghost of Christmas Future? I'm asking you again, what are you doing here?"

"I'm a student, just like everyone else." He picked a blob of dried chocolate off my sleeve. The broad shoulders of his chef's jacket burned bright white against his black Irish complexion, his unruly graying black hair peeked out in wild tufts from underneath his paper chef's hat.

"You are NOT a student here." I shouted. "You're a homicide inspector with the San Francisco Police Department." The throbbing between my shoulder blades ratcheted up several notches to an intense drum beat.

"On leave for sixteen months," he countered. "I'm in your pastry class for the next four weeks. We'll work around this…history between us." He waved his hand in dismissal, as if he were shooing a pesky fly away from his food.

"History?" I choked out in disbelief.

Was it the heat from the ovens or this conversation that was pushing my blood pressure up to near fatal heights?

"I'm here to get my life back on track, to start a new career. I don't need you here, I don't want you here," I whispered as loud as I could.

"Ryan. I'm here. Get a grip." He picked at the shoulder of my jacket again.

"Stop touching me," I hissed.

Next, three things happened. The oven timer went off, Antonello de Luca came into the room, and bone-deep mortification curled around every joint and muscle in my body. I stood there paralyzed as the oven timer droned on in an incessant whine.

All the agonizing and guilt I'd been carrying on my shoulders for the last three months had been my burden alone. A silly moment of madness for him, reduced to a grope on the front seat of his car, and he'd gone home to his wife. Based on his all-too-obvious ease, our conduct was worthy of one confession and a Hail Mary.

While me. Me.

Get. A. Grip.

Easier said than done.

A cornerstone of my rage against my ex-husband had been my conviction that no matter how bad it got, how angry or frustrated or just plain irritated I got with him, that I'd never cheat on him, that I'd never mock our private and public oath to fidelity. I'd worn that smug assurance like a hair shirt all through our separation and subsequent divorce. In the worst of my pain,

I hugged that surety to myself, smothered my own guilt about working too many hours, always putting my career first, refusing to acknowledge relationships and marriages take time and that any vows that one makes are worthless if the one uttering them is working seventy hours a week. And liking it. It took me a long time to accept that betrayal came in many forms. Mine didn't sport a nice ass. It manifested itself in a paycheck and a bonus at Christmas because I'd made *Gourmet* magazine's top ten restaurants for desserts three years in a row.

The truth of it was that as much as Jim betrayed me with another woman, I betrayed him with my career. My ambition was more important than my marriage. I'd made a choice. I am not saying that it was the wrong choice, but I definitely made a choice. I'd begrudgingly acknowledged this to myself in the darkest hours of the night when I lay there unable to sleep, when the rational part of me demanded that it takes two to destroy a marriage. But even in those dark hours I'd tell myself, well, I might have worked too much, but at least I didn't fuck anyone else. That I also wasn't fucking him somehow seemed immaterial. All that smug house of cards came tumbling down the afternoon I sat panting in O'Connor's car, and the only thing stopping me from ripping his clothes off was the beep of his cell phone. Apparently, I just hadn't found the right person.

That afternoon had plunged me back into therapy, forced me to acknowledge that it was time for Saint Mary to hang up her halo, that Jim's fall from grace wasn't an excuse for me to start screaming holier than thou, that even though I hated to admit it, I bore some responsibility for the demise of my marriage, and, Mary, that will be $130 dollars and next Tuesday?

"Cara," Antonello boomed over the oven timer. "I've been looking for you everywhere. We're all waiting. Dean Benson wants to formally welcome you to...."

Antonello saw my face stiff with shame and stopped.

"What's going on here?" he demanded over the whine of the timer, throwing a menacing glare in O'Connor's direction. "Chef Mary, is there a problem?"

I rushed past both of them and turned off the timer.

"No, everything's fine," I lied. "Chef Antonello, meet Inspector O'Connor. He was Jim's partner in the S.F.P.D. Homicide Division. He's...here...at school...a student." I mumbled, waving my hand in the direction of the kitchen.

"Pleased to meet you, Chef Antonello." O'Connor held out his hand. "Mary's told me a lot about you over the years. I can hardly wait to get into your class."

Antonello gave me a sideways glance, at which I tried to smile. The nostrils in his nose flared, his chocolate brown eyes hardened. If looks could kill. He shook O'Connor's hand with only the barest courtesy and said nothing in return.

Antonello turned back to me. "We're waiting for you at the chefs' table, Cara." He put a friendly hand on my shoulder and for a brief second pulled on my earlobe. "Are you coming?"

"Yeah, I'll be there in just a second," I assured him. "Let me get these cakes out of the oven first."

Antonello looked at O'Connor and then back to me.

"Are you sure?" he insisted. "Let me help you."

"No, no, I'm fine," and I waved a pair of oven mitts in the direction of the dining room. "Go. I'll be there in a minute."

Before Antonello left the room he made a curt nod in O'Connor's direction. "I warn you once, Mr. O'Connor."

As I opened the oven and started sliding hot sheet pans out of the deck oven onto rolling racks, O'Connor picked up another set of mitts and began helping me.

"Does he maul every woman that way?" he demanded, slamming the sheet pans onto the rack. "Jim told me that guy was always all over you."

I slid the last sheet pan on the rack. I turned to face him, now in complete control.

"Mr. O'Connor. Handle those cakes with care, if you please. They're made of eggs and air, not cement. You're here to learn pastry. You'll learn pastry. Class starts again at 11:00 a.m. I suggest you get something to eat. One final note: Neither you nor my ex-husband have any right to comment on my relationships with other men. Get a grip."

I threw the oven mitts at him and noted with satisfaction that they left soot streaks all over the front of his pristine white chef's jacket.

"Mary, we're so happy to have you with us." Dean Benson's rich basso boomed across the room as I neared the chefs' tables. Standing up to execute a dramatic flourish with his left arm, he indicated that I possessed the seat of honor next to him with the old guard. I hoped that this wasn't an indication of his position in this ridiculous conflict. Surely, he wasn't taking sides? I sat down somewhat secure in the knowledge that I had no choice but to obey the Dean's express wish that I be his guest for lunch. I hadn't realized how much time had elapsed while O'Connor and I'd been duking it out at the ovens. Everyone else had begun on their entrees. The students had finished eating, and people were going for their second cup of coffee. A pleasant buzz surrounded each table as students compared notes for the first morning of classes.

I nodded in Benson's direction and sat down, unfolding my napkin with a snap in an effort to hide my nerves. This was my first official meal with my fellow chefs, and I desperately wanted to make a good impression.

Antonello, who was sitting next to me, whispered in my ear, "Everything okay?"

I nodded briefly. Even that minute exchange had all eyes at the table on us. A few of the older chefs who'd taught when I was a student leered at me as if to say, "You and Antonello still at it, eh?" The old Mary would have stared them down. The humble and poor Mary silently muttered "frigging perverts" while checking to make sure her napkin was centered on her lap. High road, I told myself, take the high road.

Napkin safely unfolded on my lap, I turned to Benson. "Dean Benson, how nice to see you again." I shook his hand and nodded at the student chef who'd been hovering over that end of the table, dying to serve that one lone salad. Turning his body slightly away, he made a quick, sneaky swipe of his brow with his jacket cuff. I smiled in sympathy. Waiting on the chefs' table is the penalty for those who are late. His tardiness, most likely BART related as the trains always run late on rainy mornings, wouldn't make a difference. Curt, the maître'd, was merciless.

"Too much salt in this *coq au vin*, Marc. Try to keep your students more in check, if you please." Benson sniffed loudly and threw down his knife and fork on the plate with a loud clatter. This was said to the other table where the younger chefs sat. The older chefs smiled at one another in repressed glee. The briny chicken sat untouched on everyone's plates. Marc Lapin, a twenty-five-year-old *wunderkind* from Texas, hung his head in disgrace, his dreadlocks not doing a very good job of hiding the deep blush on his face.

Actually, as a dean, Bob Benson wasn't a bad choice. To his credit, although he knew nothing about running a business, he knew food. An unfortunate trait that most chefs share. Which might explain why eighty percent of all food establishments fail in their first three years of operation.

To give Benson his due, armed only with a degree from Cornell's hotel management program, he was the first to realize that what America needed was a venue that trained chefs. And what better way to get the big bucks out of people than by capitalizing on the cachet of training your juvenile delinquent in the old European tradition. With European chefs! He realized that food would become the new theater, that restaurants would become the new stage, that food magazines would start to resemble a type of Bible.

Hand in hand with this amazing, prescient idea was the grinding need to prove to his father, a real estate king who owned a baseball team back in the Midwest, that he could make it in the big bad world of corporate America without Daddy's help. When the school began bleeding money, Benson, still determined not to let Dad bail him out, frantically put the school out to bid. A pharmaceutical company snapped it up, so in addition to owning a cooking school, it was simultaneously conducting research on pills designed to let you eat what you want, all the time, when you want, without gaining an ounce. The irony seemed to be lost on everyone but me. Two years ago the school had been sold yet again to some nameless conglomerate. I could have cared less so long as the stock kept its value and they didn't ask me to bake with margarine.

Aside from his unerring ability to turn anything having to do with money into a textbook case on how to file for bankruptcy, Benson had an uncanny pulse on the food scene. What were trends before they were even trends. A fact that was not lost on the corporation that now owned the school. Benson now ran the food end of it, but had handed over the financial reins to a controller who has the personality of a cauliflower and an extremely pale and sort of lumpy face (his name exited my brain the second it was told to me). He'd also hired an office manager, Marilyn Cantucci, to run the office.

I'd been introduced to her when I'd filled out my forms. A woman whose devotion to spectator pumps was only surpassed by her loyalty to her manicurist. We sniffed around each other like dogs that didn't necessarily click but hadn't reached the stage of out and out growling and teeth snapping. Not someone I could relate to. A woman whose number one investment was herself. Manicures, pedicures, waxing, eyebrow shaping, outfits so coordinated they screeched of having her colors done—I've been dying for someone to ask me what my season was so I could say black—she never has that embarrassing white stripe of gray at her part—a fashion *faux pas* I've been guilty more times than I care to count. It seems pointless to go through all that rigmarole when you spend your life in a uniform boxy enough to fit a man or a woman.

I suspected that Marilyn was the real power behind the throne, Bob the idea man. It would behoove me to stay on her good side.

"Inedible chicken aside," Benson threw another pointed look in Marc's direction, "we'd like to formally welcome Mary Ryan to the school. Mary, in addition to her formidable culinary skills, is probably our most infamous teacher. How's the body count these days, Mary?" Dean Benson chortled at his poor attempt at wit and wagged a fat finger at me, obviously expecting some sort of equally pithy remark.

I brought my napkin up to my face and wiped my mouth, hiding an involuntary grimace. Before I'd begun teaching, I'd deluded myself that everyone would be too polite to mention last fall's murders. Fat chance. The morning was barely three-hours old, and my own dean was bringing it up. I'd have to cut this line of discussion off at the knees, or I'd be the target of dead body jokes for the next four months.

"Fortunately, Dean Benson, I left my dead body magnet at home today." I smiled sweetly to take away the sting, but hoped that would end this annoying line of repartee.

Benson bit his bottom lip, clutched the lapels of his two thousand dollar suit, and scooted his butt to the far side of his seat.

When I was a student, we all thought Dean Benson's need to puff himself up at someone else's expense more a pathetic attempt to establish credibility with the other owners because of his relative youth than any real character flaw. Here he was barely thirty, telling a bunch of seasoned European chefs what to do; guys who'd had been carving chunks of carrots into the requisite seven-sided bullets when Benson was still in diapers. Well, we were wrong. Rather than waning as he aged and his confidence grew, this arrogance had calcified so that now it was as hard as spun sugar. I'm sure they'll find a gene for it someday.

Benson's name often pops up in the society columns, which I read every day as it pays to keep tabs on your clients; who's divorcing whom so you don't seat the ex-Mrs. X at a table next to the old Mr. X and the newer, younger Mrs. X. Benson comes from money, a preliminary (but not a given) foot in the door in San Francisco society. He aims for old-money types, who find him perfectly acceptable as a dinner partner, but never consider him suitable husband material. Benson was a few hundred million short of the funds necessary to gloss over Dad's questionable real estate deals.

I steeled myself for more tasteless remarks regarding the murder when the student waiter saved the day by inadvertently trying to clear the table before everyone had finished. A big no-no. Personally, I can't stand dirty dishes in front of me, the food congealing in a lumpy mass while everyone else finishes their meal, but it's not proper etiquette.

"Young man," Dean Benson intoned deeply, stroking his red power tie for emphasis.

"Y…y…yes, Dean?" The student stuttered back in response.

"Do not, I repeat, do not remove the plates until everyone is finished. Have I made myself clear?"

"Yes, sir," the student whispered. Beads of sweat erupted on his brow, as if we were going to ask him to remove his chef's jacket on the spot so that we could flog him with giant wire whisks. With a casual flick of his wrist, Benson dismissed him, and the poor guy fled back across the dining room to the kitchen as fast as he could short of breaking into a run, no doubt in search of cooking sherry.

I'd forgotten how terrifying I found the first four months while at École. If it hadn't been for Antonello De Luca, I probably wouldn't have finished the program. Obviously, the sport of humiliating students hadn't changed over the years. I'd experienced that identical terror many times.

The first time I waited at the chefs' table I knew enough not to clear the table before everyone was finished, but no one told me that Europeans cross their utensils to indicate they're done eating, in direct contrast to Americans, who place their utensils side by side. After several chefs with accents reprimanded me, I caught on.

Once the obligatory humiliation of the student waiter was over, in an all too familiar repetition of our lunch in December, Benson began scraping his plate for the last remnants of the cherry cobbler. I pegged him as the kind of man who'd lick his dessert plate in the privacy of his own home.

I made a show of digging in, trying to muster enthusiasm for chicken *cordon bleu* at ten-thirty in the morning. Being around food all the time usually has one of two effects: either you become so sick of looking at food all day and night that very little tempts you—many chefs become vegetarians; cutting up a few sides of beef can have a real negative effect on your meat consumption—or you become entranced by it and can't stop eating. I tended to be of the eat-just-enough-to-stay-alive camp, but on my first day I should at least pretend I was enjoying the food.

Ugh, the chicken *was* too salty.

"Mary," a female voice called to me from the other table. I turned toward a petite Asian woman whose severe black crew cut highlighted her delicate bone structure and the blood red of her lipstick.

"I'm Shelley Tam. Nice spread on fruit desserts in last April's issue of *American Chef.*"

"Thanks. Didn't you open up a number of Wolfgang Puck's places? You've had a few articles in *American Chef* yourself."

"Mmmn." She acknowledged my praise with an elegant, cat-like shrug of her shoulders and twirled a spoon between her fingers. "What I liked most was your comment about how fussy desserts were becoming. How there's so much man-handling of food these days. The endless chopping, the straining, the mauling." Then she dropped the spoon on her dessert plate so that it clattered on the china.

All forks stopped. All eyes were on me.

"I didn't say *maul.* I just meant that I like my desserts simple." I babbled on, casting desperate looks at Antonello to save me. "Some fresh fruit with a little ice cream, and I'm happy. Just my personal taste."

I didn't know the rules of this war, except the more I talked the more I was bound to offend someone.

Marc, the teacher Benson humiliated earlier, interrupted me. "Hey, I know what you mean, Mary," he drawled, his Texas accent lazy and contemptuous, a lot of vowels and no consonants. "All that turning of vegetables, making stuff into unnatural shapes, pushing everything through a sieve so there's no texture left at all. Glorified baby food." He paused to push up the sleeves of his chef's jacket, like he was gearing up for something.

Marc looked directly at Étienne Broussard, who had apprenticed in Paris during Maxim's heyday. "You know," he paused, "Only the French could come up with a cuisine that makes torturing food a near religion. I can't believe we're still teaching that crap."

Marc barely got that final "pee" out of his mouth, which considering his usual drawl was quite distinct, before Chef Étienne stood up, picked up a pitcher of water, and marched over to where Marc was sitting.

"You're a disgrace to the profession," Étienne shouted. "You're incapable of even making a decent *cordon bleu*." And he threw the entire pitcher of water into Marc's face.

Chapter Four

Fortunately, the cutlery had been bussed, so there wasn't any danger of anyone getting stabbed. Unfortunately, not ten seconds earlier, in his zeal to avoid any more reprimands, the student waiter had placed fresh pitchers of water on the tables and filled all the water glasses.

The water fight started out slowly, with Marc returning Étienne's initial volley with one of his own. I thought it was going to stop there. Silly me. Because Shelley decided to up the ante and somehow, in her impossibly small hands, picked up three water glasses at once and arced a wall of water at all the traditional chefs, soaking their jacket fronts. It was all over at that point. We later found out that an enterprising student just happened to have a digital camera with him and paid his remaining school fees by putting together a calendar entitled, "Wet Chefs." My stock with the students went up several substantial notches as it was one of those haven't-done-the-laundry-in-two-weeks days, and I was wearing an oh-my-god-what-was-I-thinking leopard print push-up bra.

Memo to self: buy truckload of beige bras because you never know when you're going to find yourself in the middle of water fight and then end up being Miss July.

Plumes of water flew every which way. French, German, Danish, and English epithets accompanied each watery bullet, with blood-curdling screams from Marc that could only be described as rebel war cries. As angry chefs emptied their glasses of water at a target, they'd scramble to refill them from the pitchers on the table.

The chefs who weren't in on the water fight were pinned to their seats. Every time I made to move to get out of my chair, water came flying in my direction. I had to shield my face with my arms to avoid getting hit in the face with a wet missile.

Finally, the water ran out. As if frozen in time, the main perpetrators, Étienne and Gustav representing the old guard and Marc and Shelley the new, stood rigid with empty water glasses in hand. Étienne raised his glass an inch. Marc followed suit. Shelley hiked her glass up over her head. Gustav grabbed another glass from the table and raised his two glasses in the air. Someone was going to lose an eye—or worse.

"Stop this at once," ordered a female voice, worn down from a lifetime of smoking Marlboros. Marilyn Cantucci. I caught Antonello's eye and grimaced. Benson couldn't have stopped this before all of us weren't reduced to wringing out the hems of our chef's jackets? "Dean Benson!" she snapped.

Finally galvanized into action, Benson fussed, "Yes, yes, yes. We've got customers arriving in less than an hour."

"This isn't over, Marc," Étienne threatened, his hazel eyes all iris with fury. He slammed his glass down on the table and walked across the dining room to his kitchen. Marc watched Étienne leave the dining room, apparently unaware that his glass had slid out of his hand, rolled off the table, and onto the floor. Shelley lowered her arm and deposited her glass on the table, then leaned over to pick up Marc's glass from off of the floor and place it on the table. In a surprisingly gentle gesture, she hooked her arm through his and led him out of the dining room.

I surveyed the damage. Paper chef's hats lay in mushy puddles on the tables. Lemon slices from the water glasses were pasted to the front of several jackets. Even though not everyone had participated in the free-for-all, we were all soaked to the skin, wet hair hanging around our ears like dreadlocks. No one moved. No one wanted to be responsible for what came next.

Antonello, bless his heart, broke the impasse.

"I've got a dry chef jacket in my locker. The bidding starts at one bottle of Veuve Clicquot."

I did my bit for peace.

"I've got dry socks and dry underwear. I won't accept anything less than a bottle of Chateau d'Yquem."

The mood shifted; everyone started laughing and began picking lemon slices off of each other. Things were getting pretty festive until Curt appeared in front of the chefs' table in the tux he wore for service.

"Do I need to remind everyone we serve lunch in forty-five minutes? Get hair dryers from your lockers and designate a student to stand here and try to dry out the chairs." He sighed. "If we make a dent in the chairs, it's on to the carpets."

Ignoring the stares of the students, we all headed in the direction of the elevators to retrieve hair dryers. Marilyn had collared Benson and dragged him over to a corner of the dining room. I couldn't hear what she was saying but based on the angle of his chin and the hunch of his shoulders, she was reaming him a new asshole. He stood there taking whatever she was dishing out, shuffling his feet and trying to wring the water out of his two-hundred dollar tie. I wish I could be a fly on the wall of Marilyn's office to read the near-certain email to corporate headquarters detailing Benson's latest incompetence. There's no way to sugar-coat a water fight among your senior personnel in front of half the school.

I ran to the locker room to get my hair dryer and a dry jacket. Benson was a moron. Aside from someone possibly getting maimed or killed, our authority in the kitchen had been compromised, perhaps fatally, because this man allowed a petty spat to blow up into a full-scale war. If he wasn't in a position to demand that the chefs respect each other, who was?

Retrieving my hair dryer, I high-tailed it back to the kitchen. Students huddled together to compare notes on who threw water at whom. If we didn't get a move on I'd be here until eight.

"Hey," I called out to the room. "Rehash the gory details of the water fight in the bar across the street after school. We've lost thirty minutes of prep time."

Jake, a kid I'd privately nick-named Slouch because his center of gravity rested on his hips, piped up, "Looked to us like the chefs were just about ready to kill each other."

I groaned internally; the fall-out from the water pitchers at thirty paces had begun.

A loud cough got my attention. A miniscule smirk played on the edge of O'Connor's lips.

I shot him a look that would separate mayonnaise.

"I wouldn't say that, Jake," I lied. "Tempers are a little short being the first day of school." I raised my voice to be heard over O'Connor's irritating coughing. "We have a lot to do before the afternoon group arrives, so keep your lips zipped at least until you meet at Jack's after class. Now, I need a volunteer to help dry out the chairs. Thanks, Brad." I handed him the hair dryer. "Go see Curt and return the hair dryer to me when you're done. Remember, everyone, ask questions if you don't understand something. Move it, people."

The next couple of hours were a blur of mixers humming and whirling. We filled sheetpans heavy with *paté sucre* and *paté briseé*, the doughs used for lining tart shells; we chopped up and blended pounds of chocolate with gallons of cream for *ganache*, the chocolate standard filling for truffles and cakes; and we whipped sixty-eight pound blocks of butter with sugar to make buttercream to frost those cakes.

Pastry is precise. Chemistry dependent. It's not touchy-feely at all. Two cups of sugar, a cup of butter, and two eggs whipped just so, and you have a perfect product every time. For that reason, it attracts your classic Type A personality.

It's an anal person's game, and what that says about me I haven't bothered to examine yet.

Although the afternoon was a blur, a few things stood out. Nine of the students didn't know their asses from their elbows. I exhibited truly amazing restraint when one student added entire eggs to twenty pounds of butter—shells intact. The sound of those eggs cracking as the paddle smashed them to bits is the culinary equivalent of nails scraping on a blackboard. "But the recipe said add whole eggs," the clueless student wailed.

Brad, O'Connor, and Coolie were the only students who somehow understood that eating in restaurants for three of their meals didn't impart an innate knowledge of cooking.

As I surveyed the kitchen in a rare moment of calm, with no one tugging on the arm of my jacket or firing questions at me, I spied Coolie over at one of the enormous industrial mixers whipping eggs and sugar together for a batch of *genoise*. If I squinted I could almost envision my younger self. Her body curled over a mixer, watching the warm eggs spiral together with the sugar as the whip incorporated air. Reveling in the smells. A small hand poised over the on/off button, as she waited patiently for the eggs and sugar to reach the right volume. Punching the off button, she paused as the whip slowed to a stop. She noticed me watching her, and I got a big smile. A smile I understood. It looks right; it smells right; it's time to add the sifted flour, then the melted butter. Yeah, I know what you mean I nodded to her and smiled back. Whatever the political shenanigans brewing among the chefs, I knew I'd made the right choice to come back.

At 1:45 p.m., as promised, making a special effort not to glance even remotely in the direction where I knew O'Connor was standing, I gave everyone the *National Enquirer* version of the murders of last October. By the rapt expression on their faces, it clearly raised their opinion of me in their eyes. At 2:00, I dismissed everyone, but pulled Coolie aside before she could leave the room.

"We never would have finished all the prep work if it hadn't been for your help this afternoon. Thanks."

"No problemo, Chef Mary." Coolie talked quickly, like she was afraid someone was going to interrupt her before she finished her sentence. "I spend a lot of time in the kitchen at home with our personal chef. Plus, the caterer always let me help out whenever my parents threw parties. I love cooking."

"Personal chef?" I asked.

"Yeah. Dad's a rich lawyer. Royally pissed off when I wouldn't go to Harvard. You know. Law school. All that alma mater shit. I like being in a kitchen, the togetherness."

The money shouldn't have been a surprise. Unlike the rest of her fellow students, whose standard issue chef's jackets made them look like they were wearing white shrouds with arms, she'd had her chef's jacket and pants professionally tailored out of linen and silk.

"Sounds like your father doesn't approve of you cooking. What about your mother?" I asked somewhat absentmindedly, as I grabbed my clipboard and began tallying up the *mise en place* for Allison Warner, the night chef.

Coolie raised her chin in a defiant gesture. "Dad yelled, threatened to cut me off. Other stuff. The usual. But mom set up a blind trust for me to come here. I caught the first plane out of Chicago. Mom's very cool." Coolie paused and then amended, "When she's not in la-la land. You know. Meds. Did your father pitch a fit when you decided to go to cooking school?"

My experience couldn't have possibly been more different. I clutched the clipboard so tightly that later that night I found a charming little groove through the middle of my palm.

"No, he really didn't care." My announcement was met with complete indifference. Granted, it'd probably been the same as if I'd announced I was in line to become the next Nobel laureate. Basic nod, whatever, *vaya con dios*.

"You're lucky," she sighed.

"I suppose that one's way to look at it." I pried my hand from the clipboard. "My uncle wasn't too pleased, though. Said I was disgracing the family by going into trade, as he called it. He reminds me of this every time I see him." I grimaced. Not that I didn't take his generous birthday and Christmas checks with alacrity. It was something I wasn't particularly proud of, but couldn't seem to muster the pride to tear them into confetti and return the pieces in an envelope.

She swept her eyes around the kitchen and sniffed to catch the smell of cooling *genoise* that still lingered in the air. "They don't get it, do they?" she smiled and threw her arms up in the air. "Doesn't it smell wonderful?"

"Yeah, it does," I agreed. *Ma soeur.* "Thanks again, you were a real help."

That got a deep blush. "Got to go. We're all meeting at the bar across the street after school. See you in the morning."

"Be on time," I reminded her as she flittered out of the room, her knife roll slung over that shoulder so slim you'd think it would crack from the weight.

I was just finishing writing up my report, when the phone rang—the office with more forms to sign. I took the stairs two at a time up to the office. Cheryl, the receptionist who had yet to spell my first name right—she always put an "i" on the end—had another set of forms for me to sign. Did I need life insurance? If she'd told me this over the phone, I could have saved myself a trip and I'd be on the bridge by now. "It's a really, really good deal. How can you pass this up?" She was so insistent I began to suspect she received a percentage of the sale from every employee she signed up.

An emphatic, "No, I don't need any life insurance. No one cares if I live or die," seemed to shut her up. I silently cursed her, with a fleeting glance outside of window at the increasing traffic. Shit. It'd take me over an hour to get home in that mess.

"If you're really sure," she pouted and gathered up her purse. How can a receptionist who makes, at the outside, $24,000 per year, afford an Yves St. Laurent handbag? "I'm going to get something to eat. Allison is in a meeting right now with Ms. Cantucci. You'll see her later, yeah?" I nodded. "Will you tell her the jeweler called? Her ring will be ready next Tuesday. *She* got life insurance," she sniffed and made her way to the elevator bank.

"Bully for her," I shouted and decided to wait until she got her kick-backed ass on the elevator before I went for the stairs.

Just as the elevator doors closed I heard screaming. Screaming as in, "You fucking bitch. Do *not* mess with me."

Allison Warner came shooting through Marilyn Cantucci's door, slammed it shut with enough force to break something, then slammed the office door shut, and began pounding the Down button with her fist. She stopped short when she saw me, her shoulders heaving with the effort not to cry. What in the hell do you say when you've just witnessed a major bitch-slap fest between an old friend and Miss Spectator Shoes. I hope you won?

Without a word I tried to hand her the clipboard. She stared it as if it were an alien life form and didn't bother to take it from me. As if it was somehow inappropriate to remind her that she had twelve students to teach in about, say, three minutes.

"How about we go downstairs and we can discuss the *mise en place*, uh, away from here?" I suggested.

She nodded. As the doors opened, I remembered what the reception said. "Oh by the way, Cheryl said that the jeweler called. Your ring will be ready on Tuesday."

The transformation was amazing. Allison's shoulders straightened up, her chin jutted forward, her hands uncurled from tight fists.

"Hold the elevator for me, will you?" she said, with what couldn't be described in any other way but jubilation.

Without knocking, she wrenched open Marilyn's door, announced that, "My ring will be ready on Tuesday," and then slammed the door shut with as much force as before but with none of the rage.

After that stupendous exit, Allison's first words to me were not, "I hope that shellacked bitch's nails all fall out," followed by a blow-by-blow account of the rip-roaring argument I'd had the good fortune to hear the tail end of. Sigh. Allison's opening gambit was, "Did you hear that David Kinney got the Beard Award this year?" Catching up on old classmates until we eased back into some semblance of normal conversation was about as good as it was going to get. Damn it to hell.

Classmates at École fifteen years ago, Allison Warner and I weren't friends so much as compatriots; we happened to be in the same place at the same time and knew the same people. At the top of our class, both of us had been pastry students and both had vied for the attentions of Chef Antonello de Luca.

Blond hair that can only be described as tresses, a heart-shaped face with eyes so vividly blue they look like they're enhanced by contacts—they aren't—her hips and breasts spill out of her clothes. Allison is every Renaissance painter's wet dream. She's the only woman I know who looks sexy in a chef's uniform. Constantly on a diet in a futile attempt to ape the anorexic waifs that parade across the media, Allison was oblivious to the power of her own sensuality. I'd never heard any gossip about her dating someone, and yet every guy I knew had a hard on for her.

Once we arrived in the classroom, Allison gave me a warm hug, "Good to see you, Mary. I see you survived the baptism." Her heavy perfume wrapped itself around my vocal cords. I coughed discreetly in a bid for fresh air. Her liberal use of perfume always surprised me. Most chefs don't want artificial smells competing with the natural odor of cooking. Often I know when something is done by the smell coming from the oven. "I heard about the water fight even before I got out of my car. How are you? I heard you've had a rough few months," she murmured in a polite nod to the murder case I'd been involved in.

"Really happy to be back," I replied, hoping against hope that I wouldn't have to repeat any of the gory details of (a) finding my employee beaten to death by a frying pan; and (b) finding my employer shot to death in my bed. "I'm dry by now, although the elastic on my underwear is still damp." I grimaced. "It got real ugly there for a minute. I thought someone was going to get hurt."

"Idiots," she spat out. Allison expertly twisted her long hair into a chignon, secured it with a clip, and fitted her chef's hat on top. If her uniform was any judge, she'd allied herself with the old guard; classic checked trousers and white, boxy, polyester jacket. "Fortunately the night chefs all get along."

"Clue me in on what's happening around here. Here," I handed her the clipboard with the *mise en place* listed on it. "I asked Antonello about it and he just waved his arms and pinched my cheek."

She sighed. "Basically, it's a few twenty-five year old brats who think they invented cooking. Marc's the ringleader. He's singled out Gustav and Étienne for the majority of his nasty remarks, calling them culinary dinosaurs to their faces. Last semester, in a voice loud enough for the entire dining room to hear, Marc announced that he'd rather be roasted on a spit and served for Christmas dinner than admit to being trained at Maxim's. That it's little more than a training school for culinary terrorists where they learn to torture and maim food. Can you imagine?"

I'm surprised that remark didn't give Étienne a stroke. In his mind, nothing was equal in taste, finesse, and elegance to a meal *à la* Escoffier, the nineteenth-century French chef whose name is synonymous for classic French cuisine.

"What about Antonello? Where does he fit in all this?"

She snorted and made notes on my list. "Thanks for making all those extra *genoise*. You know Antonello. He's friends with everyone. He actually likes some of the new ideas."

I raised an eyebrow at that tiny note of criticism. Normally, Allison worshipped the ground Antonello walked on.

"I can see where he's coming from, Allison. When these kids graduate and look for jobs, they need as much experience as possible," I pointed out. "Food has changed. The school needs to change with it." I took off my apron and arched my back. Christ, it was hard to believe this was my first day.

"Perhaps," she said in a conciliatory tone, but threw the clipboard down on the desk and then wrapped her arms tightly around her body.

"Oh, you'll need to order more eggs from the storeroom. An entire case ended up in the trash. A student actually put whole eggs in the mixer. In their shells, believe it or not. Anyway, do you know Benson's take on this? He sat there mute during the water fight while we all got drenched. He should put up Lost and Found posters, with a big reward for the first person who finds his spine."

Her arms went down and her hands balled up into fists.

"Robert's got enough on his plate without these chefs making trouble. The curriculum here has been perfectly adequate for twenty years."

I stared at her in amazement. Although I disagreed with Marc's methods, he did have a point; the school wouldn't maintain its student population if it didn't keep up with the times. A new cooking school seems to pop up every month, competing for tuition dollars.

"Oh come on." It was my turn to snort. "How can you say that? American cuisine of the last twenty years has undergone a total revolution. It's no longer jello for dessert; it's fresh fig and marscapone tart. The tuition here is ten thousand dollars a quarter. The students deserve to learn both the traditional and the trendy."

"What do you know?" she hissed. "This is your first day on the job and already you're making pronouncements from on high, acting like you know better than anybody else. As usual." She jabbed my shoulder blade with a pointed finger. "You always had to be smarter and faster than anyone else. Always running to Antonello to brag how competent you were."

What? I never saw her as a rival. Our strengths lay in entirely different areas. My forte was execution and organization; she was exceptionally creative. Paradoxically, I went into restaurant work, which would have been the perfect venue to showcase her talents, while she stayed to teach at École, a job that was tailor-made for me. And as for Antonello, he flirted with both of us. I admit, sometimes the sexual innuendo got pretty thick, but I never crossed that line between flirting and fondling. Nor did I think he wanted any more than trading lascivious comments. I was engaged and he was married.

People who cook are intense. I know this. But I'd never stepped on so many toes in such a short period of time in my life. Okay, there was that hotel where I walked out after only two hours on the job, but other than that....

"Allison, I'm sorry. I didn't mean—"

"Why don't you work here for a month or two before trying to solve all our problems."

I tried again. "I'm sorry. I—"

She cut me off with a wave of her hand and averted her head. The rage and jubilation of ten minutes earlier had faded. Her classic peaches and cream complexion was the color of old croissant dough, and stress lines framed her forehead and mouth.

"Are you sick, Allison? You don't look well. Do you want me to take your class tonight?

"No, Mary. I'm fine. I'd hoped that everything would be...taken care of by now. I thought that by Christmas..." She grabbed her apron. "By the end..."—she wrapped her apron around her waist—"of the week..."—tugged on the strings and cinched it tight around her waist—"all this will be solved." She secured the apron with a perfect bow. "One way or another."

I opened my mouth to ask another question, but our conversation was cut-off by the afternoon class shuffling in the door.

One way or another. That sounded ominous.

Chapter Five

You can always tell what kind of day I've had by where I leave my car keys. A great day and the car keys actually get hung up on the hook just inside the door. A so-so day generally means they get thrown in the general direction of the dining room table. A bad day and they end up getting dumped on the sideboard where I keep a bottle of Remy V.S.O.P. This makes hunting for car keys at 5:30 a.m. always a challenge.

The minute I got home, the keys barely hit the sideboard before I grabbed the neck of the brandy bottle, twisted the cork out with a practiced yank, and sloshed a hangover-sized amount of cognac into a Waterford crystal brandy snifter. I used to have two of these glasses. Wedding present, of course. When my marriage became the kind of statistic lamented by those promoting family values, Jim got one, I got the other. Sometimes I didn't have the heart to use it and just poured the brandy into a coffee mug. Nothing screams, "Danger, Will Robinson, danger, danger!" potential alcoholic more than only one brandy glass. I seriously have considered ordering another one to give myself the illusion I'm not drinking alone.

Not even bothering to find a chair. I leaned my back against the wall and slid down to the floor, my knees offering my elbows a convenient shelf, which left my hands free to cup the glass and warm the booze. I drank half of it before I had the energy to begin what I knew was a pointless debate with myself about the wisdom of calling my ex-husband.

Two years later and seriously expensive overtime with a therapist, Jim and I'd finally reached the point where we could talk to each other without the conversation spiraling into a screaming fit on my part, a defensive whine on his.

Unfortunately for me, it didn't mean I'd reached the point where I could do this fully sober. Which explains getting half-toasted before having the nerve to call him. But dammit, he was the only person I knew who could give me the scoop on O'Connor.

"Inspector McCreery, Internal Affairs."

"Jim, it's Mary."

"Who's dead?"

"Nobody's dead."

"Well, it must be that or the second coming of Jesus Christ for you to voluntarily call me."

I ignored his pathetic attempt at sarcasm.

"The scoop on O'Connor. Give. He's a student at École. Doesn't he have a mortgage, kids, and car payments? Plus a wife that doesn't work."

There was a pause.

"What's the big deal, Mary? He's on medical leave from the department."

Medical leave?

"Let's try this again, Jim. At École he's going to be lifting sixty-eight pound butter blocks, hoisting twenty-gallon stock pots from one burner to another, and standing on his feet for hours on end, working diligently on those varicose veins that no amount of surgery will repair. I have trouble envisioning Workman's Comp rationalizing that O'Connor training as a chef would be appropriate after suffering several gun shot wounds to his chest. Bullet-proof vest notwithstanding."

Silence for a couple of seconds and then…

"I don't feel comfortable telling you this, Mary, but when O'Connor got shot, it did something. His docs put him on disability for post-traumatic stress syndrome. Anyway, why are you calling me about him? Didn't you see him today?"

Sooooooooooo desperate. In feint and attack mode. Lie first and then turn the tables.

"Stop. Can I put you on hold for a minute? The bullshit is getting so thick on my end of the line that I'm going to need to get the shovel from the garage to clear a path from the phone to my front door."

Silence again. Which in hindsight was a sign Jim was making a real concentrated effort not to push my buttons; however, I was well past the point of no return. The metaphorical smell of bullshit tends to do that to me.

"O'Connor doesn't get stressed. He just runs another six miles. Please stop," I reiterated and gave the receiver a little shake in lieu of smacking him on the arm in frustration. "And yes, I did see him. We got into a fight. I didn't get the whole story."

Jim laughed. "Sounds like the status quo, Mary. When aren't you and O'Connor fighting?"

Which enraged me because it was true.

Back in October when we were slobbering all over each other. A distinct change in the status quo.

For years, O'Connor and I suffered each other. As Jim's wife, I barely tolerated, with ill-concealed poor grace I must admit, his supremely annoying best friend, and O'Connor easily matched my sarcastic remark with sarcastic remark, the subtext of his not so subtext; his utter astonishment that his best friend had chosen such an *über* bitch for a wife. Facing each other across a stovetop was literally the only time we weren't arguing, yelling, and insulting each other. Our camaraderie *in* the kitchen was as infamous as our incessant snarking at each other *out* of it.

The murder investigation last fall whisked us out of the comfort zone of mutually satisfying antagonism. Suddenly cooking amicably together and verbally abusing each other the rest of the time, morphed into cooking amicably together, but please shut up now so that I can jump you. Before we could investigate any further, was this lust, was this love, we tacitly agreed to stay away from each other. I needed to cobble together a new life, now that Jim's and my declarations of "till death do us part" turned out to be as real as the ridiculous claims that tofu has a taste. O'Connor needed to go back to his wife and three kids. Where he belonged.

"What's the big deal?" Jim complained, a trifle testy. "The only time you two get along is *when* you two are in a kitchen. I think you'd be ecstatic to have someone who knows what he's doing. Aren't you teaching freshman pastry?"

Evil Mary emerged. Really, she'd been waiting in the wings for several minutes whispering, nagging, "Now? Can I come out NOW?" I'd been keeping her at bay until I realized I'd been unconsciously gripping the brandy snifter—the single brandy snifter without its mate—and the cut glass edges were ripping into my palm.

"You been checking up on me again, Jim?"

"Maybe. No law against it."

And we were off and running. The lessons learned from thousands of dollars of therapy vanished into nothing more than a signature on a bunch of checks as I began to yell. We slid easily into the me screaming/him whining mode, bringing with it a certain comfortable predictability, both of knowing the script of this particular play backwards and forwards. I played the sarcastic shrew who put more energy into her career than her marriage and yet resented it when her husband complained that working eighty hours a week seemed a tad much. The other actor in this sad little repeat performance was Jim, whose portrayal of the cheating husband who justified his infidelity because of abject loneliness was destined to get a nod for Best Actor. We'd thought this performance had closed, but apparently it'd been brought back for a limited run.

We both ran out of steam at the same time, an exhausted silence on his end of the line complimenting mine.

It wasn't cathartic. Or even satisfactory. Just pathetic.

"Let's stop," I begged, trying to keep the quiver out of my voice. If I started crying, he'd keep me on the phone forever. Then when I'd finally force him to end the conversation, he'd call my mother and tell her he was worried about me. And then she'd call me....God, I couldn't go there tonight. "Need to go."

"You okay?" he insisted.

"No, I'm not, but I'm going to lie, and say yes, I am. Then I'm going to ask you if you're okay, and you're going to lie to me and tell me that, yes, you are. Because if we don't, we'll end up saying even more hurtful things, and I don't really feel like drinking my dinner tonight. So, are you okay?" I asked in a deadpan voice.

"Yeah, I'm okay," he replied with equal enthusiasm and defeat.

"Good," I managed to mumble and hung up.

"Make dinner, Mary," I ordered out loud and moved my legs in direction of the kitchen, forestalling the temptation to pour myself an entrée.

‹›‹›‹›

I shoved Puccini opera highlights into the CD player and cranked up the volume to full blast because cooking alone can be almost as soul destroying as drinking alone. Filling a pot with water, slopping in a goodly amount of olive oil, followed by a generous helping of salt, covering pot with lid, I upped the gas. I zested an entire lemon, minced parsley and the lemon zest together very fine. I tossed ridiculously expensive salad mix with balsamic vinegar and oil. Threw angel hair pasta into roiling water. Cooked it precisely two and one-half minutes. While the pasta was cooking, I sautéed garlic until it smelled nutty but not burned. The heft of the knife in my hand, the tart smells of lemon and parsley, the heavy scent of cooked garlic, the soprano in mourning, all brought me back to myself, or at least a part of me that felt halfway human and somewhat hungry. I drained the pasta. Tossed the parsley, lemon zest, garlic, and more olive oil with the pasta. I forced myself to sit at the kitchen table, light the candles, use a cloth napkin, and three forkfuls of pasta later, the muscles in my neck stopped jumping sideways.

Having cooked an actual meal and seated myself at a table with appropriate accoutrements, I rewarded myself and poured a glass of Pinot Grigio.

Review of the evidence. O'Connor on stress-related leave?

Bullshit.

Did he exhibit any signs of physical illness? Hands the size of hams. Check. Skin its usual Black Irish swarthy cast. Check. Poor fit of the chef's jacket notwithstanding, shoulders firm and broad. Check with a cherry on top. Mental attitude? Business as usual. Which meant loaded for bear. On a bad day, O'Connor packed enough attitude for five people. After our little encounter today, I'd say his attitude meter was off-scale.

In other words, bullshit, again. I didn't believe it. If he was so damn stressed, what was he doing in the pressure-cooker environment of a kitchen? Prying anymore information out of Jim was out of the question. Another stroll down that not-so-garden path would ensure flunking out of Therapy U.

In four weeks O'Connor transferred to another section. I'd say some sleuthing was in order.

Mary Ryan meet Nancy Drew.

Oh, I see you've met.

Chapter Six

Every time I cross the Bay Bridge and see the city lit up, the arc of lights following the curve of the water, I get a nice shiver down my back. San Francisco's my kind of town. I love the mishmash of different ethnic groups, the odd mix of liberal politics and Brooks Brothers suits. I love the elegant Victorians painted garish colors and the old hotels, the Mark, the St. Francis, the Fairmont, presiding over the downtown like stuffy elegant dowagers who know how to pound back a few drinks and always have a bawdy joke to tell. And I love the Golden Gate and Bay Bridges, embracing the city in their arms like a protective mother.

After my divorce from Jim, we'd sold our mold-prone house in the Sunset, divided the profit, and I'd bought a tiny two-bedroom cottage in Albany. I hated commuting, and the Bay Bridge was becoming more of a transit nightmare every day, but I was near my mother and I had a yard. In my immediate post-divorce state, those were defining criteria.

Now that I was getting back on my feet, the pull to get back to the city was strong. Like the children hearing the Pied Piper, it was tea-smoked duck in Chinatown, fresh pasta in North Beach, and more restaurants per square mile than any other city in the United States that snared me with its siren song. Maybe it was time to consider moving back to the city.

I arrived at school a little after six. Shelley was still changing. We had the locker room to ourselves.

Although our paths had never crossed until now, Shelley Tam's reputation had preceded her. One of these size-two women who compensate for their size and sex by being twice as aggressive as anybody else, she'd opened up a number of the big name restaurants in the northwest. She never stayed longer than six months. Shelley's the type of chef who thrives on the chaos and hype of a new restaurant. Like most high-profile chefs, she's an adrenaline junkie. I'd have thought École would be way too tame for her.

On the drive home, Allison's criticism still ringing in my ears, I'd vowed to stay out of this conflict. Do my job. Get paid. Teach pastry.

Who was I kidding?

As we were alone, surely a few questions wouldn't hurt. And I really wouldn't be nosing around or trying to solve the situation. If I knew the lay of the land, I might stop stepping on people's toes. Apparently, my capacity for self-delusion was at an all time high. Right. I'd just ask her a few questions. Just a few.

Trying to ignore the tight little somersaults roiling my stomach, I grabbed a clean jacket, pants, and apron from the laundry closet and began to change out of my street clothes. I know it's stupid, but petite women intimidate me. Maybe because I'm tall with big feet, but when I'm with someone whose waist is the same circumference as my thigh, I revert back to being a gangly, awkward fourteen-year old; clumsy and always saying the wrong thing.

"Good morning, Shelley. You dried out yet?" I shivered as I leaned against the bank of lockers to thread my legs into my chef's pants. Although the dining room and kitchens were state-of-the-art, the chefs' locker room was a little Dickensian. Drafty, with barely enough light, at certain times of the day it smelled of sewage.

She looked up from tying her red high tops; her crew cut was moussed into tiny sharp spikes, like the tines of a fork. "Whose side are you on, Mary?"

Shit. I gulped. Nothing like cutting to the chase.

"Sides? Do I have to choose s...s...sides?" I stammered with cold and hurriedly pulled on my pants. "I know that Chef Étienne can be a little pompous with the Maxim's stuff, but he's harmless."

"The man should be fired," she snapped. She finished tying her shoes and stood up. "Or shipped back to France where he can continue making that old-fashioned crap that nobody wants to eat anymore."

"Don't you think that's a little harsh?" I reached for my chef's jacket. It's hard to prove a point when you're arguing in your bra. "I agree his style of cooking is passé, but the techniques underlying classical French cuisine are an excellent basis for any cooking program." The minute I said it, I realized how trite I sounded, like a dated brochure.

Shelley's eyes narrowed. "I'm surprised at you, Mary. I thought you'd be on our side."

"I'm not on anybody's *side*," I emphasized. "There's room here for many cuisines, many methods. Étienne is just one teacher out of twenty. Why do you and Marc dislike him so much?" My fingers, cold and nervous, fumbled with my jacket buttons.

"I don't dislike him," she said, sounding surprised. "I just think his time is over." Her voice lost its hard edge. "It's more personal with Marc. I don't know why. He won't tell me."

Something in her tone made me realize that she and Marc were a little more than just co-workers.

"You and Marc?" I hinted.

"Of course." She slammed her locker door shut. "I wouldn't stay at this hellhole of a school for more than two weeks if it weren't for him. I told him only four more months. Then I'm out of here. He can stay if he wants."

I made one more appeal. "I don't think this in-fighting is in the best interest of the students."

"Fuck the students. You'd better decide on which side your bread's buttered, Mary, or butt out," she warned. She turned on her heel and walked out of the locker room: ninety-five pounds of pure hell.

⟨⟩⟨⟩⟨⟩

A letter addressed to all the chefs appeared in our mailboxes that morning. In it, Benson admonished us to not have any more fights and to "keep in mind that we were beacons of culinary knowledge to these students, and we shouldn't jeopardize the glorious traditions established at École by petty grievances."

If this were Benson's sole response to that water fight yesterday, we'd all better take out life insurance. I'd have to get the scoop from Antonello later on whether more drastic measures had taken place behind the scenes.

Whether it was Benson's letter or the water fight, most of the chefs seemed to realize that some horrible line had been crossed. The tables were still segregated between the old guard and the new, but aside from Étienne, Marc, and Shelley, who wouldn't speak to any one at the "other table," everyone else was at least polite to each other. I made a point of sitting at the old guard's table at breakfast and the new guard at lunch. Antonello did the same.

When I found myself side by side with Marc in the hallway, I decided to not say anything. What would be gained?

"Shelley says you're trying to talk some sense into us."

About six four in height, he slowly came to a stop and leaned against the wall and turned toward me, demanding an answer. He was like Antonello; a man who wore his sexuality with ease. Didn't beat you over the head with it, but if you were looking—and I was—it was there. Maybe not for the taking, but it was there. For the first time in ages I found myself physically responding to someone—aside from O'Connor and that wasn't so much as a response as a full-blown sex attack. I opened my mouth to respond and nothing came out. His eyes did a minute one-two up and down my body and the shy smile that accompanied it told me that the kick between us was mutual. It wasn't offensive; as flattering as all hell if the truth were told. If they're all like this down in Texas, I'm moving next week.

"Need to choose your poison, Mary," he drawled.

A little nonplussed by the pheromones this man was radiating, I stuttered, "N...n...no, I don't." If I ignored the slope of his waist and how his apron rested nicely on his hips, I might be able to get out a complete sentence. "Can we talk about what happened yesterday? We're all professionals, right? It got pretty ugly. Why not—"

"You want to whup some sense into us all?" he interrupted.

I blushed. When he put it like that, Allison's accusations of me acting like God All Mighty seemed a little too close to home.

"No," I back-pedaled. "I just think there's room for both types of cuisine. We don't need to start throwing water glasses at each other. Food is a fluid art. Next week Étienne's style might be all the rage."

"You're probably right," he agreed, and his face lost that come-here-you-sexy-thing look. He scrutinized me with a sharpness and energy I hadn't noticed in him before. For a split second, I understood what an effort it must be to hold his own with older heavyweights in the field. "Next week someone's going to present that old tried-and-true French shit and give it a fancy name, like retro-nouveau cuisine, and I'll have cow pie all over my face. But Étienne and I are on a collision course that you can't stop, darlin'. So if you don't plan on signing the petition I'm circulating requesting that Étienne's ass be canned, you can just go back to piping out éclairs."

He didn't wait for me to respond, but turned away and resumed his stroll down the hall.

Étienne was one of the original owners of the school and still had plenty of clout, if not stock, to guarantee his job. Marc had better brush up his resumé; it wasn't Étienne's ass that was going to be in the proverbial sling.

That made three people in the last twenty-four hours who had told me to mind my own business.

Memo to self: stop trying to solve everyone else's problems and get down to teaching pastry.

Second memo to self: this celibacy thing is getting old. You need to get laid.

Chapter Seven

The next week was a blur of activity, culminating in the buffet on Thursday and Friday nights, often called the Last Supper, a slur in reference to the amount of food people consumed. Some things hadn't changed; the students still nominated Pig of the Night, the one individual who piles salads, cheeses, patés, and slices of meat on his or her plate in one gigantic, gravity-defying mound. When I was a student standing in officious attention behind the buffet table, I actually saw someone take a hunk out of a tallow carving and add it to her food mountain.

A buffet has no redeeming features other than being an excuse for sheer gluttony. Part of the sensual ambiance of eating is having your food arranged on your plate, each dish framing the other like a painting, not piled on top of each other like kitchen scraps about to go down the disposal.

Buffets are the secret culinary code for "emptying out the walk-in refrigerators before next fresh produce delivery." To this day, I will not eat at buffets unless it's Mother's Day and I have no choice. Then I stick to the cheese platters. Cheese is supposed to be aged.

Marc and Shelley ignored me. I ignored them.

Devoting all my energies to my students, the first week flew by as I tried to simultaneously assess the experience level of the students, still produce what we needed to produce, and not make too many mistakes. Many of the kids in this group had never been in a kitchen before and the potential for injury was enormous.

Some classes are a mix of novices and seasoned restaurant professionals who want the credential and contacts that École provides, other classes are constituted of students just out of high school and can barely turn on a mixer. This class was very green; O'Connor, Brad, and Coolie were exceptions to the rule. Despite all my intentions to do otherwise, I found myself depending on O'Connor constantly. The students came to look up to him as my assistant, and I didn't dispel them of the notion. Often I'd turn around and find him watching me, no expression on his face. I'd return his stare, blank expression for blank expression. I always turned away first.

Two thirty on Friday found me pleasantly tired. The students had packed up their knife rolls and headed for the bar. As soon as I connected with Allison about the inventory and researched a few things in the library, I'd be across that bridge. For the first time in ten years, I'd have weekends off, the perks of teaching. The latest issue of *Fine Gardening* had arrived the day before, and I was itching to read all about setting up a potager's garden.

I dreaded conferring with Allison for an end of the week wrap-up. What in the hell was going on between her and Marilyn Cantucci? The strain she was under was physically evident; everyday the stretch of her neck tightened, like a horse with a sadistic rider pulling hard on the reins. By her own admission, this was to be the day of reckoning. I didn't know whether I wanted her confidences or not.

Imagine my shock when she almost waltzed into the pastry kitchen. Her cheeks were as flushed as a shiny ripe apple, and her eyes had a satisfied gleam in them, like a kid-in-the-candy store who's just eaten a handful of gumdrops behind his mother's back.

"Hey, Allison, you sure look happy," I greeted her.

"Oh, hi, Mary. We all set for tonight?"

"Yep, plus we made a fresh batch of fondant for the petit fours, and the four sheetpans of croissant dough have had all four turns. They just need to sheeted and cut."

"Oh, the sheeter?" she asked, as if she'd never been in a pastry kitchen in her life.

"Yeah. You know. The thing that automatically rolls out dough so you don't have to use a rolling pin?"

She blushed deeply. I extended the clipboard. Instead of taking it, she ran both hands through her luxurious hair, in a motion redolent of the bedroom. I used to make those sort of post-coital motions myself when I had hair down to my waist. Like a cat stretching itself after a particularly wonderful snooze in the sun, it's an affirmation of pleasure. During one of our bitterest fights, Jim told me that when I cut my hair off, I effectively ended our sex life.

The green finger of jealousy stroked my cheek. My sex life these days might be reduced to gratefully accepting leers from twenty-six year old co-workers, but it *is* like riding a bike, you don't forget. If Allison hadn't just emerged from having the time of her life, I'd eat my kitchen clogs. I knew I sounded snippy and churlish, but the words were out of my mouth before I could stop myself.

"Allison, I'd like to get out of here. Could you come back down to earth?"

The sharp tone in my voice penetrated her carnal reverie.

"No need to snap at me. Something bothering you, Mary?"

I couldn't really say, yes, I'm as jealous as all hell that you have someone to fuck, someone to argue with, someone to connect with.

"No," I denied. "I want to find some historical tidbits in the library for next week's lessons. Except for one or two, the students seemed bored."

Having taught freshman pastry for many years, she shrugged her shoulders in resignation.

"You know how it is, people either love pastry or they hate it. There's no middle ground."

Pastry is a culinary animal all to itself. Chefs de cuisine look down their noses at pastry chefs. It's never accorded the same respect as the other disciplines. The pecking order in the kitchen is as follows: chef de cuisine, saucier, *garde manger* chef, and pantry chef. Off in the corner chopping up blocks of chocolate all by themselves are the pastry chefs. The prevailing attitude is that those who can cook, do, and the rest became pastry chefs.

"I know, I know, but I'd at least like to try to make the effort. I'd like to get on the bridge before it gets backed up. You know what Friday afternoons are like."

As Allison's students began shuffling in, I noted with satisfaction that they didn't look any more awake than mine did. At the sound of knife rolls hitting the tables, she whirled around and then looked at her watch.

"God, I didn't realize it was so late. Mary, do me a big favor will you? Here are my keys. I've got a bottle of vitamin supplements in my locker. Would you get them for me?"

Before I could answer she handed me the keys and turned to her students. In penance for being so snotty to her, I went to fetch her vitamins. As I crossed the pastry kitchen, I spied Antonello marching across the empty dining room. His face looked flushed, too. Hmmm.

Memo to self: you're not supposed to butt into other people's lives.

I turned away and headed straight for the locker room.

The locker room isn't much lighter at three o'clock in the afternoon than it is at six o'clock in the morning. Damn, I'd tucked the clipboard under my arm and forgotten to give it to her. Fumbling with the key to her locker, I swore, prayed, and wiggled that key in every permutation I could think of. I might be a wizard with a whip, but I'm a klutz with a key. My father always told me that there was no greater force than gentleness, but obviously he never opened a locker at École. True to type, the school spent ten thousand dollars last week on new wine goblets, but they bought the cheapest-shit lockers available for the chefs. As I gave the lock one last vicious turn, the door flew open, the clipboard went flying, and a pill bottle rolled across the floor.

God-dammit, this was turning into a scavenger hunt.

I got down on my hands and knees and found clipboard at one end of the locker room and the bottle of vitamins lodged under a bench at the other, near the lone window in the room.

What sort of vitamins was so all-important that she had to have the pills ASAP?

Holding the bottle up to the meager light, I read the label. Vitamins my ass. They were some sort of herbal diet pill: VitaLife. What sort of crap was the answer to Allison's imaginary weight problem? The front of the bottle guaranteed that these pills would give you more energy, increase your circulation, and, by the way, melt away twenty pounds in two months. Just take one pill one hour before you eat. I shifted the bottle to my left hand to open the door and the bottle pulled at my hand. I peeled it away from my palm and little bits of old glue dotted my skin. I turned the bottle over. Odd, the label on the back seemed to have been peeled off.

When I returned to the kitchen, I caught her eye and tucked the bottle in her purse. She gave me the high sign, her cheeks still faintly aglow. I was just about to leave when I remembered I still had the clipboard with the inventory on it.

I scooted by her students, who were lined up along the long stainless steel tables like soldiers, icing cakes with a military precision, and said in a low voice, "Allison, I forgot. Here's the inventory, plus on the front of the clipboard is a copy of Marc's petition asking for Étienne's resignation. I crossed out my name. Marc is being ridiculous. Étienne's not going to be—"

I never finished my sentence. At the mention of the word petition, her cheeks reflamed.

She snatched the clipboard from my hand, ripped off the petition, crumpled it into a ball, and threw it on the floor. Students stopped, their spatulas suspended in mid-air; globs of buttercream dropped onto the floor as they watched her, their mouths open.

"That's what I think of Marc's petition. If he asks you where it is, send him to me."

Her indignation as potent as her sensuality had been not thirty minutes earlier, she was never so beautiful as she was at that moment. The next time I saw her she'd be covered in gigantic red welts and gasping her last breath.

Chapter Eight

Despite all intentions to hit the road, I spent more than an hour and a half leafing through cookbooks and magazines comparing ten different recipes on how to make the authentic Sacher torte, something only a true foodie can understand.

When I looked at my watch it was almost four thirty. Cars would be packed on that bridge like sardines. Having blown my window of opportunity, I decided to have something to eat on the school's dime. The students would just be sitting down to their evening meal, two hours before the onslaught of buffet addicts.

I loved Fridays; it was buffet day. Which might seem like a paradox because I hated the buffet. But unlike Monday through Wednesday, when the students cooked for the school's restaurant (which had a menu just like a traditional dining room), and Thursday (when everyone was gearing up for the buffet), on Fridays the students were free to experiment and make what they wanted for the student lunch. More often than not they'd make something ethnic: curries with nan, mole with handmade tortillas. My lips twitched in anticipation.

The dining room was filled with the happy sounds of students and chefs gossiping and eating. The scene brought back memories of when I was a student. I lived on bad coffee, gossip, and the hype you get from people savoring something you've cooked. Talk about instant gratification/depression. I'd peeked through the glass to see if diners liked the desserts I'd made; a frown and a pushed away plate sent me scurrying back to the kitchen to do it again, a smile of pleasure filled me with a high that lasted all night. I'd go home to Jim and regale him with my culinary triumphs. The aroma of baking bread permeated my hair, driving him crazy with desire. He'd rip off my jacket and we'd make love in the hallway of our cramped apartment, the yeasty smells of bread and sex the ultimate aphrodisiac.

Crossing the dining room, I noticed that Antonello, who was seated next to Allison, had stayed late as well and was speaking to Benson. If the hand-gestures and table pounding were any indication, Antonello was furious; Benson's attention was focused entirely on his plate.

I stifled the jealousy I felt percolating as I saw Allison and Antonello sitting side by side. Although Antonello and I had done some pretty hot and heavy flirting, we both knew it'd go no farther than innuendo. It was petty on my part to resent his relationship with Allison, more like she got the bigger piece of cake that I really didn't want until she got it; it was fifth grade sort of behavior that should be beyond me. Well, maybe not beyond, but at thirty-five you should be mature enough to relegate it to the mental trash bin.

Recalling those hot and heavy scenes with Jim had sent my libido up to broil. I contemplated different locations in the school suitable for a nice after lunch romp. My imagination went hog wild wondering where Allison and Antonello could commit sexual acts without detection in such a public place. Obviously, their sexual acrobatics had taken place at school, but where? The garage was pretty dark, but Antonello drove a Lancia sports car so small that wouldn't accommodate two mating cats, never mind Allison's voluptuous curves. Her car? Again, no way, she drove one of those smallish Japanese imports. A deserted classroom, perhaps?

These licentious thoughts carried me all the way across the dining room when I realized I still had Allison's keys in my pocket. Scooping them up in my hand, I turned toward where she was sitting. I knew the symptoms right away. Even from fifteen feet away I could see angry red welts popping out on her face and hands. My throat constricted in complete terror. I squeaked out a scream, but no one heard me over the chatter.

Shellfish. Why in the hell had she eaten shellfish? She knew she was allergic.

Allison, her nails digging into the tablecloth, her lips a black blue, was in full-blown anaphylactic shock. The panic in her eyes haunted my dreams for months. Her chest heaved in staccato humps in a desperate bid for air. With a shudder she slumped unconscious against Antonello.

I ran into the pastry kitchen to search her purse for an epi pen, found it, raced back to the dining room, and jabbed her with it. It was too late.

To this day I remember Allison's death in choppy, short, black and white segments, like five-second cuts from a film: Antonello ripping off her chef's jacket to administer CPR; Benson hovering over her and screaming, "Oh my God," his hands fluttering in a spastic twitch; Étienne running to the first aid kit cabinet, gauze and bandages spilling onto the floor as he frantically searched for Benedryl; the horrible silence of dining room as we realized she was dying; and the absolute worst, Antonello ordering Allison to breathe and trying to pour Benedryl down her throat, the pink liquid dribbling out the corners of her slack mouth; her limbs lay splayed in haphazard abandon against the gaudy floral dining room carpet.

After the paramedics had strapped Allison to a gurney and wheeled her away, Curt posted himself at the front door. Like the theater, the show must go on. He lied to patrons that we'd suffered a burst water main and that their reservations would be honored next Friday.

After the ambulance left, everyone was at a loss as to what to do next. Students milled around in disparate groups drinking coffee and smoking cigarettes. Benson sat alone in a corner of the dining room and stared into space, slowly emptying a magnum of wine, a coffee cup at a time. When anyone would get within three feet of the table he'd growl, "Go away." The chefs parked themselves at another table in the dining room far away from the scene of Allison's death, never again to claim that part of the dining room as their turf. Finally after Antonello whispered in his ear, Étienne, the most senior chef, ordered the chefs and the students to put the food away and clean up the kitchens; then we could all go home.

I took one look at the hollow, red-rimmed eyes of Allison's students and dismissed them. On autopilot, I cleaned up the pastry kitchen myself. I found some comfort in putting things away. It was silly, but although I couldn't save her life, I'd make Allison's kitchen clean.

Antonello came to check up on me around nine o'clock. Like tending to a child, he wiped my cheeks free of tears. I hadn't even known I was crying.

"What's this with your pocket?"

My right pants pocket was bloody.

"Oh the keys," I muttered. I held up my hand; I had one long cut along all four fingers. When I saw Allison choking to death, I'd squeezed her keys so hard that I cut my fingers on the edges of the saw teeth. He led me over to the first aid cabinet.

"That needs to be cleaned. Cara, you shouldn't carry your keys like that, you'll put a hole in your pants," he fussed, more to say something than anything else. As if either of us gave a good goddamn about the pants.

"They're not…" I started to say that they weren't mine, they were Allison's, but I couldn't finish the sentence. Looking into his face, I realized that time hadn't passed him by at all. I'd been fooled by his quick step and his general joie de vivre. The skin around his eyes was parchment paper-thin with that hint of gray that circles the eyes of older Italian men. And watching him apply bacterial ointment to my cuts, I saw the gnarled hands of the older chef, the knuckles puffy, the skin folded on itself with thousands of microscopic wrinkles from washing your hands and handling too much acidic food. Just what my hands would look like in ten years.

He finished bandaging me up, put the first aid kit into the cabinet, and turned back to me.

"You will be okay." It wasn't a question. "I tell Allison's parents." Whenever Antonello gets excited or upset, his English deteriorates. "I don't wan' that drunken Benson or the police doing it. You go home and get some sleep, eh?"

I nodded with more confidence than I felt. "Thanks for the first aid. Are you all right?" I hoped that sounded fairly ambiguous. If he didn't want to confide in me I understood. Maybe he was worried I'd feel betrayed, who knows? If he wanted to have an affair with Allison that was between him and his wife.

For the tiniest of seconds his shoulders slumped and his eyes scrunched as if in pain. Then he adjusted his hat and smoothed his apron.

"Cara, I call you, tomorrow. I must make my phone call." He hugged me and walked out of the kitchen, across the dining room, and in the direction of the office.

The specter of Allison's parents made me realize I needed to find her purse in the supply cabinet, return her keys, and then give it to Antonello to give to her parents. Unlike me, whose purse could easily hide a small child, Allison had a small leather backpack-cum-purse affair, just large enough for a coin purse, checkbook, pen, keys, a small vial of perfume. When I opened her purse, the scent of Chanel No. 5. wafted out.

I sprayed a little perfume on my wrist and inhaled it. Smell is the ultimate memory jogger for me. The smell of pine trees make me think of Christmas; the thick scent roast beef sizzling in an oven recalls Sunday night dinners at my mother's house. And the smell of that perfume unleashed a hundred memories of when Allison and I were students. The Christmas she and I won a citywide competition for the best gingerbread house. The spring we'd made a spun sugar replica of the Conservatory of Flowers for the mayor's charity ball. Good memories, memories to replace that horrific death in the dining room. We should have been better friends; there was so much we had in common.

I took one last whiff of my wrist and snapped her purse shut.

Crossing the dining room, I saw Dean Benson slumped over a table in a drunken stupor, his arms cradling his head. The magnum was empty. He was mumbling over and over something into his arms that sounded like "Mama."

When I reached the office I stopped. Antonello sat in the receptionist's chair; his body and arms hugged the top of the desk in an imitation of Benson. But through the glass door I heard deep, harsh sobbing.

I turned away and went down to the locker room and put her purse in my locker. I couldn't deal with Allison's funky lock right now. I'd give him the purse later.

I called my mother from my cell phone and spent the night at her house. There were too many people alone in their grief that night, and I didn't want to be one of them.

Chapter Nine

A morning spent drinking tea with my parents, Ed and Roz Grant, did a lot to blunt the shock and grief of Allison's death. My parents are retired and live on a cul-de-sac in Kensington, a tiny enclave squeezed between the Berkeley and El Cerrito hills that butts up against the flats of Albany. No one on the block is under seventy.

In contrast to my crisis-to-crisis life, their lives were enviably calm and orderly. My stepfather devotes his day to reading three newspapers and communicating with POW groups online. He was in the Royal Air Force in World War II and spent four years in a Japanese prison camp. His POW group is campaigning to get reparations from the Japanese and British government before they all die off.

Mom's passions are her family, gardening, swearing, her dog, and gambling, not necessarily in that order. Everyday she visits the local seedy liquor store to buy daily scratchers and bi-weekly lottery tickets. Just about the time the family starts quizzing her on exactly how much money she spends on the lottery, she wins a five hundred dollar jackpot that shuts us up for a while.

Their house is always clean and the tea's sharp and sweet. This morning a heavy, cold mist obscured the garden, only accentuating the sense of sanctuary I feel at their home. When I think about not having their kitchen as the ultimate refuge when I'm upset or just want to gossip, I start to hyperventilate and panic.

I repeated all the details of Allison's death before our tea had a chance to cool. Mom used to be an ER nurse and secretly relishes details about death: decapitations and dismemberments being personal favorites.

"She must have been a severe allergic reaction," my mother asserted, with an authoritative shake of her head. She wore her "nurse" face; chin firm, brown eyes sharp. Even her hair had authority. I used to pity the doctors she worked with. Mom never surrendered her opinions and knowledge honed over forty-five years of nursing to some mere doctor. "Was Allison allergic to shellfish, like me?"

"Yeah, super allergic. She even had an epi pen in her purse." I threw up my hands in frustration. "Everyone knew about it. The students were given a warning about it the first day of school. If it had shellfish in it, you had to warn her."

"I hope to God some poor student wasn't responsible. Poor girl. Remember what happened to me last summer? Maybe the same thing happened to her. Scared the shit out of me."

My stepfather lowered the *New York Times*, leaned his bald head forward, and wriggled his forehead in remonstration. "I warned you about that crab, Roz."

She stuck her tongue out at him.

Mom has been routinely avoiding crab for years after one particularly nasty reaction. Recently, however, she'd been nibbling little bits of crab here and there and nothing seemed to happen. Last summer we were at a family get-together at my aunt's house and ten minutes after downing a crab cake my mother sprouted hives nearly as virulent as Allison's were. Fortunately my cousin Sam is a doctor and injected some antihistamine in her right away. Sam surmised that the iodine in the shellfish accumulated in my mother's system until that last near-fatal bite turned the iodine level toxic.

"I know just how she must have felt. Her poor parents." Her voice was somber. She reached across the table to squeeze my hand, as if to reassure herself that I was indeed alive and not an apparition.

My chest tightened with tears remembering the panic on Allison's welt-poxed face as she fought for the tiniest bubble of air.

The ring of the telephone made me jump. I leapt out of my seat to grab it before the second ring.

"Grant residence." I said.

"I thought I'd find you at your mother's place. You okay?"

O'Connor. I turned my body away so that my parents wouldn't see me blushing. I glanced over at the oven to see if it was on; the kitchen felt awfully warm all of a sudden.

"Yeah, I'm fine. I didn't want to spend the night by myself. It was pretty ugly."

"You two were students together, weren't you? That must have been tough. I'm sorry."

As soft as marshmallow, O'Connor's voice held none of that businesslike, brusque tone he'd adopted since becoming a student.

"Thanks, O'Connor. Yeah, we went back a long way." I could hear my voice start to shake and squeak. I cleared my throat. "Sounds pretty quiet at your place. Where are Moira and the kids?"

"Stevie has a field hockey game this morning. Why were you at the school so late?"

Mom began mouthing "Hi" in the background. I rolled my eyes in acquiescence. She and O'Connor have a mutual admiration society going on.

"My mother says hello."

"Tell your mom hello and that I hope she's doing well."

"Mom, O'Connor says hello and hopes you're doing well," I repeated in a rush.

"How come you were there so late?" he repeated. "If there was more prep you should have told me. I could have stayed late and helped you."

The thought of O'Connor and me working in tandem, alone, not buffered by nine other students was a scary proposition. I undid the top two buttons of my nightgown.

"I was up in the library doing some research. I lost track of time and when I checked my watch it was four thirty. I thought

I'd eat dinner at the school, hoping the traffic would have died down by the time I'd eaten."

"Did you see anything unusual before Ms. Warner went into shock?"

He'd been doing a pretty good job until he slipped with that "Ms. Warner." The wonderful heat causing my wrists and underarms to sweat evaporated, leaving me chilly and cold.

"Is this a professional phone call?"

Silence.

I walked out of the room and into the bathroom so my parents wouldn't see my face or hear my voice. Despite all my grousing and complaining, the sick feeling in my stomach, disappointment the size of a casaba melon, made me realize I'd secretly been celebrating O'Connor's surprise appearance at the school. I whispered to myself that he was there for me. He faked a disability, put a second on his house, all so he could legitimately be with me, all in the name of true love.

Could I get any more pathetic?

Although my fingers dug so fiercely into the plastic of the phone that I broke two nails, I forced my voice to be calm.

"I thought you called to inquire about my welfare. It's merely the prelude to an interrogation, isn't it?"

More silence, then, "You're paranoid, Mary."

Bracing myself with one hand on the counter top, I refused to let it drop.

"Are you investigating Allison's death?" I demanded.

"No," he snapped back.

"Don't insult me, O'Connor. I was married to a cop for ten years, god-dammit. I know what a preliminary investigation sounds like. What's wrong with Allison's death?"

O'Connor heaved a sigh ripe with frustration.

"Get a life, Mary. Last fall's murder has you looking for bodies everywhere. This is not a murder investigation. You and I are not teaming up together and doing Nancy Drew again."

The snide reference to Nancy Drew was like putting a blow torch to a pot of oil. I sat down on the toilet and pressed the phone to my forehead. How was I going to make it through the next three weeks with this man in my classroom?

All of a sudden I heard the chatter of his kids and wife in the background. The game must have been called for weather.

"There were over fifty people in that dining room. You want the gory details of Allison Warner's death, start dialing. I'm going to hang up now. But before I do I want you to know, O'Connor, I'd rather stick both hands in a deep fat fryer than work on another case with you."

I punched the End button, cutting him off. I looked in the mirror.

Liar.

Not only a liar but a fool as well.

My feet dragged against the cold linoleum as I slunk into kitchen and put the phone back. I felt, rather than saw, four eyes begging an explanation of why I had had to secret myself in the bathroom with the phone.

Avoiding eye contact, I announced to the kitchen cabinets, "I need a hot bath." I shuffled back to the bathroom to scald clean my foolish desires. I filled the tub to the very top with blistering hot water and raked a soapy washcloth over my legs, arms, and back.

What in the hell was I thinking?

With every pass of the washcloth I forced myself to visualize Moira's face again and again. I reminded myself that she wasn't a non-entity that O'Connor could or would discard like an orange peel, but his wife, mother to his three children. Someone he's been married to for seventeen years. Someone whose house I know nearly as well as my own. Someone whose kids call me Aunt Mary. Someone who under no circumstances should be betrayed, even in fantasy.

The hot water and brutal scrubbing left my skin mottled and raw like a sausage, but my state of mind resolute and determined. I dressed slowly, each maneuver accompanied by a resolution. Pull on underwear—no more delusional fantasies about O'Connor and me reenacting the food scene from *Tom Jones*. Struggle into bra—fill the gaps in my own life, without the benefit of swarthy, sexy, married, Irish cops. Pull on jeans—do sit-ups, stomach looking flabby, can't compete against twenty-somethings on dating scene with squishy middle. Force turtleneck over head—join organizations to meet men, no cops and no chefs allowed. Pull on socks and boots—don't let biological clock propel you into situations that humiliate and debase you. Comb hair—sue Clairol for convincing you that Radiant Ruby was the hair color for you. Check hair in mirror—go back to therapist to find out why you have this thing about aging. Brush teeth—O'Connor had another reason for being at the school and it didn't involve you, so get over it.

Mid-stroke I stopped. The foam from the toothpaste dribbled down my chin.

If O'Connor wasn't a student because of my undeniable charms, why was he there? I dismissed out of hand Jim's hints that O'Connor was on medical leave. Nonsense. If O'Connor weren't conducting an undercover investigation of the school, I'd eat lima beans every night for a week. I loathe lima beans.

I finished brushing my teeth with so much vigor that my gums bled. The little angel of common sense whispered, "Don't snoop around, Mary. Last time it nearly got you killed." The devil of pride, appealing to my wounded vanity, sneered, "Oh yeah, who solved that case, you or O'Connor? Who was two steps ahead of the game the whole time?"

No contest who won that battle.

Gathering up my nightclothes and toiletries into a ball, I crushed them into my overnight bag. It was time to get moving, time to find out what was so damn interesting about École d'Epicure that O'Connor would go undercover.

Chapter Ten

Two minutes after I'd wiped the toothpaste from my chin, I was out the door and driving to San Francisco.

With my eyes focused only on body parts below the neck, I kissed my parents goodbye, thanked them profusely for their hospitality, and exited the kitchen with some asinine excuse about buying bananas.

I didn't need bananas. What I really needed to do was to hunt through Allison's purse and locker for clues.

Which were at École.

Heading up the Bay Bridge incline to Yerba Buena Island, I turned on my windshield wipers. It was after eleven, but the fog still hadn't lifted. Some days it doesn't. Like a tired dowager settling her gray skirts, it sits over the region all day and doesn't budge. Landmarks had disappeared, swallowed up by the misty curtain, and visibility was about twenty feet. Whenever I drive in that kind of fog, I get a tickle on the back of my neck warning me I might be entering the Twilight Zone.

The deck of the Bay Bridge was slippery. Cars hugged their lanes and crawled along at about forty miles an hour. With headlights on and wipers in lazy mode, people were driving as if their trunks held cartons of eggs. Seasoned Bay Area drivers never use their high beams in that sort of fog. If you do you're pegged as a tourist or an asshole.

The fog suited my purpose. I wanted to be invisible. The ex-wife of a cop couldn't claim ignorance about basic law. What

I was planning was illegal, and I knew it. Technically, I could be charged with aiding and abetting if an actual crime had been committed. I had every right to be at École; but rummaging through a dead woman's locker and handbag was another matter.

I prepared my alibi. If I ran into anyone, I'd say I was collecting Allison's things for Antonello so that he could give them to her parents. Which was absolutely true; the part about searching her purse and locker *before* I handed it over to Antonello the rather illegal part. I wasn't particularly worried. I doubted I'd see a soul. The school was closed on weekends except for private events, and traditionally January was a slow month. Holiday burn out. Things didn't pick-up until February. Besides, who'd want to return to the school so soon after Allison's death?

Unless you were like me.

Obsessed, driven, and pissed off.

As I anticipated, my car was the only one in the underground garage. I did have a fleeting moment of common sense. Suppose there was something fishy about Allison's death. The killer might have the same idea about looking for incriminating evidence. How wise would it be to return to the crime scene? No one would hear my screams for help.

Nonsense. O'Connor was right; I was manufacturing dead bodies out of thin air. First of all, it was highly unlikely that Allison's death was anything other than anaphylactic shock. I'd seen those symptoms too often in my mother to think it was anything else. Second, there wasn't a hint, a soupçon of evidence that O'Connor was there for any other reason than attending classes. Two hours ago I was dead certain he was surreptitiously interrogating me about Allison's death. Now I wasn't so sure. Maybe he was legitimately attending the program. And if he hadn't called to see how I was doing after Allison's death, I'd have labeled him a complete cretin. Plus, if I was going to be completely honest, I seemed to be the only one trying to shake off covert sexual longings. All I got from him was either attitude or a blank stare big enough to lose myself in.

By the time I had reached École, I'd almost convinced myself this was a wild goose chase. I'd collect all of Allison's belongings and drop them off at Antonello's place in North Beach.

But not until I had searched through everything.

I used my elevator key to reach the basement. The elevator doors opened to absolute pitch black. Damn, this hallway had always been lit when I'd been here before. The storeroom where the dry goods were kept was on the left and down a few feet, on the right, was the door to the locker room. That Twilight Zone twitch at the back of my neck came back. Nothing, nothing was going to make me negotiate that total dark.

Memo to self: if you are going to pretend to be Nancy Drew, have the goddamn sense to carry a flashlight with you.

My hand fumbled along the wall for a light switch. A flash of bright light blinded me for a second. I squealed in fright, then relief. A motion sensor had flipped on the fluorescent light overhead. Of course, the light would be on a sensor. When did a bunch of twenty-year olds remember to turn off lights? Not until they started paying electricity bills.

It felt about thirty degrees down here. I shivered and zipped my down vest up to the limit.

When I opened the door to the locker room another flash of light greeted me. A second motion sensor. This settled my internal debate whether to be as blatant as possible about my presence or to skulk around. With lights announcing my every movement, I'd better look like I had a good reason for being here.

The locker room was tiny, roughly twenty by ten feet. One bank of lockers was propped up against the north and south wall, and one bank of lockers and a long wooden bench bisected the room. The entrance to the bathroom was at the far side of the room.

When I stepped into the room the stench of sewage was overwhelming. I walked across the room and peeked into the bathroom. Christ, the toilets had overflowed again. That was twice in one week. By Monday afternoon the janitor would have pasted crudely lettered signs up on the wall berating us for flushing feminine hygiene products down the toilets. I guess it was easier to write signs than replace the ancient plumbing.

My locker was located in the middle bank of lockers, Allison's in the far south corner against the wall. Cuffing my nose against my sleeve, I opened my locker, found Allison's purse, and grabbed her Chanel No. 5. I spun around, spraying a two-foot arc of protection against the smell so that I could check out Allison's wallet without gagging.

I'd gone through the contents of Allison's purse the day before in the pastry kitchen: the only thing I hadn't searched was her wallet. I sat down on the bench and laid out its contents. Her wallet was as neutral as her purse. Bills were carefully arranged according to denomination, the heads of the presidents all in the same direction. There were no credit card or ATM receipts bulging out from the billfold like in my wallet. Her only items of identification were one credit card, a gas card, and a driver's license.

This neatness spoke of a need for order so compelling that life's everyday clutter had been ruthlessly erased as it happened. No checkbook even. Strange. And not a single clue, unless one was searching for an insight into Allison's rigid nature.

No wonder she'd blown up at Marc's petition. Her orderly, little world was about to be rocked. For someone obsessed with being in control of the smallest minutiae of her life, the events of the past few months must have been unbearable. It certainly explains why, in spite of her phenomenal creativity, she'd never left the comfortable fold of École for the crazy, rollicking world that food had become in the last ten years.

For a few seconds I felt smug about the clutter that seemed to accumulate around me. I'll shove one bank slip in my wallet and overnight ten more will have sprung up. With money—completely hopeless. If I ever get desperate before paychecks, I can always find a few fives and ones hidden in every coat and sweater pocket I own. And you'd better believe that they aren't in any sort of order in my wallet, denomination or direction-wise. I'd always considered this sloppiness a deep character flaw. But despite the best intentions, I never seemed to get a handle on it. Looking at Allison's wallet made me feel almost saintly by comparison.

Then I tried to envision what my life would look like if someone decided to search my purse. They'd think I was a disorganized mess of a woman who wrote far too many checks under $5.00 and seemed to buy an inordinate number of shoes. All these things were true, of course, but it was such a small, mean picture.

Come on, Allison. You are so much more than the sum of this wallet. Help me out, I implored her mentally. I studied her driver's license picture, as if that would give me divine inspiration. She had listed her weight at one hundred and ten pounds—at least fifty pounds off the mark.

If I hadn't have been staring at her license so intently I'd have missed it. The tiny point of a business card peeked out from behind her license. I pried the license out from under its plastic cover. Beneath it was a business card from a jeweler in North Beach. I turned the card over. Written in Allison's ornate script was a time and date: January 12th, 10:30 a.m.

This Tuesday. The phone call reminding her that her ring would be ready.

Okay, this was something to work with.

I scrounged around in the bottom of my own purse, found my wallet, and hid the business card under my own license for safekeeping. Then I put everything back into her purse and stuffed it into the enormous black sack that I use as a handbag. With such a pristine wallet, I'd no hope that her locker would yield any clues. I rounded the end of locker bank to the corner where Allison's locker was located and stopped short. I didn't move a muscle.

Her locker door hung open wearily on one hinge. The locker was empty.

The door and the frame had been pried open until the lock had snapped. Despite the cold, I began to sweat. Up to that point I realized I'd been playing a game, trying to prove to O'Connor how smart and sassy I was. I hadn't really believed that Allison had been killed. It was a necessary by-product of my fantasy. Like reading a mystery novel, none of it was real.

Until I saw the locker.

Whoever had trashed that locker it wasn't the police. Someone needed something in that locker. Someone so desperate he beat it open with a crowbar, not caring who saw his handiwork. At the very least something had been terribly wrong in Allison's life. At the worst, she'd been murdered because of it. I don't know how long I stood there trying to accept the real possibility of Allison's murder as it beat like a tom-tom into my brain.

The light went out.

Terror stuck my feet to the cold cement floor. I was too afraid to even blink. Then my brain started to thaw and began screaming at me, "Move, idiot, and the light will go back on."

Before I could move, I heard the lock turn.

The door opened.

The light came back on.

Chapter Eleven

I slipped into the bathroom and lodged myself behind the door, cell phone in hand poised to dial 911. With my free hand I pulled the band of my turtleneck over my mouth and over the bridge of my nose as a makeshift mask so that I wouldn't suffocate from the noxious fumes emanating from the floor. It didn't help.

"Yuck, it stinks in here. The toilets are clogged again."

"I'll be two minutes. Tops."

It was Marc and Shelley. What was Marc doing in the ladies' locker room? And two minutes for what? From the snotty tone of their voices, they were gearing up for a fight.

"You still haven't explained to me what we're doing here," Shelley complained. "After what happened yesterday I'd just as soon never come back here again."

Silence.

"Marc, why are we here? You promised you'd take me to brunch and all of a sudden you pull into École's parking lot."

There was a pause and then Marc said, "I need to check out Allison's locker."

I heard the sharp intake of breath.

"Marc, the woman is dead and you want to rifle through her stuff? What in the hell is going on?" Shelley was clearly outraged. Our brief encounters hadn't exactly endeared her to me, but her sense of propriety in this instance was right on the money. How dare Marc violate Allison's privacy.

That was my job.

Marc's voice was sullen, the southern drawl more pronounced. "It's got nothin' to do with us. Just somethin' I need to take care of before I quit."

God, it was cold. I clenched my jaw tight to stop my teeth from chattering. I was so aware of their presence, every high and low of their voices. If they discovered me, how was I going to explain myself? Think, Mary. Why would you be hiding behind the door of the bathroom, cell phone clutched to your chest, your hightops mired in two-inch deep sewage.

"You promised me you'd quit *last* semester. Fuck it, Marc. I'm giving my notice on Monday. I'll stay until the end of the semester and that's it. Wolfgang's opening a new restaurant in Paris this spring. I told him last Monday I'd take the job."

Three beats and then Marc asked, "And when were you goin' to tell me?"

"I didn't think you'd care," she countered.

"Of course I care," he sputtered.

"Then come with me." Shelley had thrown down the gauntlet.

Silence.

"Marc, are you coming with me or are you staying here at this total dead-end? This place can't even keep its sewer lines clear."

Still no answer.

"Marc, I want an answer. Now," she demanded.

It amazed me that someone who was only sixty inches tall could have such a big voice.

"I don't know." I could hear the desperation in his voice. "I'd like to, but I got something going on here. It's got nothing to do with us. You know I love you."

Shelley's voice boomed throughout the locker room. "You promised me this was a two-semester gig. We've been here four semesters. And that petition to get Étienne fired—what do you care if that French fart works here or not when you're leaving? Next, you want to search through a dead woman's locker. What is going on here?"

I cringed listening to this. Shelley's cranky, take-no-prisoners tone was a little too familiar. Jim and I'd had variations of this fight numerous times. It wasn't selfishness so much as my unwillingness to be second best—at anything. I'd never wanted my career to be *more* important than my husband's. I only wanted it to be *as* important. A job opportunity would pop up that was stimulating, with more prestige, more money, and lots more hours. I always took it, thinking that somehow we'd make it work.

We didn't.

After Jim walked out on me I spent the next six months blaming myself for being so driven. A year of therapy—perhaps I should slip Dr. Robinson's business card in Shelley's locker—made me realize that Jim needed a wife whose main focus of attention was him. Unfortunately, that wasn't me. We both felt cheated. Me, because I was constantly justifying my need to excel at what I did best, and him because he always felt like he came in a distant second.

"Come with me," Shelley cooed. "Just think, Marc. Paris in April. We'd have such fun."

She said "fun" in a husky, deep tone that promised satin sheets, red lingerie, and whipped cream in strategic places.

Next, I heard the unzipping of a zipper and the rustle of clothing. This couldn't get any worse. Please, oh please control yourselves, I begged silently.

Shelley continued her siren song. "With a last name like Lapin you must have French blood in you somewhere. We could drink Beaujolais Nouveau the minute it's released." More rustling and another zipper was freed from its teeth.

There was a pause in the action, then Marc barked, "Stop it, Shell."

"Oh, come on," she teased. "Let's pway. Just the way you wike it."

The Elmer Fudd voice put me over the edge. I slipped the cell phone into my pocket. I couldn't listen to their verbal foreplay for one more second. Just as I was about to stick my fingers in my ears, the sharp tone in Marc's voice stopped me.

"I said stop it," he bellowed.

Then I heard a loud bang, as if someone had pounded an angry fist into the side of the lockers. There was more frantic rustling and zippers being rezipped. Someone wasn't in the mood.

"I get the message, Marc." Shelley's voice was sulky.

"I can't. Not here." Then he tried to woo her with food. Always works for me. "Let's have brunch like I promised and then go back home. Then you can tell me about Puck's new place and we can pway. Okay?"

I heard leather squeaking, like he was rubbing the back of her coat.

"Yeah," she agreed, mollified by the back rub and the promise of chow. "How about Anjou? We can eat and pretend we're already in Paris."

"Great, but first I need to check out that locker."

"This is illegal, Marc, and I want no part of it. I'll wait for you outside."

Shelley might not have a problem with sexual high jinks in public places complete with cartoon voices, but apparently she drew the line at breaking and entering.

Marc didn't wait for an answer. I heard his shoes squeaking against the cement floor and then stop.

"Shell?" His voice displayed all the disbelief that I'd felt seeing Allison's locker.

"Marc, I'm not being a party to any of this."

"Come *here*."

"What is the hell is the matter with you…."

They stood in silence for a few seconds.

"Marc?"

"I swear I had nothing to do with this. You've got to believe me."

"You're going to explain everything to me. No stalling this time. I want…Wait a minute. Don't you smell it?"

Shelley's voice was an octave above her normal contralto.

"It's Allison's perfume!" she shrieked. "It's that Chanel crap she was always squirting on herself."

"Calm down, Shelley," Marc said. "You're imagining it. I don't smell...."

Then I heard little sniffling sounds.

"We're out of here," he yelled.

The sharp tap-tap-tap of her boots was followed by the muffled thuds of Marc's sneakers.

I'd waited another ten minutes to make sure they'd left and then walk out after them. Using the tweezers from my Swiss Army knife, I untied my shoes. Getting my socks off with the tweezers was trickier but I finally managed. I dropped everything in the first garbage can I could find. First I'd go home to get some new socks and shoes, then I'd go to Allison's apartment. My bare feet made no noise as I negotiated my way back to the garage. Lights greeted me as I rounded every corner.

I was alone.

Chapter Twelve

As I drove back across the Bay Bridge, the specter of Allison's locker kept reappearing again and again in my mind. Such undisguised fury or desperation is the stuff murder is made of.

After last fall's murders I didn't take anything for granted anymore. O'Connor's sneer about me seeing bodies behind every tree wasn't so far off the mark. When you're a casualty of evil, it opens a door that can never be shut. It's the adult version of realizing there's no Santa Claus.

A co-worker I had trusted, a person I actually liked, killed two people—over money. The first victim's face was bashed-in so violently with the flat side of a frying pan that I wouldn't have recognized him if it weren't for his unusual buzz cut. For the coup de grace, they wrapped a kitchen apron around his neck and pulled the strings tight until he died. The second victim was shot execution style in my bedroom, his brains splattered all over a quilt that Jim and I had bought ten years ago as a wedding present to each other.

Number three on the killer's list, I'd been so close to death that razor sharp images of everyone I'd ever loved seared my brain in a desperate attempt to carry them with me into eternity. Every nerve I possessed focused on the barrel of that gun poised to rip a fatal hole in my body. The millisecond before I was nearly shot, a primal scream of fear roared from my soul in outrage at my own mortality.

Allison had been my friend.

I couldn't bear the thought that she, too, had screamed that final cry of frustration and fear. I prayed she wasn't the victim of someone who, as she fought for every molecule of air in that room, held his breath hoping she would die.

My killer hadn't succeeded.

Hers wasn't going to either. If she had been murdered, I was going to find out who and why.

When I reached my house in Albany, the first thing I did was scrub my feet and ankles in anti-bacterial soap. Then I changed into gray sweats to blend into the fog-drenched landscape. I'd bought them last year in the hope new clothes would motivate me to go the gym for some much needed exercise.

Another fantasy bites the dust.

Pulling the strings of the hood tightly around my face so no trace of Radiant Ruby stuck out from beneath the edges, I zigzagged through the flats of Albany—the suburban solution to urban living—to Hopkins, up Hopkins to Berryman, down Berryman where it turns into Shattuck, past the Gourmet Ghetto, and up Virginia to Allison's apartment. I was a little surprised that with her meticulous sense of order she'd chosen to live in Berkeley. Not only had we ended up in career paths more suited to the other's talents, Allison would have heartily approved of the manicured and homogeneous character of my Albany neighborhood, while I felt more at home with the wacky, envelope-pushing, eclectic nature of Berkeley culture.

Gradually the neat houses with trikes parked on the front porches and playsets dominating the backyards were replaced by the older, bigger homes in Berkeley, which in turn gave way to the hodge-podge of housing that characterized the north side of campus.

Northside is student country. Over thirty-thousand of them. With little official university housing, the scramble for even a large closet into which to throw a futon is fierce. Berkeley is a perennial hostage to the housing crisis. Northside, in particular, has lost much of its original charm. Tacky apartment buildings are crammed among older homes that have been chopped up into awkwardly shaped flats. Most places need paint jobs, the yards weeding. Old maple trees line the streets, hinting at an earlier time when stately houses sat in every lot, not yet balkanized in the frenzied need for student housing. Every now and then a home sits back on a well-tended lawn with only one mailbox and a fairly new Volvo in the driveway, and you wonder how in the hell it escaped.

Even if I hadn't memorized Allison's address, I wouldn't have had any trouble finding her building. An older, newly painted four-plex, it was the only building on the block without leaves littering the front porch. Yellow and blue primroses lined the path up to the front door. Allison had clearly found a landlord whose passion for order complimented her own.

On the drive over I'd decided I'd march up to the front door and act like I belonged there. If anyone challenged me, I'd say Allison's parents had asked me to drop her purse off at her apartment. It was shocking at how easily I was manufacturing lies out of thin air.

Must be that Catholic school training.

My usual ineptness with keys was my undoing. Instead of blithely turning the key in the lock and slipping unnoticed into Allison's apartment, I stood there swearing under my breath for several minutes, turning and jiggling the key every which way except the right way.

The apartment door to the right of me opened. A woman not a day under eighty stood in the entryway, a broom in one hand and a dustpan in the other. Little patches of pink scalp peeked through the rigid, tight pin curls of her home permanent. She wore a shapeless housecoat with buttons down the front that women of her generation wore when they "cleaned house." My grandmother had owned about twenty of them.

"Can I help you?" she asked politely.

I thought I could bluff my way out of this until I met her eyes, sharp and intelligent behind the quarter-inch-thick lenses of her glasses. The lies I'd rehearsed died on my lips. As erect and straight as the broomstick in her hand, her body language had a firmness to it that suggested she belonged there and I didn't, and I better have a good explanation why I was on her front porch.

The same degree of guilt and dread I'd felt when the nuns had caught me sneaking a smoke in a secluded section of the high-school rose garden washed over me.

"I, uh…" While I fumbled for words, the keys slipped out of my sweaty hands and fell on the concrete with a tinny splat. After I'd bent over to pick them up, I smiled in a futile gesture of respect, as if this would expiate my sin.

Like the nuns, she wasn't placated.

"Young lady, what are you're doing at Miss Warner's front door with her keys?" she demanded, glaring at my hand clutching Allison's keyring.

She may have been old, but she sure was feisty.

"I'm sorry, Mrs…?" I began.

"Horne. Bridie Horne," she snapped. "I'm the owner of this building, so don't try to pull any funny stuff."

"Mrs. Horne," I mumbled, half expecting the ghost of twenty-year-old cigarette smoke to waft up between us. "I'm returning Allison's purse."

I held up the purse as evidence.

She was not mollified.

"And why are you returning Miss Warner's purse? Doesn't she need it?"

She didn't know.

I guess Allison's parents were too grief-stricken; they hadn't called her landlady.

"I'm so sorry, Mrs. Horne. I thought you knew. Allison had an…accident at work. I teach at École, too."

A patchwork of worry lines creased her forehead. "Is she all right?" Her voice had lost all its spunk. She sounded every bit of her eighty-plus years and more.

My eyes smarted with tears remembering Allison's last horrible moments. I shook my head no. Her blue eyes, distorted by the thick lenses of her glasses, also filled with tears. The broom and dustbin fell to the floor with an awful clatter. Looking like she was about to collapse. I stepped forward and cupped a hand under her elbow to make sure she didn't fall.

Looping Allison's purse over my left shoulder, I put my right arm around her and led into her apartment. I immediately felt a sense of déjà vu. This apartment was a near replica of my grandmother's flat. A piano hugged one wall, covered with school photos of grandchildren. All the furniture had elaborately carved legs, polished to a shine. The aroma of Lemon Pledge hung in the air. Spying two chairs parked at an angle in front of the fireplace, I steered her toward a high-back Queen Anne and gently pushed her into it. I placed Allison's purse on the floor next to her chair.

"Now you stay there," I ordered. "I'll make you a cup of tea."

She started to protest and then stopped. Pulling an ironed handkerchief from her pocket, she began dabbing her eyes with one hand and waving me in the direction of the kitchen with the other.

I picked up the broom and dustpan, closed her front door, carried them into the kitchen, and put them back into the broom closet. Once I was in the kitchen, Mrs. Horne began barking orders to me from the living room in between loud honks into her handkerchief.

"Tea's in the cupboard to the right of the sink. The Irish Breakfast. You'll find a teapot on the shelf above the kitchen table. Don't use the Blue Willow one; the brown one makes better tea. I like my tea plain, but most people don't. A creamer and sugar bowl are in the cupboard to the left of the sink, second shelf. You'll find a tray in the cupboard above the fridge."

Like most strong-minded people—code for obnoxious, take-charge types—you know when you've met your match. In five minutes I'd loaded up the tray with a teapot, creamer and sugar bowl, two teacups with saucers, and a plate of cookies. I placed the tray on the coffee table in front of the fireplace and sat in the well-worn, brown leather club chair opposite hers.

"Give it a minute. I like my tea strong. Something tells me you do, too. Now what's your name? No shilly-shallying." Her eyes were red from crying, but the spunk had returned full force.

"Mary Ryan. Allison and I were old friends. We went to school together at École."

"Ryan, eh?" She sniffed that little snort of approval when the Irish officially acknowledge each other. "Nice Irish name. My maiden name was O'Sullivan." I wouldn't say she beamed at me, but her face lost its look of mistrust. She pushed her glasses up the bridge of her nose and peered at me to get a better look. "Allison's talked about you. You're the competitive one, right? She told me you were coming back to teach. Made her nervous. She didn't say so, but I got the impression that she was afraid you'd steal her thunder. You can pour that now," she ordered, pointing at the teapot.

"I'm not *that* competitive," I complained, as I poured the tea. "We had some good times when we were students. I was looking forward to working with her."

"Oh, she liked you well enough. Just thought you were pushy."

What could I say?

"How did she die?"

"The paramedics said it was a fatal allergic reaction." I tried to blank out the image of Allison's face pocked with welts.

"She was very allergic to crab, shrimp, anything like that."

"Yeah, I remember that from when we were students. She must have eaten something with shellfish in it."

Or someone knowing her sensitivity to shellfish slipped some into her food.

"She was good people." Mrs. Horne's hand shook a little as she placed her teacup back onto its saucer. "Don't know what I would've done without her when Frank died a couple of years ago. The kids wanted me to move in with them. I got two daughters; one in Tucson, one in Dallas. I told my girls, 'Thanks but no thanks.' Too hot. Plus I like my independence. I've got my church, my quilting group; I didn't want to start all over again in a new city. Allison was a peach. Got me through the really bad patch. We would have been married sixty-two years next month."

"This must have been Frank's chair." I patted the arm and shifted in my seat. Over the years the chair had molded itself to Frank's body, and judging by the lump hitting the small of my back, Frank wasn't very tall.

"Almost threw it away when he died. Couldn't bear to see it empty." She gazed out the window for a moment as if to collect herself, then her eyes returned to me. "Allison persuaded me to keep it, that one day I wouldn't mind. She was right. Now I set my quilting frame in front of his chair and pretend he's sitting there. Tell him about my day. Neighbors probably think I'm nuts. Any hoo, I'd better call her parents. Give them my condolences. Nice girl. I'm real sorry. Can just imagine how I'd feel if something happened to one of my girls. I don't know if I have the heart to finish her quilt." Mrs. Horne sighed and looked at a quilting frame nestled against the wall to my right behind Frank's chair.

Stretched tight across the quilting frame was a nearly finished Wedding Ring quilt. The quilting was even and fine, the kind of expertise with a needle that takes a lifetime to develop.

"You're quite a quilter, Mrs. Horne. It's beautiful."

"Well, it was appropriate at the time. Don't know any other young women getting married though."

Thank goodness I'd just put down my teacup.

"Getting m…m…married? Allison was getting married?" I stammered.

"Sure. Her fiancé had hemmed and hawed for months. Thursday night she told me they'd finally set a date. Have never seen her so happy." She shook her head.

Thursday night. And Friday afternoon she waltzes into the school kitchen looking like the cat that ate the canary.

"You look surprised, Mary."

Nothing got by this lady.

"I didn't know she was engaged. Didn't even know she had a boyfriend to be honest," I said slowly. "Did you ever meet her fiancé?"

"Nope," she said. "Come to think of it, she never even mentioned him by name. Just said that they'd finally come to terms."

"To terms?" I repeated. That sounded like Nations Bank taking over Bank of America. Not very romantic

"Those were her very words. Sounds odd, I admit. I assumed her fiancé was that good-looking Italian-looking guy who came over sometimes. The chef at your school. You must know him. Looks like Dean Martin in his younger days."

"Chef de Luca? He's married," I protested.

Her lips pursed in disapproval. "Doesn't seem to bother people these days, does it? I don't truck with that sort of thing. I thought Allison had more sense."

Me too.

"I appreciate you sitting with me." She patted my hand. "I'm okay now. Leave Allison's purse there on the floor. I'll tell her folks it's here."

"Thanks, Mrs. Horne." I guess searching Allison's apartment wasn't going to happen.

She hoisted herself out of her chair with a little difficulty.

"Call me Bridie. Don't get old," she advised. "It's hell."

I leaned over to pick up the tray.

"Nope, leave it. I'm going to have another cup of tea with a couple of inches of whiskey in it."

I pulled a business card out of my purse, scribbled my home phone number on the back of it, and placed it next to the teapot.

"Call me if you need me, Bridie."

"Will do." She grabbed my arm. "Should have never have stopped moving. This damn hip of mine is acting up." Leaning heavily on me, she led me to the front door. "No wedding ring. How come?"

I'd thought I was past the age of blushing, but apparently not. "I'm divorced. My husband couldn't handle having such a pushy wife." I tried to sound jocular, but it came out bitter.

She folded her arms across her chest and gave me a long, hard look. "Some men are weak. They need a weak woman to make them feel strong. I'm a pretty good judge of character."

She pointed a finger in my direction. "You, missy, need someone who'll give it right back to you. Otherwise you won't respect him. Did you respect your husband?"

I'd never thought about Jim in those terms. I had loved him, but had I respected him? I shook my head.

"I was lucky. Found a man who wasn't afraid of my intelligence and spunk. Said I kept him young." She glanced over at a photo on the piano. It must have been taken shortly before Frank died. Bridie was staring straight into the camera, as if daring it to expose every wrinkle and flaw. He was looking at her, an amused smile on his face. "You need someone like my Frank. When you find him, you'll know. And don't let go. They're as rare as hen's teeth. On second thought, would you mind taking Allison's purse up to her place? Every time I see it'll remind of her death. I don't need those types of reminders at my age. I'll tell her folks it's there. She's above me on the second floor. My hip gives me trouble when it's damp like this."

I coughed to hide my glee. "I'd be happy to." I walked back across the room, scooped up Allison's purse from the floor with eager fingers, and returned to the front door.

"Lock up when you're done and put the keys in Allison's mailbox. I'll get them later. Remember what I said about finding the right man. He's out there." With a gentle pat on my cheek, she shut the door behind me.

Damn you, O'Connor.

Chapter Thirteen

I hated deceiving the old lady, but if I was going to conduct a decent search I had no choice. Unlocking Alison's door, I bounded up the stairs, counted to ten, and then bounded down the stairs, stomping forcefully on every riser. Slamming Allison's door shut so Bridie would think I'd left, I untied my shoes, stuffed them under my armpit, and crept back up the stairs in my stocking feet. With Allison living directly above Bridie, I couldn't make a sound.

When I rounded the corner to enter her living room I blinked several times, my eyes on sensory overload. It was like walking into a spread in *Apartment Beautiful*, the feature article being "Chintzpah—Go for It." All her furniture, upholstered in fabric emblazoned with large yellow and pink flowers, was oversized, with plump rolled arms supporting gigantic pillows in the same busy fabric. At five-nine I'm rarely overwhelmed in physical settings, but the combination of the large floral design and the sheer size of these pieces crammed into a relatively small space made me feel like Alice in Chintzland after she ate the wrong side of the cookie. If I'd been the slightest bit claustrophobic, I'd have had a panic attack on the spot. Naturally, it was spotless.

Where to start? No checkbook in her purse or locker; hunt for the checkbook. Look for clues to the identity of the commitment-phobic boyfriend. Allison being such a neatnik limited the potential for clue finding, but I had to start somewhere. I doubt whether I'd find any miscellany giving insight into Allison's past. (I cringed, thinking of last year's Christmas cards still on propped up on my mantle). But I might find something about her present and what she thought might be her future.

Fortunately, the blinds were drawn so I didn't have to skulk around under the windowsills. The only piece of furniture that didn't match was a plain utilitarian desk almost hidden in the far corner of the room.

Eureka.

Allison's checkbook was on top, flanked by two pens and a roll of stamps. Everything was in order to pay her bills.

The checkbook didn't hold too many surprises. Allison's passion for lingerie matched my obsession for shoes. She'd bought something at Victoria's Secret at least once a month. The rest of the entries were standard, checks to Bridie, the utilities, etc. There were two interesting entries: one was a check written three weeks earlier for $1000 to Garibaldi's Jewelers in North Beach—the same jeweler whose card had been hidden under her driver's license—and the other was a check written on the same day to Trips Out Travel for $4000. Her desk drawers yielded a bunch of travel brochures for tours of Tuscany but nothing else. She'd circled a couple of tours coinciding with school break at the beginning of April. It didn't take a genius to realize Allison was planning her honeymoon.

Every inch of kitchen counter was covered with cooking paraphernalia: a waffle iron, a Cuisinart, a Kitchen Aide mixer, a bread machine, an ice cream maker, just to name a few. Allison had been a gadget freak.

In contrast to my fridge, which usually houses six different types of mustards and nothing else, hers was filled with cheeses, packages of fresh pasta, and an abundance of vegetables and fruits in the vegetables bins. Ditto for her cupboards: chock-a-block with staples. I could have fed Napoleon's army with the bounty in that kitchen. I stuck my hand in the sugar and four different kinds of flour, but came up with nothing but dirty hands. Not wanting to turn on the taps in case Bridie might hear the water running, I wiped my gritty fingers on my pants.

Two narrow bookcases, squeezed into the spaces between her kitchen window and the walls, were filled with most of the same pastry cookbooks I owned (another personal obsession), as well as a number of Italian cookbooks. I remembered Bridie mentioning Antonello De Luca's visits. I removed Marcella Hazan's *The Classic Italian Cookbook*. On the flyleaf was an inscription: "Cara, to Tuscany." Opening another Marcella Hazan book, I found the same handwriting, different inscription. "One day, Cara." The same person had inscribed every Italian cookbook I opened. All written in fountain pen with peacock blue ink, some of the inscriptions were faded, indicating this affair had gone on for a long time. Had Antonello and Allison had been carrying on this affair when we were students? Flirting with me, bedding her?

Maybe the bedroom might tell me the identity of this boyfriend with the penchant for giving Allison Italian cookbooks inscribed with empty promises. I still wasn't convinced it was Antonello. Or maybe my ego wasn't.

None of the excess so prominent in the living room found its way into the bedroom. Whether she just hadn't had time to overdo this room or realized she needed a respite from all those loud flowers, there wasn't a single overblown rose in sight. The bedroom was done in tasteful beiges and whites. The only mark of excess was her bed, a king-size brass bed with a plethora of wrought iron flourishes.

On the top of her dresser were several bottles of Chanel in various numbers and a cluster of photographs: her parents; a charming picture of her around age ten, even then all cheeks and hair; a picture of me, her, and Antonello De Luca celebrating at a bar in North Beach the night we'd graduated from École; another graduation picture of her and Dean Benson. I hadn't remembered Benson there that night, but then again I'd gotten shit-face drunk, and Jim had had to fling me over his shoulder fireman-style and carry me back to our car.

Two dresser drawers contained the usual shirts and pants, and the other two were stuffed with expensive lingerie. One drawer had a month's worth of underwear and bras. The second drawer was chock-a-block with negligees. I ran my hands slowly, guiltily, and carefully in and out of the neatly folded piles of negligees with their matching peignoirs. Befitting a person who adored chintz, Allison's negligees were festooned with acres of lace. As careful as I was, sachets of Chanel No. 5, the most sensual perfume ever concocted, released their scent as my hands glided easily over the smooth silk, my fingers careful not to catch on the delicate lacework.

Why had I steadfastly denied myself these frivolous sorts of pleasures? Over the years, I had demoted everything to whatever took the least amount of effort. Chopped off my hair because I didn't want to spend the time blow-drying it. Made a uniform out of tee-shirts and jeans because they never needed to be ironed. Aside from the lingerie I'd worn on my honeymoon, I wear oversized men's tee-shirts and leggings to bed in the winter, and for the summer one-size fits all nightshirts that my sister picks up for me in Disneyland. My current favorite has all the bad girls of Disney on the front: Cruella de Ville, the witch from Snow White. Amusing? Yes. Sexy? I don't think so. Crushing a sachet in one hand, I reveled in one final whiff of Chanel before I closed the drawer.

Lecture to self: perhaps your lack of love life might be related to the type of underwear you buy.

A yin-yang thing. You own underwear that meets the approval of the Pope. Perhaps this dry spell is actually God's way of sparing you a humiliating episode. Think about the first potential date—okay, a fuck—for the first time in two years. Your intended playmate might just flee the room at the first sight of your Jockey for Her picked up at the local drugstore, the tired elastic barely hugging your hips.

Memo to self: a trip to Victoria's Secret is in order.

Now where was I? On to her closet.

My socks slipped a little on the hardwood floors as I made my way over to the closet. I opened the door just in time to see a blouse sleeve sway, as if someone had just brushed by it.

Uh-oh.

I stood there for a second, letting my eyes adjust to the dark inside. In the back corner, on the floor behind some long garment bags, were two black, size twelve Nikes.

Attached to ankles.

I slowly slid my hand over the outside of the door, hoping against hope for a thumb-turn lock.

No lock.

I sprinted like a gazelle across the area rug framing Allison's bed. The socks were my undoing. When I reached the doorway separating the bedroom from the living room, I began running in place as my socks fought for purchase against the hardwood floors.

He caught me. Grabbing the fabric at the back of my neck, he pulled me toward him.

Thank God Jim had taught me some rudimentary self-defense skills.

Before he could get an arm around my throat, I rammed a vicious elbow into his ribs and stomped on a foot.

He grunted in surprise and let go.

As if on ice skates for the first time, I wobbled and slipped my way to the entryway. If I hadn't been wearing socks I would've made it.

The second time he caught me he was much rougher.

Bringing an arm around my neck, he pulled me up against him, and then clamped a large hand over my mouth. His other arm wrapped around my body, pinning my arms. I tried to stomp on his feet, but my stockinged heels were totally ineffectual. I wrenched my body back and forth trying to break his hold over me.

Thrashing my body back and forth as he dragged me through the apartment and back to the bedroom, I dug my toes into the floor, the carpet, anything to stop him from reaching the bedroom. I swung my legs out trying to connect with the furniture, hoping that something would topple over, Bridie would hear it, and call the police. Nothing worked. Powerless to stop this awful dance, we slowly made our way back to the bedroom.

We fell on the bed on our sides. Bringing one of my arms up over my head, he shifted his weight and pinned it with his knee, his other knee pinned me to the bed. He grabbed my other arm and pulled it up, imprisoning both my hands in one of his. I flailed my legs trying to connect with any body part but he was too strong. Shifting his weight again, he was on top of me. Coarse black hair scratched my cheek as he tried to pin my head to the mattress using his head.

Oh my God, was he was going to rape me before he killed me?

I tried to wrench my mouth free to bite his hand when miraculously my hands were freed. The hand lifted off my mouth.

"If you bite me, Mary," he whispered in my ear. "I'll break your neck."

Chapter Fourteen

The heat of O'Connor's breath seared my ear. The adrenalin fled my body as fast as it had come, leaving me limp except for a horrific hammering of my heart that squeezed my chest and filled my ears with its unrelenting pounding. The second I'd stopped fighting him, O'Connor jumped off me like I was made of lava. He sat on a corner of the bed, a cool, gentle finger stroked my forehead as I lay shuddering, my hands covering my face, trying desperately not to cry.

After a few moments he leaned over and whispered, "Mary, we have to get out of here. It's getting late."

Taking my hands from my face, I looked up at O'Connor. In all the years we'd known each other, we'd spent most of it arguing. I don't think I'd ever allowed myself a moment of rest to really look at him. His eyes, the deepest of browns without being black, gazed down at me with such tenderness and concern that it lifted for one small second the aftermath of fear and angst gripping my chest. The broad plain of his forehead was, for once, not wrinkled in frustration or impatience. His pug Irish nose, marooned in a face with such strong features, snuggled up and was lost in the crest of his cheekbones. The soft curve of his bottom lip, usually a compressed thin line, was full and sensual.

The blinds were drawn, the room dimming slowly in the late afternoon light. A faint hint of Chanel still lingered in the air. The bedroom began warming up from the sticky heat of the radiators as they chortled and hissed. If I didn't get myself off that bed, I'd do something I'd regret for the rest of my life.

I rolled over slowly, got up, and fetched my shoes from the landing.

We snuck out of the apartment through a backdoor off Allison's kitchen and tiptoed down a narrow wooden staircase. When we'd reached the bottom, I pointed to the back of Bridie's apartment, mouthed "landlady," and motioned we should exit the backyard on the opposite side of the building to avoid her windows.

Once on the front sidewalk and a few doors down from Allison's, O'Connor said quietly, "I think we both need a drink."

I nodded.

"I'll drive. Foghorns?"

O'Connor's car was down the street and around the corner. We walked side-by-side, matching strides, shoulders so close together our clothes occasionally scritch-scratched against each other.

Once in his car, we began screaming at each other.

"You are sick, O'Connor. You did that pseudo-rapist thing to scare the living shit out of me. To punish me for being in Allison's apartment."

O'Connor lifted his eyes toward the sky and clasped his hands together in mock prayer. "Sweet Jesus, give me patience." Then he turned to me. "Goddamn it! I didn't know it was you. I thought you were the landlady. I ran into the closet and closed the door. When I heard you opening and closing dresser drawers, I peeked out and saw somebody rifling the place. A little aside here: if you ever decide to take-up a life of crime, learn how to search a place with a little more finesse."

"What about when I opened the closet? Couldn't you see my face?"

"I was behind those frigging garment bags. I couldn't see anything."

"Liar. What about when I ran across the bedroom? You *must* have known it was me."

"How in the hell was I supposed to know it was you? The hood of your sweatshirt covered your hair. Your back was to me the whole time until we fell on the bed."

"We didn't *fall* on the bed. You *dragged* me there. You knew it was me."

"Did not!"

"Did too!"

It continued in that vein as we barreled through four stop signs and a red light. O'Connor reached the bar in a record two minutes. Breaking for a brief hiatus to order our drinks, we began bickering before the barmaid had a chance to finish writing down our orders.

Foghorns is a Berkeley drinking institution. Run by a father and son team for over fifty years, it ostensibly has a full bar, but no one orders anything but martinis. The bar was empty except for a young couple across the room from us who kept touching each other in that shy wonder of first love. It was a little early for the serious drinkers, the type who have gin for dinner and pretzels for dessert.

The décor is what could only be called Victoriana *à la* Monty Python. Chairs, old bicycles, musical instruments, anything appealing to the older Foghorn's sense of whimsy hangs from the ceiling. Unfortunately, the seating is equally eclectic. The ancient Victorian settee had emitted little clouds of dust when I'd sat down on it. We'd parked ourselves in a dark corner, began guzzling martinis, and fought, I insisting O'Connor had pulled that commando stuff to scare me straight, O'Connor claiming he thought I was a burglar.

I'm a hard liquor wimp, and my rules for martinis are written in stone: no martinis on an empty stomach, no more than two, and none until after seven o'clock. I was batting two for three. The first two martinis hadn't touched me. It wasn't until the fourth sip of my third one when the gin finally lifted the weight off my chest. Foghorns has fish bowls filled with aspirin on every table. I tucked three packets into my pocket, insurance against the inevitable hangover I was courting with a vengeance.

"You all right? You haven't yelled at me in, oh," O'Connor looked at his watch, "ten seconds."

"Yeah, I'm fine." I drained the rest of my drink, relishing the gin as it scoured a hot path into my stomach.

"Can we have a normal conversation?" he demanded and finished off the remainder of his third drink.

Ignoring his question, I leaned my gin-soaked body against the back of the musty-smelling settee. I was beginning to feel sleepy. Too many martinis and no lunch.

The bar had gradually filled up during the time we'd been slinging back the gin and yelling at each other. A group of soccer players, their jerseys and shorts smeared with mud, had taken over the bar area and were bouncing soccer balls off their heads in between gulps of martinis. They'd begun to build a pyramid out of the empty martini glasses. The pseudo-intellectuals with the bad haircuts and nerdy-style glasses either had their noses parked in books or were huddled close together in intense (and, I was sure, absolutely brilliant) conversation. Students with the blackest of hair, black sunglasses, black clothes, black gumboots, and lots of piercings filled the rest of the tables.

When I was young, I thought Foghorns was the height of sophistication. Fifteen years later it didn't look so much cool as tired and dirty; however, the martinis hadn't lost their wallop.

Memo to self: nap time.

"Mary, don't fall asleep on me. I knew the third martini was a mistake." He sighed. "Wake-up," he ordered and reached across the table to give my shoulder a gentle shake. "So," he said softly, "tell me what were you doing in Allison Warner's apartment?"

I blinked a couple of times to clear the alcohol fog. I had a momentary evil thought he'd purposefully gotten me snockered to make me less argumentative.

"Are you at the school because of me?" I asked, talking to the table that was scarred with rings from thousands of martini glasses.

"No." He sounded angry, but somehow I knew it wasn't directed at me.

I looked up. Much grayer and thinner than he was last fall, the chef's whites and toque had masked how much he'd changed. Sitting in Allison's apartment in the dark glow from the late afternoon sun had softened the sharp cut of his cheekbones. O'Connor was of Irish farmer stock and being thin didn't suit him. His face was devoid of expression, as if any emotion would be a betrayal.

A betrayal of what or whom I asked myself.

"Why are you a student? I need to know," I said quietly.

He picked up his empty martini glass and twirled it, the delicate stem disappearing in the folds of his fingers. "I told you, I'm on leave."

"Bullshit," I said in a loud voice. The voices around us faded to nothing. I lowered my voice. "Jim tried to convince me you were on medical leave. Do you two think I'm a complete moron? And if you're not undercover, what were you doing in Allison's apartment?"

Silence.

"I'm on leave," he repeated.

That nice, martini-induced sense of well being was in serious danger. I stood up.

"I need some honesty here. When you are ready to stop this farce, call me."

I turned to leave. One of his giant hands encircled my wrist; his thumb pressed the inside of my palm as he gently pulled me toward him.

"We need to talk. Don't go."

I strained to hear his voice above the whoops of the soccer players. His voice was soft with a gentleness I'd only heard him use with his children, and his mouth had relaxed into that sensual fullness that made my heart skip beats.

I slowly pulled my hand away and sat down. Gulping a few times to dislodge the large lump that suddenly appeared in my throat, I said, "Okay, but don't, don't continue with this ridiculous story about being on medical leave. You're on some sort of undercover assignment."

He sat there mute, which I assumed was as close to a "yes" as I was going to get.

"I think Allison was murdered." I said, bracing myself for more comments about my pathetic Nancy Drew complex.

His dark eyes flew up to my face. "Why?"

"After cleaning up on Friday night, I noticed Allison's purse in the chef's cupboard in the classroom. I didn't want to leave it there, so I put it in my locker for safekeeping. I realized this morning that her parents probably would need it, so I went over to school to get it so Allison's landlady could give it to her parents."

The waitress re-appeared with a tray and the hard smile you get when you've been waiting on drunks too many years.

"The check, please," O'Connor said.

"I'm not done," I protested.

"No more for you. I've been around you after four martinis. You either pass-out or get weepy, and there's nothing worse than a maudlin Irish woman." He tossed a two twenty-dollar bills on the tray. "Keep the change."

She gave me a defeated shrug of apology and went on to the next table.

O'Connor leaned toward me, the cop was taking over. "Did the landlady tell you anything?" His voice clipped off the edges of his words, the question all staccato, no legato.

"Allison was supposedly engaged. All the Italian cookbooks in her place were inscribed to her by the same no name guy. And based on what I saw in her checkbook and desk, she—"

"I saw the checkbook. Just for the record, I actually had legal permission to case her apartment. Unlike you. She was planning on going to Italy for her honeymoon. De Luca was going to dump his wife and take Allison back to meet the relatives."

Despite seeing no less than a dozen inscriptions to "Cara," I rejected outright the idea Antonello and Allison had been having an affair. I'd known Antonello a long time. I wasn't ready to condemn him as an asshole and philanderer until I had positive proof. I jumped to Antonello's defense. "There was nothing in those cookbooks to indicate who they were from."

"Oh, please, Mary," O'Connor scoffed. "'Cara,'" O'Connor imitated Antonello's Italian accent. "'I've been looking for you everywhere.'"

"I still don't think it was him. He's happily married," I protested and yawned. Where did that yawn come from? It was only 6:00 p.m.

"We'll pass on determining De Luca's marital bliss for now. Knowing you, you went through Allison's purse with a fine toothcomb. What did you find?"

My neck began to feel very heavy. I propped my head up on my chin trying to focus on O'Connor's face.

"Nothing but a North Beach jeweler's business card with an appointment at ten o'clock Tuesday morning."

"The same jeweler she wrote the big check to?"

"Yeah. Do you think she was murdered?" I asked, now using both hands to keep my chin up. My eyes began to close into slits, against the smoke I told myself. Although we were in the no-smoking section of the bar.

"I think so," he admitted. "Just a hinky feeling I have. The autopsy confirmed anaphylactic shock, but there were no traces of shellfish in her stomach. All of the food from the garbage cans tested negative for fish as well. Hey, are you falling asleep on me?" he demanded.

Uh, who me? I sat up. It was getting harder and harder to sit up straight. "You tested the garbage?"

He had the grace to give me a small smile. "Routine. I just don't get it. It doesn't fit. You still haven't told me why you think she was murdered."

One more sentence and then I need to take a little nap. I yawned and arched my back against the couch back. "When I went to École this morning to get her purse, her locker looked like it had been busted open with a crowbar."

O'Connor's face dropped that blank, no comment, look. He metamorphed into his cop persona, the lips tight, the eyes on high-beam.

"Tell me everything," he ordered.

I opened my mouth to speak and then gave up the ghost, embracing the gin full force. Nothing came out but yet another yawn. And gee, it was getting hot in here. Really hot. It took three tries before I actually got my sweatshirt off. I kept losing steam and taking little gin-soaked catnaps in between attempts. Once I finally got it off, I found that my eyes wouldn't open. They were deliciously sleepy, like I hadn't closed them properly in an entire year. Wonderful. I wadded my sweatshirt into a makeshift pillow, put it under my arms and fell forward on the table in front of me already for a nap. This felt good. When was the last time I really slept the sleep of the dead?

Memo to shelf: ssshhhoouulddnnn't drink thish muccssshhh. Maaaayyyybbeee IIIIIIIIIIIIII sshhhhhhhouuuullldd nnnnntttttt dddrrrriiiikkk...

Even in my drunken stupor I heard the expletive.

"Shit, I knew I shouldn't have let her have that last martini. Hey, could you get me a big cup of coffee and some french fries, please."

Who is he talking to, I wondered? I tried to raise my index finger to ask who the coffee was for. I certainly didn't need any coffee. It was nap time.

Three minutes into the black hole of my nap, strong fingers gripped my shoulders and began to shake me awake.

"Wake-up, Mary. I have a nice big cup of coffee for you. Time to sober up," he ordered.

I buried my head farther and farther into the sweatshirt. It was so soft. Just one more minute, I pleaded silently.

More rough shaking and then the sweatshirt was pulled out from under me and my shoulders pinned to the back of the couch.

"Come on, Mary. I need you to tell me about the locker. Wake-up! Drink some coffee and eat these fries. They'll soak up the gin."

My ears perked up at the mention of drink and then promptly closed up again at the mention of coffee and fries. What a revolting combination.

Somehow I kept myself upright against the couch back, but still managed to luxuriate in the drunk. This really did feel good, and a small part of me was very much frightened at how I was chasing this numbness. The bigger part of me, however, the one normally tied up in six different kinds of stress knots, heaved a sigh of relief as those knots began to unravel in quick successive. This is how alcoholics are born.

"Please, Mary. I need to know what's going on at École. You're the only one who can help me," he said.

I ignored him and tried to sleep sitting up.

"Someone else is going to get killed." He said this quietly, but I heard it. It was enough to make me open my eyes and look at him. He was close yet far away and while the words registered, they didn't quite get all the way inside my eardrums. They sort of floated around my ear canal.

And yet another reason why I don't tie one on too often is that I can get incredibly selfish and mean. This is when evil Mary runs amok.

"Didn't think you were undercover. Didn't think you knew who I was in that room," I sing-songed and closed my eyes again. "If you lied about the one, I bet you lied about the other. Bet you knew it was me." I waggled my finger in his direction. At least the direction I thought he was sitting.

"Fuck it," he said, his voice gritty with some emotion I couldn't fathom. That penetrated. I opened my eyes and he was staring at me grim, resolute. He grabbed both my hands and squeezed them so hard that they ached for days afterwards.

"If I'd known it was you, I wouldn't have clamped my hand over your mouth. I'd have traced my fingers around those beautiful lips of yours. If I'd known it was you, I wouldn't have wrenched your arms above your head. I'd have kissed the white of your arm until I reached the base of your neck. I knew it was you because when I lay against your long, lovely body I smelled chocolate. You're the only woman I know who always smells like chocolate."

Chapter Fifteen

That confession consumed all the alcohol in my system. The drink just left me. Clearly, I had wanted to be carried away, using the flimsiest of excuses (okay, three double martinis on an empty stomach isn't flimsy, but even so, it didn't explain why I was so hammered). I wanted to float away on my little raft made of gin and olives and just go where the tide was taking me. I was so tired of taking care of myself. That's the real tragedy when a relationship fails. There's only you to pick up the pieces of, well, you. I let the gin take me because I knew O'Connor wouldn't let me fall, let me drown. And now, because of my stupid behavior, he was placing the responsibility for drowning us both on the Titanic of betrayals on my inebriated shoulders. God, what was he thinking?

O'Connor's face twisted with anguish, all eyebrows and lines, his hands continued to crush mine, as if I must pay physically for what unholy hell he was suffering emotionally. This confession hadn't given him any solace.

O'Connor wanted me. And did my victory taste sweet? Were violins metaphorically serenading us as we sat facing each other, O'Connor never easing up one iota his passionate grip on my hands?

No.

My devil of pride hopped up and down on one shoulder gloating, "I told you so. It's just like Bridie said. You found him.

Hen's teeth, Mary. As rare as hen's teeth. Bridie knows. I told you so." I couldn't deny that this was true.

With a patronizing and rather stern shake of her head, the little angel of common sense and goodness insisted, "You mustn't."

Sometimes I truly hate myself. Goodness won out.

I couldn't take what wasn't mine. And despite the passion in his voice, once his martinis wore off he'd hate himself for betraying his wife and his children. Eventually he'd hate me. No matter how much he loved me, he never would have betrayed Moira if it hadn't been for our intimate tussle in Allison's apartment, my badgering, and the fatal third martini. I couldn't confront that anguish any longer. With a nobility and strength I very much regretted I possessed, I took those proverbial hen's teeth and scattered them to the winds.

Turning my face toward the soccer players, I told O'Connor everything I thought might support my theory that Allison had been murdered. I told him about the fight between the chefs. Allison's horrific argument with Marilyn. The mysterious problem that would be solved by the end of the week. Marc's petition to get Étienne fired. Allison's uncharacteristic rage when she saw the petition. The scene in the locker room with Marc and Shelley. And, finally, Allison's death in the dining room. I told it all in detail.

When I was done, I allowed myself to savor this last touch for five more seconds. Then I pulled my hands away. They ached as if branded by essence of O'Connor, immense strength interwoven with deep gentleness. I looked at him for the first time in twenty minutes.

"Go home, O'Connor. If you hurry you'll be home in time to read your sons a bedtime story." Black eyes upbraded me, hated me, chastised me, loved me, and finally seemed to thank me. "Go," I begged to the table and then turned my attention back to the soccer players.

I heard a chair scrape, saw a blur of black sweats walk briskly by the table, and that was that.

Bringing my hands up to my face, I licked across both sets of knuckles and sighed with pleasure. So this is what decency tastes like: vanilla, salt, and gin. I didn't care who was watching me, I licked my knuckles again and then the back of my hands in an attempt to keep that delicious flavor from dying in my mouth. When it was all gone and I could only taste the salt from my own pores, a desolation so complete almost robbed me of my ability to breath. I thought, if I don't move, I'm going to die in this chair. I grabbed the table with both hands and heaved myself up to a standing position.

I caught the younger Foghorn watching me, a cloth in one hand, a glass in the other, embarrassment and concern on his face. He'd had a crush on me since high school. Since my divorce he'd make half-hearted passes whenever he saw me. Nothing offensive. Just a nice guy trying to get a date.

I made it over to the bar and parked myself on a barstool. "Dave, I'm going to get absolutely toasted. I want you to keep pouring martinis until closing time. Then put me in a cab and pay the cabbie to take me home. I still live over on Neilsen. Call me tomorrow and let me know what I owe you. Okay?"

"That guy you were with. He screw you over?" Dave's shoulders began jerking in that bantam rooster, defend the womenfolk, sort of way.

"No, he's an old friend." I gave his arm a gentle squeeze. "Just like you. Thanks for looking after me."

He began furiously polishing glasses, checking for non-existent spots. "You still carrying a torch for that ex-husband of yours, Mary?"

"Sorry, Dave. Maybe another time. You know what a fool I am for those Irish cops. Start pouring."

‹›‹›‹›

There are still some gentlemen left in this world. Despite the repeated brush-offs I'd given him over the years, Dave drove me home and made sure I got in the front door. I must have been semi-conscious because I was able to tell him where I kept the

Hide-a-Key, my original set of keys being hidden in the wheel-well of my car parked near Allison's apartment.

When I woke up I was curled up in a fetal position on the entryway floor, my back pressed against the front door. I must have pretty much passed out in my entryway because there my sweatshirt was neatly folded into a square and my head was under it. He'd gone into my bedroom and removed the quilt from my bed and wrapped me up in it. I tentatively moved a leg. It hurt like hell. I got up on my knees and tried to untangle myself from the quilt. The room began to whirl so fast I felt like I was on some out-of-control merry-go-round about to take off into orbit. After a couple of minutes the spinning slowed down. Crawling across the room, I pulled myself up on the couch. Everything hurt. Even blinking hurt. The weather front had dissipated and from the angle of the winter sunlight as it streaked across my living room, I guessed it was about eleven o'clock.

Dave must have been watering down the martinis at some point, otherwise by all rights I should be dead from alcohol poisoning. The only thing I remembered past ten that night was Dave grabbing me by both shoulders, shaking me out of my alcoholic stupor, and he telling me he'd take me home. Before we got in the car, he forced me to take six Excedrin P.M. he'd stashed behind the bar for special occasions, followed by an Alka Seltzer chaser.

Inside the front door was as far as I got.

As I lay splayed on the couch trying desperately to stop the room from spinning, the phone rang. Its high-pitched chirp shattered what little equilibrium I had left. I grabbed two pillows and crushed them against my ears to blot out the noise. After a couple of minutes I gingerly removed one pillow to make sure all was quiet. The machine blinked a bright red digital 4, chastising me to pick up the phone. People needed to speak to me. I didn't even know if I could speak. Perhaps I'd permanently fried my larynx. It would serve me right, the woman who always has to have the last word pickles her voice box.

Get a grip, Mary. First, turn off the phone. Then take a shower. Then get dressed. Then get something to eat.

By two o'clock I was dressed and sitting in my kitchen with the remains of cinnamon toast and hot chocolate in front of me. I'd scoured every pore in my body with a nail brush in a futile attempt to remove the stench of old booze, but I could still smell traces of gin. Which made eating slightly problematic; however, what few carbohydrates I'd been able to force down my throat had reduced a potentially fatal hangover to merely permanent brain damage.

Not only did I physically feel like shit, I hadn't felt this sort of self-disgust since the night Jim had walked out on me, and I'd gone on a similar sort of bender—also, unfortunately, at Foghorns. Despite the scalding shower and the clean clothes, I felt dirty and debased, like I broken all ten of the commandments all at once.

Next I did something I hadn't done in twenty-two years. I walked to the nearest Catholic Church and went to confession.

With Sunday services over for the day, the church was deserted. The ornately carved pews, marble statues, and a gilded altar all spoke of a time when people still believed a church's beauty was a reflection of your love for God. A few candles still sputtered, lit earlier in the morning by parishioners in that age-old tradition of saving a soul. If anyone needed a candle lit for them it was me. As a sign of our times, the donation box for the candles was outfitted with a Schlage lock and tied to the altar with a heavy metal chain to deter theft. From a cavalcade of stained-glass windows depicting the Stations of the Cross, a canopy of red and blue light arced over the nave. And like some fifteenth-century criminal frantically searching for sanctuary, I almost wept with relief, knowing I'd come to the right place to be forgiven.

Heading straight for the nearest confessional, I entered and knelt down, my knees sinking into the deep dents in the leather made by the knees of untold thousands of others seeking redemption. The grill on the other side was empty, but that didn't matter.

I didn't need formal absolution. Both priest and penitent, I castigated myself for every scene in that bar. Motivated primarily by pride and my pathological need to always be right, step by step, I'd cajoled O'Connor into making his own confession—a declaration of love I had no right to. My only consolation was that in the end I'd done the right thing and refused him. I didn't know how he and I were going to handle the next few weeks, but I was determined to end this dangerous game of one-upmanship that had been our pathetic cover-up for romance. Before I left the church I lit a candle for Moira. If anyone deserved my prayers it was her. I turned to leave and, on second thought, lit a candle for myself.

By the time I walked back to my house it was six o'clock. The walk to and from the church had cleared my body of most of the poisons contaminating my system. I called a cab, got my car from Allison's neighborhood and returned home, steeling myself for the messages on my machine.

Chapter Sixteen

Message one was from my mother. She'd called yesterday afternoon, "Just to make sure everything is okay." I knew from the tight, high-pitched endings to all of her vowels that my behavior the previous morning had tripped those mommy-alarm bells. That she'd waited until the afternoon was a token nod to my status as an adult. "Mom" I wrote on the notepad, and added, "be chirpy," underlined three times.

Message number two was from Dean Benson. "Mary, Benson here." He spoke in that slow, clear diction of the drunk pretending to be sober. To compensate for blowing it on the esses, he over-enunciated every tee and dee. "I need you and Shelley to cover Allison's classhes until we hire another chef. If the two of you rotate one day on, one day off it meanshs fourteen-hour days every other day. Shelley is unable to take the Monday night shift so the first shift is on you." Click. "SHIT," I wrote in capital letters. I'd gotten out of the restaurant business to end those fourteen-hour days.

Message number three was from Dave. He had called around 9:00 a.m. while I was still passed-out/asleep in my hallway. "Mary, this is Dave. You know, Dave Foghorn. You make it to bed all right?" Well, sort of. "You were pretty toasted last night. I…ah…was a little worried about you. Give me a ring at the bar will you? I'm on tonight." "Dave" I scribbled. Nice guy. Why didn't I find him attractive?

I hit play for the last message. Nothing. Another telephone solicitor thwarted by modern technology. Sometimes I get six hang-ups a night. It has gotten to the point where I never answered my phone after five o'clock; I let the answering machine pick it up. If by chance I pick it up and hear a human voice pleading for money for some worthy cause, I'm sunk. I can't say no. Everyday I receive letters reminding me of my phone pledges and would I cough up the cash I'd promised?

My finger was about to hit the delete button when a flat, androgynous voice threatened, "Leave the school." I dropped my pen and stabbed the replay button. Punching the volume button as far as it would go, I listened to the message again and again. Besides the voice, the only discernible clue was a sound in the background at the very end of the message, like a victory whoop, something you'd hear at a ballgame. Then the caller had hung-up.

Why were ex-husbands such pains in the ass? This was so typical of Jim. No doubt the cop toms-toms had beat their rhythm before Allison had arrived at the morgue. "Hey, Jimbo, heard someone died at that fancy cooking school your ex works at." That's all it would take for Jim to get on the horn and do something as inane as try to get me to quit my job. During last fall's murders, he'd tried to protect me and almost got blown away by S.F.P.D. His interference was as welcome now as it was then.

I dialed his house hoping his wife number two wouldn't answer. I gotten over most of my rage toward him, but it was still a huge effort trying to be civil to her.

"Yes," a female voice answered.

Shit.

"Hi, Tina, it's Mary. May I speak to Jim?"

She paused and then said, "Well, it's dinnertime. Is it important?"

I wanted to scream, "Of course, you bitch, do you think I called just to chat?" but my knees were still sore from all those Hail Marys and Our Fathers; a not-so-subtle reminder to turn the other cheek. "Please, if you wouldn't mind. I won't be long, I promise."

I heard several children giggling in the background and Jim's gentle warning to keep it down while he was on the phone.

"Mary, is everything okay?"

Funny, in the beginning of a relationship you can't say enough to each other. As the relationship sours, even the simplest statements become marital landmines so you stop talking altogether. The simple phrase, "Did you stop at the store and get something for dinner," in reality is, "Did you stop at the store because as usual there's no food in the house because you work an eighteen-hour day and you are too tired to cook and I don't want to eat out or have chicken pot pies for the fourth night this week." When the relationship is really over you've come full circle and you can't stop talking. You say all the nasty things you've warehoused for months and months in an attempt to keep the relationship together. I'd always been contemptuous of couples whose divorce deteriorated into a series of ugly shouting matches until I'd had a few dozen of those myself.

"Jim, I know you're eating, so I'll keep it short. I have no intention of quitting my job. I appreciate your concern, but I'm staying at École. So no more phone calls, please."

Silence for a few seconds and then, "Mary, what in the hell are you talking about?"

Goddamn it, he was going to act all innocent until I dragged it out of him. Well, my dinner wasn't getting cold.

"You know, the phone call telling me to leave the school."

"Mary, it wasn't me. I swear."

"Stop it, Jim. After trailing me last fall, your track record on this stuff isn't too good."

"On my honor as an altar boy it wasn't me," he insisted.

Jim never invoked the altar boy stuff unless he meant what he said. It'd been our last refuge of honesty when our relationship was falling apart. The heebie-jeebies began marching down my spine. If it wasn't Jim, who was it?

"Tell me more about the phone call," he demanded.

"Someone said, 'Leave the school.' Nothing else. And before you start doing your cop thing, I didn't recognize the voice. I've saved it on my machine if you want to hear it."

There were a few beats that there shouldn't have been, like he was thinking, like there was a whole background on this that I wasn't privy to.

"You need to call O'Connor. Tonight," he insisted.

After that scene in Foghorns? Not an option. "I can't do that," I insisted right back. "I need to go to work tonight and prep for tomorrow. I'm working double shifts for a while until the school replaces Allison. I'll see him tomorrow and I'll tell him then." Maybe I could slip him a note?

"Do you promise you'll tell him?"

"On my honor as the ex-wife of an altar boy, I promise. Now go eat your dinner."

I hung up before he could say anything else. I'd had a horrible thought when I'd realized it wasn't Jim. What if it had been O'Connor trying to get me to leave the school? What if he was afraid I was compromising his undercover work there? What if he just couldn't stand to face me after that scene in Foghorns but had no choice about remaining undercover at the school? I'd have to tell him about the phone call if only to make sure it wasn't him.

If I had to work a double shift tomorrow, I better get moving. I didn't want to walk in and be blind-sided. I hoped Allison had a production schedule hidden somewhere.

Clearing all the messages except for the threat, I cranked up the espresso machine for a triple mocha with extra chocolate and made my phone calls before I drove to the City. I phoned my mother and by faking happy was able to get off the phone in less than ten minutes. Next I phoned Benson to let him know that I'd gotten his message, and then called Foghorns and thanked Dave for saving my life by watering down the martinis. I cut him off before he could ask me for a date.

You'd think dinnertime on a Sunday night would mean I'd be able to zip across to San Francisco in twenty minutes. An hour later I'd paid my toll, and like all the other frustrated, angry drivers, crawled my way up the incline. Although I'd desperately needed my parents' support after my divorce, the ready cup of tea in my mother's kitchen was beginning to pale next to the daily grind of negotiating the bridge.

Maybe what I really needed to completely heal from my divorce was a drastic change. A complete amputation. Move to another state, another coast, maybe do a stint in France. I'd never lived and worked farther than a twenty-five mile radius from where I was born. I was an anomaly in the food business where skipping from job-to-job, state-to-state was *de rigeur*. On the other hand, why leave an area that was at the forefront of every food trend before it was a food trend? But maybe, a little voice nagged, maybe it was also a good excuse not to push that envelope.

A headache the size and weight of a watermelon began pounding at the back of my head, warning me that this was dangerous mental ground. I pulled into the garage of École just in time to avoid a stress migraine.

As I exited the service elevator into the production kitchen, the perfect aroma of baking chicken and garlic banished all traces of my headache. I hadn't eaten since that morning when I'd forced miniscule bites of toast down my throat to give my body something to live on other than old gin. Now my stomach began whining "feed me, feed me" and rumbling in grateful anticipation of decent food.

Marc's long body hovered over one of the big black stovetops as he sautéed green beans, the hot flames licking the sides of the pan as the vegetables and butter tumbled over each other at the flick of his wrist. It was with a jolt that I saw Marc out of his chef's uniform. He wore jeans, a white tee-shirt, and black cowboy boots as shiny as the waxed fender of a Cadillac. No longer hidden by the boxy chef's jacket, his waist went on forever with that slippery, rubber band quality young men have, starting under the armpits and swooping to a graceful end at his knees.

Singing that Edif Piaf song, *C'est Lui Que Mon Coeur A Choisi*, at the top of his lungs, Marc seemed not to notice me standing there. Like a high-wire artist in the circus, his every movement was fluid, balanced, as he'd give the beans a shake in tempo to the music. Then he stopped singing, popped a couple of beans into his mouth and closed his eyes, as if afraid that it wouldn't be cooked to perfection. It was. His lips, shiny from the buttery beans, curved in a smile of satisfaction. He opened his eyes.

The smile vanished to be replaced by what looked like the most severe of disappointments.

"Oh, Mary, it's you. I heard the elevator...."

Clearly he was expecting someone else. Flanked by two barstools, one of the stainless steel tables was set with china, linen, and glassware. For two. A bottle of Pouilly-Fuissé stood chilling in a bucket of ice. He'd even remembered candles. It was terribly romantic. Marc was truly turning on the heat. No one had tried to woo me in a hell of a long time. I'd be in tears if I didn't get out of there.

"Hey, I'm not going to rain on your parade," I assured him. "Looks like you and Shelley have quite an evening ahead of you. I need to see what Allison had planned for tomorrow then I'll be out of here. Smells fantastic." I made an inane thumb's up sign.

I moved in the direction of the pastry kitchen when I heard Marc slam an oven door shut and say, "Fuck her," in a low voice.

"Mary," he called out to me. "You want some dinner?"

Turning back around toward Marc and all that lovely food, I watched him cut up the chicken with the skill of a surgeon, the smell of baked garlic filling the kitchen. He plated up two dinners, the leg of each chicken forming an arm for the fan of chicken breast. A high pile of *pommes frites* nestled next to an equally high pile of green beans.

Ignoring the nasty rumblings coming from my stomach, I said, "Wait a couple of minutes. If she sees me sitting here it'll spoil this romantic feast you've planned. She'll show."

"Nope. She ain't coming. She's more than an hour late. Had a bust up fight so loud I'm surprised the neighbors didn't call the police. Thought my groveling on the phone set things right. Guess not." He took a big swig of wine and refilled his glass. "Tough merde, as they say in France." Marc perched himself on a barstool and filled the other glass to the brim with the wine.

"Dinner," he announced, thrusting the wine glass in the direction of the other barstool, "is served."

I looked back over at the elevator. The panel showed no activity. No Shelley. I didn't want to get in the middle of Marc's and Shelley's fight, but I was near to keeling over from starvation. "I'll take you up on your offer." I smiled and sat down on the other barstool. "I never turn down forty-clove chicken."

"You know your Julia Child." He toasted me and the ping of the crystal echoed off of the stainless steel tables like a church bell.

Halfway through the meal we turned off the lights and lit the candles. By dessert we were feeding each other raspberries dipped in melted chocolate and swigging champagne directly from the bottle. At the end of the meal we were dancing an excruciatingly slow two-step, my bare feet resting on the tops of his cowboy boots while one free arm encircled each other's waists, the other held a snifter of cognac. We sang Gershwin songs to each other in between sips of cognac.

"Mary, I like feisty women. I like you," he whispered. The alcohol on his breath sent shivers down my neck. I ran a hot hand down the long length of his back. It went on forever. Desire danced a marathon up and down my body. I wet my lips with the last of the cognac and pulled him toward me.

You can't always get what you want. But sometimes you get what you need.

Chapter Seventeen

"You're one great piece of ass, Mary."

Marc nibbled on my ear for a few seconds and then nestled his head between my left ear and my shoulder blade. Following the curve of my body, he shimmied even closer to me, sealing every possible air pocket. A searching hand found my breast.

In my twenties that type of remark would have raised my feminist ire to just short of nuclear. I'd have ranted and raved for ten minutes, thrown on my clothes, and exited with some well-placed insults. At thirty-five, I basked in the knowledge that I was still an object of desire, that a young stud muffin whose entrance into a room caused every female student to lick her lips twice found me, dare I say it, hot.

In the back of Marc's VW camper van, the clean, spanky aroma of Tide detergent mingled with the musty smell of fresh sex. We lay spoon-fashion on top of every piece of clothing Marc owned, snuggled under a trench coat for warmth, with my bunched-up clothes for a pillow.

Earlier, we'd raced through the kitchen scooping up plates, silverware, pots and pans, and thrown everything into the dishroom. After a perfunctory wipe-down of stainless steel tables, we'd repeatedly punched the elevator button between frantic, hot kisses. I dropped my keys twice as I struggled to unlock the elevator to ride down to the garage where Marc's van was parked. Only the elevator's security camera stopped us from ripping each other's clothes off right then and there. As the elevator made its slow descent into the garage, we'd faced each other, panting with anticipation.

Sex at my age is no longer that long road of wonder and discovery that makes young love so poignant and unforgettable. Thank God. Now I know what I want and how to get it. It's more mechanical, but it's also a hell of a lot more fun.

I'd been celibate for over two years, three counting the last year of my marriage. Jim and I'd had sex only as a pathetic attempt to tell ourselves that the relationship couldn't be over. We were still having sex weren't we?

Now I was like a vegan who, walking by The House of Prime Rib, suddenly finds herself almost crazy from a deprivation she didn't even know existed. Storming through the front door, she lunges for the first piece of prime rib she can find and begins tearing it apart with her bare hands, stuffing the hunks of meat into her mouth to satiate a wild, painful hunger. We rumbled, we tumbled—my Pandora's box of a sex drive more than a match for Marc's raging young male testosterone. I wouldn't be surprised if all of Marc's clothes weren't covered in scorch marks.

Finally, after two hours of sexual acrobatics that left me sore and smug in a gee-I-didn't-know-my-body-could-do-THAT kind of way, we were satiated. I stretched my arms and back in a cat-like, post-coital grace and linked my hands behind my head. I was a very happy camper.

"Must have been some fight for Shelley to dump all your clothes in the hallway," I said, wriggling to escape a shirt button poking me in the butt.

"Yep. Shelley's got a temper." It didn't seem to bother him; in fact, he sounded wistful.

"Don't worry, by tomorrow she'll have calmed down. Surprise her with two dozen roses and a bottle of French champagne."

"Not this time, I blew it," he sighed. "She's going to France."

"Oh?" I said, in what I hoped was appropriate surprise. No need to broadcast how much I knew about her travel plans.

"I probably shouldn't tell you this," he said sheepishly. "But she's planning on ditching school at the end of the semester. She's got a gig lined up in Paris. Wants me to join her."

Early in our marriage, Jim and I spent three weeks eating our way through France. Did we visit Versailles? No, we ate at Alain Chapelle's. Did we climb to the top of Notre Dame? No, we sipped frothy cappuccinos at Deux Maggots, searching in vain for the ghosts of Hemingway and Fitzgerald. Young love, eating warm baguettes as only the French can bake, espressos in cafes, sex in the afternoon. And the food, the food! I practically had another orgasm just thinking about it.

"Sounds like a lot of fun." Now it was my turn to sound wistful.

"Told her no."

I raised myself up on one elbow and stroked Marc's chin once before raking my lips over his for the last time. "Marc, you hate it here." I waved a hand in the general direction of school. "You're not cooking the food you want to cook. How many more times can you order students to plate up *Duck à L'Orange* without going barking mad?"

"It's personal. You wouldn't understand."

His sulky whine put a pinprick in my bubble of contentment. Ugh. How young he sounded. Time to get dressed, go home, and wake-up in my own bed. I wasn't going to beat myself up over having sex in the back of a van like a drunken sixteen-year old on prom night. It'd been a lot of fun. But in the blur of our sexual escapade, it'd been very easy to forget the ten years between us. What if we woke-up in the back of the van and Marc spent the whole morning squirming with embarrassment, privately blaming our passion solely on the gallons of wine and champagne we'd consumed? Maybe if I left now what we'd both remember would be the taste of our kisses, sweet from the cognac and raspberries.

"Hand me my clothes, will you?" I ordered. "They're under your head. I need to get home and get some sleep. I've got a double shift tomorrow." He dutifully lifted his head and handed me the bundle. I began to unravel my clothes, searching for my underwear and socks. A hopeless endeavor in the dark. "Is there a light in this thing?"

Marc reached above me and flicked on the overhead light. Climbing out from under the trench coat, I slipped on my jeans and shirt, then balled my underwear and bra and shoved them in my pockets. I pulled on my socks and laced up my hightops. I tucked the trench coat under the length of Marc's body and gave his waist one last caress.

"See you later," I said and kissed him gently on the lips, all passion gone. In the faint, yellow light with the trench coat up to his chin he looked about six years old.

"Don't go," he asked with enough quiet desperation to make me feel a little bit like a sexual heel.

"I have to," I lied. "I have a bunch of material at home I need to bring to school. It was…"—I was going to say fun, but it was more than that— "…lovely, Marc. Truly lovely. Thank you for a wonderful evening. But it's time for me to go home." I looked at my watch. Two a.m. "The flower mart down on Fourth Street opens up in an hour. Go scrounge up two dozen roses and make nice to Shelley. I'm telling you from experience. There are people who come into your life who are irreplaceable. It's like you share the same DNA." The stiff hurt on O'Connor's face when I told him to go back to his wife flashed in front of me. "When you find them, grab them, because they're as rare as hen's teeth. Is Shelley like that for you?"

"Yeah," he mumbled and then pulled the trench coat even tighter around his neck, as if embarrassed by this confession.

"Go to Paris. You're young. You've got no worries, no mortgage, no kids. Some things can't be put on hold." I flung back over one shoulder and put a hand on the door handle, poised to make my exit.

I'd never before experienced claustrophobia, but the back of this van was getting smaller by the minute. Perhaps if we'd been in a normal-sized room, my impatience and Marc's immaturity wouldn't have seemed so apparent. When thrashing around like teenagers in a confined space only heightened the sexual tension, sniping at each other in a space roughly three feet by four feet was akin to throwing a gallon of light fluid on a bunch of coals and then igniting it with a blowtorch.

"You sound like Shelley. Have you two been comparing notes?"

The bitter tone in his voice made me stop. With a savage jerk, Marc threw off the trench coat and after rifling through the pile of clothes, grabbed a pair of jeans.

"We're young. Why won't you come with me? What's going on?" Marc sing-songed in a vicious parody of Shelley. He pulled on the jeans, muttering. "Nagging bitch."

I was halfway out the door when I heard him add "...es."

I climbed back in the van and slammed the door shut. I don't know what made me lose my cool so completely. Maybe it was because now I'd be driving across the Bay Bridge not remembering the taste of those raspberries; instead I'd be fuming the whole time how I'd wasted four hours of my life screwing some guy with the maturity level of Bart Simpson.

Crouching in front of Marc, I screamed at him, "You, asshole. This had been one of the nicest nights I've had in a long time, and you had to go ruin it with your little temper tantrum. I should send Shelley a note congratulating her on ridding herself of such a jerk. Clearly, your immaturity extends to all aspects of your life. Shelley. Étienne. He might have the students carve vegetables into little shapes for hours, but the first spoonful of his soup, *any* soup, will bring tears of joy to your eyes. He doesn't deserve your scorn anymore than you deserve his respect. Cooking is a very small world, Marc. Menu by menu you're building a reputation for being a cocky *prima donna* who is way too big for his chef's whites. This school graduates a hundred students every four months. Lots of those students like Étienne. Your petty shenanigans at the school are already making waves in the industry. Who's going to hire a trouble-maker?"

I hated him. Perhaps a one-night stand isn't the healthiest of barometers for getting back into the dating scene, but tonight all I needed was for someone to tell me I was beautiful, desirable.

Nothing more. So instead of looking back on this night and patting myself on the back that I'd crossed an important threshold, I'd be berating myself for being unbelievably stupid and desperate. That's the last time I'm going to be spontaneous. If I didn't leave, I'd smack him. I turned and was once again halfway out of the door when Marc grabbed me by both arms, spun me around with a force that knocked the wind out or me, and pulled me down on my knees and toward him until our faces were eight inches from each other.

"Trouble-maker?" he sneered. "I heard you wrote the book, darlin'. A new restaurant every six months until Brett Brown hired you. Heard you had him nicely pussy-whipped. Jumped when you said jump."

Our insults ricocheted off the thin walls of the van. The inside of the van reeked of Tide, motor oil, and sex. I grabbed a deep breath, fighting back an ever-increasing sense of claustrophobia.

"Don't you dare insult Brett Brown," I spat back. "He'd wipe the kitchen floor with you. That chicken you served for lunch the first day? He'd have jumped off of the bridge before he'd serve shit like that." I tried to wrestle free but he only tightened his grip. "I don't know what your secret agenda is—"

"What secret agenda?" he demanded and gave me a shake.

I might be skinny, but I'm strong. You haul sixty-eight pound butter block around for a living and you build some upper body strength. I wrenched myself out of his grip. But instead of making a break for the door like I should have, my temper, as always, got the better of me. I shoved my face even closer to his, the hot breath of his anger mixed with mine.

"Making the chefs choose sides in your one-man war to get Étienne fired. Strolling your sexy body through the corridor trying to woo everyone into signing your petition. And worst of all, trying to rifle through a dead woman's lock…"

Shit.

He grabbed me again, this time his arms locked around me in a vise so strong I thought my lungs wouldn't have room to move.

"What do you know about me and Allison's locker?"

Chapter Eighteen

Will I ever learn to keep my big mouth shut?

Marc clamped me to his chest, our kneeling bodies pressed against each other in the cramped cab of the van, faces two inches apart, both of us panting in rage. The faint smell of cognac filled the interior of the van. Funny, how not two hours ago this position would have had me shaking with desire and the panting would have signaled mutual unbridled lust.

Okay, Mary, the best defense is a good offense.

"First of all, I had a right to be there. It is the *women's* locker room. Second, let me go. Now," I ordered. "You're hurting me."

Surprisingly, he did. I flexed my arms and rotated my shoulders. The park rangers tell you when you meet a bear try to make yourself big. Didn't think this applied to being on one's knees, but I crawled backwards a few inches, straightened my back, and thought "TALL."

"Yeah, so why didn't you say anything when you heard our voices," he countered, doing some very adequate verbal maneuvers of his own. "Were you spying on us?"

Think fast, Mary. Why wouldn't I have said anything? "I'd just used the bathroom and…it started overflowing. No mop, nothing." He grimaced, remembering the stench in the locker room. "I was dancing trying to save my shoes from getting covered in shit, if you really want to know. By the time you and Shelley arrived I was about to scream for the lifeboats. The overflow was nearly up to my laces."

When in doubt gross out. A trick I learned from my nine-year old nephew.

He cocked his head to one side, apparently trying to determine whether I was telling the truth or not. I greeted his study with nonchalance born out of years of lying. Brazen I do very well. Visual dueling is child's play to a Catholic girl. I'd faced nuns who'd have had the masterminds of the Spanish Inquisition quaking in their robes.

Marc didn't stand a chance.

"Why didn't you say anything when you heard our voices?" he demanded again. But I heard the waver in his voice. I had him.

"Told you, I was up to my ankles in sewage. The school was closed for the weekend. I think I'm alone and all of a sudden I hear a male voice in the women's locker room. Pardon me, if I decided to keep my mouth shut and stay put. And then, if you remember, Shelley started grabbing at zippers and buttons. Would that have been the optimum time to announce my presence?" He had the grace to blush. "So. What's your story? What were you hoping to find in Allison's locker?"

Marc shoulders slumped. Victory. Sitting back against the wall of the van, he rested his head on his knees and then wrapped his arms around his legs. He began shivering, his torso pale and thin in the weak yellow light from the ceiling.

"Shut the door, will you? It's cold," he said.

I slammed the door closed, sat back against the door, and rubbed my arms in an attempt to numb the bruises while waiting for his answer.

He looked up and saw me rubbing my arms.

"Did I hurt you?"

"No," I lied.

"I…You have to believe me. I wasn't going to steal anything. I wanted to see if she had anything I could use against Benson. Then when I saw her locker all trashed I freaked out."

"Back-up," I ordered. "What do you mean, 'use against Benson?'"

"You know what a kiss-ass Allison was. Always twittering around Benson and Antonello. Chef this and chef that," he intoned in falsetto. "Acting like some horny sixteen-year old all the time. Always in Antonello's kitchen. Or up in Benson's office complaining. Mostly about me." He grimaced. "Hand me that sweatshirt would you. It's colder than fuck in here." I threw the sweatshirt at him, and he slipped it over his head and then knees in an effort to get warm. "She pulled a lot of la-di-da shit on me right off the bat, sort of I'm Queen of the May in this place and you'd better watch it. I came this close to sabotaging her butter with fish stock. Could she even cook?"

"Take my word for it, Marc. She could cook. I admit, she might have been trapped in a time warp. If it was good enough for Escoffier, it was good enough for her. Showpieces were her true forte." I remembered all the showpieces Allison and I had put together, the sharing of recipes and meals, I leaned my back hard into the wall of the van to blunt the lump swelling in my chest. "Spun sugar, pastillage. That's where she truly shone."

"Why the flack, then? I'm a good cook." he protested.

I thought for a moment, the different career paths the two of us had chosen. One determined to take on the world, the other thinking the world wasn't worth taking on.

"She probably felt threatened by a chef like you. Someone not classically trained, just kitchen smart and talented. At the school she could do the showpiece crap, be a big fish in a small pond. The kitchen hustle wasn't her type of dance. She knew her limitations. In a real kitchen, she wouldn't have lasted two weeks."

"Well, she wouldn't give me the time of day," he grumbled.

"Perhaps your physical charms didn't work for her. That Elvis Presley-like swagger, the lazy grin. Just didn't pull her chain."

"Maybe not," he grinned. "But I pulled your chain, honey, didn't I? Man, did I pull your chain."

Normally, that sort of cheap remark would have enraged me. I must be getting old. I didn't feel indignant, just tired, and only confirmed to me how horribly young Marc was.

Memo to self: do not sleep with men under the age of forty.

"Allison was made of sterner stuff. I'm easy pickings," I admitted and added silently, *apparently*. Considering how sexually deprived I was, one of the three stooges—well, perhaps not Shemp—could have propositioned me and I would have pulled. "Back to the issue at hand. How does this tie in with Allison, her locker, and Benson?"

"Uh, the light's hurting my eyes, mind if I turn it off?" he asked, but didn't wait for a response as he reached over and flicked the switch. "I heard them arguing," he said to the dark. "One day in the hallway near the store room. Classes were on, and I guess they figured no one could hear them. I couldn't hear them very well, they were whispering, but it was definitely angry sort of whispering, and at one point Allison lost it and said really loud, 'I'm tired of waiting, Bob. I know what's going on. One month, I'm going to give you one month.' Then she stalked off. I knew it was a long shot, I thought she might have a notebook or something to blackmail Benson with. So he'd fire Étienne."

"Blackmail Benson? Fire Étienne?" I repeated in horror. "Are you out of your frigging mind?" I snapped the light back on. "No wonder you wouldn't tell Shelley what was going on. Last time I checked, blackmail was illegal. Not to mention that little B and E thing."

He shrugged.

"It wasn't really illegal," he protested weakly and reached again to off the overhead light. I pushed his hand out of the way. Like a small boy who's been caught stealing the last cookie, he shoved both arms under his armpits wrapped his arms around himself even tighter, as if compressing his body would legitimize the rationalization.

"Bullshit. I was the wife of a cop for ten years. This might not apply in the state of Texas, but here in California breaking and entering means prison time with cellmates nicknamed the Terminator."

Silence.

"Out with it, Marc. I need to know. Otherwise I'm reporting you to Benson. I'm serious. Tell me." I extended my foot across the length of the van and kicked his ankle—hard—to make sure he knew I meant business.

"I'm still cold." Marc shivered. Grabbing the raincoat we'd snuggled under after our sexual high jinx, he wrapped himself up in it, his eyes moving everywhere around the van but where I was sitting.

"Quit stalling," I demanded. "I want to know what's going on. You have five seconds. One, two, three—"

"Okay, okay," he sighed. Closing his eyes and taking a big breath, as if what he was going to say required a tremendous amount of energy, he mumbled, "Étienne's my father."

That was truly the last thing I expected him to say. It takes a lot to leave me speechless, but I couldn't say a word. He opened his eyes a crack to gauge my reaction.

"Don't tell anyone. I don't want it spread around," Marc admonished.

Ah, yes, I thought. The nose. That Gallic nose that looked so foreign on his perennially sleepy looking face. Rather like a finding a mushroom on top of a chocolate cake. The infallibility of genetics aside, I was still confused. I hadn't work with these men for more than a couple of weeks, but I definitely didn't see signs that they knew each other. Quite the contrary, it had been water pitchers at fifty paces.

"There's something seriously wrong with this equation, Marc. Why would you try to get you own father fired?"

"As a kid, I never knew who my father was. You know how kids are. Pestered my mama and got vague bullshit. He was French, couldn't come to this country. His family wouldn't let them marry. Never any details. When I started high school she told me I had the right to know who he was." The eyes closed again, the pain too private to share with me. I got up and crawled over next to him, moving my shoulder hard against his to help him bear this burden that in reality could only be borne by him. I reached up and turned off the light. Groping in the dark for his hand, I brought it up to my warm cheek and cradled it there. It was cold and lifeless.

"Did you contact him? He must have been here teaching by then."

"Nope, didn't really care. We had a pretty nice life, my mama and me. She taught French in the high school, encouraged me to cook, said it was a gift from my father. Bastard. Mama died a couple of years ago, and when I was cleaning out her stuff I found a bunch of letters she wrote him. First telling him how much she missed him, then she was pregnant, then begging him to marry her. He dumped her. God knows why he returned those letters or why she kept the ones he wrote her. Only showcased the true turd he is. He wrote a few checks over the years. That was it."

I tried to ignore the tight knots forming in my neck. "How'd they meet?"

"She was an exchange student. Junior year abroad. Texas girl from a town with maybe three thousand people going to Paris and having some young French guy make love to you. It was like shooting fish in a barrel." He rested his head against my shoulder, as if its weight were too much to bear. "Anyway, she got pregnant, didn't know until she got home, and from that point on he ignored her. I was okay with not having a father until I read those letters.

"The cruelty and the selfishness, Mary. All the time he's making a name for himself, earning the big bucks, while she's a high school French teacher in a hick town where a gourmet meal is having green leaf instead of iceberg in your salad and ninety-five percent of the population speaks Spanish. This," and he pointed in the direction of the school, "is important to him. Really floats his boat. Well, my mother was important to me. I'm going to get him fired if it's the last thing I do."

He pulled his hand away from my cheek and pounded the floor of the van with his fist; the cheap metal reverberated with his rage.

Sometimes you let people talk, sometimes you feel it's necessary to say something to ease their pain, and sometimes you need to say something and know you're going to get smacked in the chops for it. I knew I was opting for door number three on this one, but I couldn't sit there and say nothing.

I reached over and followed the path of his arm to find that fist I knew would be clenched tight. I very gently wrapped my own hand around it and brought it up to my face and kissed it with extreme tenderness.

"Marc. Give this up. Go to Paris. If Shelley goes to France, you've lost her." That hit home; he stiffened.

"I told him who I was, Mary. My second day on the job here." He said these words so softly that with my free hand I cupped his head even closer into the well between my ear and shoulder blade in an effort to catch every quiet word. "I thought he'd be proud. You know, I'm a pretty good chef. Made a rep for myself already. Christ, I'm only twenty-six years old, and I've got television producers trying to hook me for cooking shows. He looked at me like I was yesterday's dog shit. I went berserk, screaming at the top of my lungs what was so fucking wrong with my mother and me that he ignored our very existence. He said nothing. Just adjusted his chef's toque and walked out of the locker room."

I shifted my weight and wrapped my arms around him, pulling him into my chest, trying not to crush him with my own rage. To throw away a child like that. I'd undergone fertility treatments for several months with no success. As our marriage disintegrated, Jim and I tacitly agreed that continuing them would be profoundly irresponsible. Part of my horrible anger toward Jim when our marriage fell apart was the fear that my one chance for having children had walked out the door. To throw away a son. Fool.

I gave him a chaste hug. "Buy two planes tickets. One for you, one for Shelley. Getting Étienne fired is not going to get you the father you want. You play poker?"

He nodded.

"Then fold this hand. He doesn't want to play, and the cost of you playing is too high."

"Don't know if I can," he murmured.

"This is the voice of experience talking. I've played this game with my own father and you can't win. You'll get a shitty hand every time. Trust me."

As with most of my advice, I'd be a much happier woman if I ever followed it. My dad walked out the door when I was three and for many years I played this emotional poker, losing every time. One thing my father did, however, ultimately saved me from the bitterness Marc was holding on to for such dear life. One memory that was sort of his salvation.

There's an old-fashioned restaurant out on Hegenberger Road near the Oakland Airport called Gino's. It's had the same menu for thirty years. One Sunday before my father remarried, we were playing family, even though my parents had been officially divorced for years. My mother was in the front seat, sister and I in the back. I guess I was about eight, my sister six. We drove past Gino's. God knows why we were even out driving that day; it was pissing outside like you can't believe. The wipers were going full bore and all the windows were fogged up from the heat of our breath. Suddenly, my father swerves over the highway median and does a U-turn like Steve McQueen in the chase scene from *Bullitt*.

Dad begins yelling about freeing the donkeys from the rain. The poor beasts were getting drenched, he shouts. None of it made any sense. With a squeal of breaks he pulls up in front of Gino's, jumps out of the car, not even bothering to slam the door. Rain's pouring in from the open door. My mother rolls down her window trying to figure out what in hell was going on. Using our sleeves to wipe the windows clear, my sister and I see my father wading through the ice plant. He stops, waits a few seconds, and then with his head down, returns to the car. He gets in, nobody says a word and we drive off.

They weren't real donkeys, of course, just Gino's idea of landscaping. Stone donkeys chained in ice plant. They're still there. Now they are painted red, white and green, the colors of the Italian flag. I saw them a couple of months ago. But when I was a child they weren't painted, and on a rainy winter's day, to a man with rather bad eyesight, they looked like real donkeys.

I dust this story off and replay it in my memory banks whenever I don't get a birthday card or think about playing the kind of hate poker Marc had been dealing himself. Not a bad man, perhaps a terrible father.

After a few minutes, Marc and I lay back down on the makeshift bed of laundry and nestled each other spoon fashion to grab a couple of hours of sleep before school began. But neither of us slept. Occasionally one of us would move an arm to check the luminous dials on our watches and then sigh. I don't know what kept Marc awake, but whenever I closed my eyes all I saw was an eight-year old girl with brown eyes and braids, nose pressed against the rain-splattered window, watching her father trying to free stone donkeys from the iceplant.

Chapter Nineteen

At 6:00 a.m. the alarms on our watches went off simultaneously. If I ever spend another night on the floor of a VW van, I'll be crippled for life. I couldn't help but moan as I tried to raise myself up on my elbows. Every muscle hurt. And not in the ways that I liked.

"Here." Marc cupped my elbow and helped me into a sitting position. "You look pretty tired. You okay?"

I figured "pretty tired" was code for "total shit," but I managed a small smile. After being up all night, Marc merely looked sleepy, eyes tight around the edges. I probably looked like an extra from *Night of the Living Dead*.

"Let's get out of here. It's going to be a long day," I sighed. A double shift on maybe fifteen minutes of sleep. It would be eleven tonight before I'd have a chance to even think about my head touching a pillow. I sniffed, the smell of sex and Tide still lingered in the air. Pointed my nose toward Marc and sniffed again. Sex, no Tide. "We need to hit the showers before anyone else comes in." I forced one knee to follow the other across the floor of the van, realizing that the only way to get through this day was a minute at a time.

Marc hung back as if not sure how to play this. Post-coital remorse? Most likely, post-coital confusion. Like he was supposed to say something about how great it was, or how pretty I was, and then segue into vague, clumsy hints about how this will never happen again.

I didn't need to hear it, didn't need to be given the soft landing, but I guess Marc was young enough that he hadn't lost all of
his innocence. He was probably a little puzzled to wake up, the
heavy aroma of mutual passion clinging to his body, but in the
cold morning light, no romance to disguise what was basically
a screw. His brow creased in confusion. Perhaps he still believed
that you had to be a little in love with someone to bed them.
And who's to say he wasn't right? Maybe we had been a little in
love. The memory of the raspberries, the dancing, the music.
Was I going to begrudge myself six hours of love?

So although I really didn't feel like picking up the slack here—I
desperately needed to get out of the van and get to a shower—I
decided to acknowledge that innocence, pay tribute to it. I turned
around and ran a gentle hand along the stubble of his chin.

"Hey, it was good. I felt desired." This was said with a slight
catch in my voice because it was true. It had been so very long
since I'd desired and been desired. "I can't tell you what this
meant to me." I ran my thumb along the plane of his jaw. Such
a nice jaw. "Thank you. But you have someone you love." For
emphasis I kissed him lightly, pulled on his bottom lip just a
tad, and then let go. "Now make nice with Shelley and dig out
that passport."

I got back a grin of relief. We could dine at the chef's table
together, meet in the hallways, no sweat.

Poking a head around the door of the van, I checked out the
parking lot before I climbed out. Coast clear. The last thing I
needed was for a student to see Marc and me exiting the van,
hair wild, clothes wrinkled, looking like we'd just auditioned
for a porno flick. Marc followed me, his eyes shifting left to
right with his own sneaky little glances. I wasn't the only one
concerned about the stupidity of making our little tryst public
knowledge. All of a sudden remembering that that were cameras in the elevators, I spit in my hands and smoothed my hair
back. It's times like these when I realize I will *never* grow my
hair back again.

Our clogs clip-clopped across the concrete in a slow, tired gait.

Hellish. The day was going to be nothing short of hellish.

Reaching the elevators, I barely had the energy to push the Up button. As the doors began to close, someone shouted, "Hold the door." Oh. My. God. No. I lunged for the Close button, but O'Connor just managed to squeeze-in before they wheezed shut.

I said nothing, staring ahead, refusing to make eye contact. Marc greeted O'Connor with a lazy, "Hey."

That "hey" went nowhere; the word hung in an embarrassed limbo. Silence from O'Connor. As the elevator rose, I tried to inch my way toward Marc so O'Connor wouldn't smell sex in my hair. Pointless really, the entire elevator car reeked of old sweat and sex. He knew, oh, he knew. If his disapproval had been any stronger, I would have had to hack it back with a machete.

One half of me wanted to grab his shoulders, face him, demanding that he voice this disgust so that I could fling that disgust right back at him. How dare he? The other half of me shrank from confronting him, afraid I was forever diminished in his eyes.

When the elevator door opened, I fled to the security of the women's locker room. Once inside, I moved on auto-pilot to the far corner of the room. Shit! Humiliation so ripe that my cheeks felt like they were on fire, I first leaned one red cheek, then the other against the cool steel of a locker door. Why did I feel like some fifteen-year old whose father has caught her with her boyfriend's hand down her pants?

The door to the locker room slammed back against the wall.

"Mary!" O'Connor's voice demanded.

I didn't reply, shrank into the corner. Maybe he'd go away.

"I saw you come in here. Where are you?"

I waited two beats. Please go away, I prayed.

"Goddamn it, Mary," he growled.

Finally, the feisty, I-don't-have-to-take-this-shit-from-you genes kicked in. You know the Irish really have an unfair advantage. Except when it's Irish facing down Irish.

"I have nothing to say to you, O'Connor. Nothing." My voice echoed throughout the room, bouncing off the metal lockers. I sounded defiant. Excellent. The fact that I was propped up against the locker to brace my weak knees was immaterial.

In the five seconds it took for him to find me, I'd bucked up and thrown my shoulders back. I had done nothing wrong. He wasn't going to shame me. I had no intention of acting the penitent.

Take the high road, Mary. Ask him to leave. Nicely, if possible and then try to manufacture out of thin air the energy you need to get through this day.

Turning the corner, he stopped short when he saw me. My height, plus the couple of inches my clogs gave me meant we were staring at each other eyeball to eyeball. The weak fluorescent light cast a green glow over his skin. His lips pressed together with suppressed rage, he took two steps toward me and stopped.

"How old is he?" he sputtered. "I thought you had more sense."

Okay, high road not an option.

"You have no right." I tried to control myself but my response was only a little bit shy of a shout. "None." I sliced the air with my hand.

He came two steps closer. "Aside from the age thing, do you know how stupid it is to fuck your colleagues?"

I stepped back two steps. To stop myself from hitting him. "What I do and with whom I do it is *my* business. I don't need your goddamned approval, O'Connor. He made me feel sexy, beautiful, feelings I haven't felt for months. Years even. It might seem like settling for leftovers...." I was so cold and getting colder, like some essential spark was dying in me. I wrapped my arms around myself to try to stop the shivering. "Do you understand? I go home at night and I'm alone. Nobody's in my bed asking me about my day. Nobody rubs my back. Nobody hugs me hello or good-bye. Aside from the fucking," at this he winced, "it felt wonderful just to have someone hold me."

I bit my lip in an effort not to cry. Smug, Catholic bastard. So easy for him. The wife, the children who adore him. "I...I haven't had a man want me in a very long time." The memory of Marc's passion as he mouthed his way down my body with such obvious enjoyment warmed me just a little; God, how long had it been? "You face an empty house with an equally empty bed for two years and then you have the right to judge me," I countered.

"I'm not judging you, Mary," he said stiffly.

"Utter bullshit. It's on the tip of your tongue just how many Hail Marys and Our Fathers I should say to atone for my sins." I turned around and shuffled to my locker. A shaking hand fumbled uselessly with my combination lock. "Get out of here. I got fifteen minutes of sleep last night and have a double shift ahead of me. I need to pull it together." I leaned my forehead against the locker. It was the only thing holding me up.

A hand, so gentle I barely felt it, turned me around. I twisted my head to the side, scrunching my eyes shut.

"Look at me, Mary."

I shook my head.

"Please."

Knowing this was a mistake, knowing I would hate what I saw, disgust, disappointment, the how-could-you in his eyes. I opened my eyes, steeling myself for his scorn.

What I saw was far worse.

"That's not true," he whispered. "He's not the only man who…" and his face crumpled. His voice broke, followed by a deep breath so heavy with profound sadness that it threatened to bow him, to crush him under its weight.

I closed my eyes. "I know," I whispered back. "Please go."

Chapter Twenty

Forcing my feet to move, I stumbled into the shower and scrubbed away all traces of my desperate grab for desire. I dragged a toothbrush across my teeth, the mint-flavored toothpaste stamping out the last remnants of raspberry and cognac. Once dressed, I manage to negotiate my way to the dining room without breaking an ankle. I lifted a weak hand to greet the chefs' table, the other gripping a coffee mug steeping with three tea bags of maté. I thought, fucking hell, I'll never make it through this day.

Handing out assignments, my voice raw with exhaustion, I told my students I was fighting the flu, and if they had any questions I'd be at my desk trying not to barf. About 8:00 a.m., the maté kicked in full force. I pulled my aching body upright and found I could walk without feeling like my knees were missing.

I paired the people who'd worked in kitchens with people who'd only eaten in restaurants, praying that this would minimize the mistakes. O'Connor and I successfully avoided all contact. Right off the bat, I asked that he man the ovens (a completely ludicrous request as the person filling the oven should be responsible for unloading it), but he'd looked relieved and parked himself up in the little ante room containing the ovens.

Shortly after I'd pulled myself into a standing position, a student asked me if I'd check to see if his cookies were done. A quick sip of yet more maté (why is there never a double shot of tequila at your fingertips when you really need it), I followed her back to the ovens. Cupping a delicate paper cone filled with melted chocolate, O'Connor stood over a table practicing writing, those thick, strong hands engulfing the delicate parchment, hands that were meant to grasp a gun or a shovel. The hands of an Irish cop or farmer. And yet for all his strength, there was a sweet grace to that broad back as he gently pinched the paper cone so that the chocolate oozed out onto the stainless steel table in a continuous flow, forming letters as he moved the cone up and down.

"Are they done, Chef Mary?"

I coughed, trying to erase the hitch riding my voice. "They'll taste better and won't get stale as fast if you let them go another couple of minutes. You want to caramelize the sugar a little."

At the sound of my voice, O'Connor's back stiffened. With a swift scrape of the spatula against the stainless steel table, he wiped away all his handy-work. But not before I saw in perfect Catholic school cursive, the phrases, "Happy Birthday Aidan," "I cannot," "Happy Anniversary," "Duty," "Marriage," and "Love."

I returned to my desk, propping myself up on one elbow sipping maté, eyes open but seeing nothing. Physically and emotionally wrung dry, a student could be in flames and I wouldn't have noticed. The words, "passion," "loneliness," desire," and "sin," formed and reformed in my mind, and every time I tried to wipe it clean they reappeared in perfect Catholic school cursive.

Because of my near state of insensibility, I didn't notice until it was nearly time for break that Coolie was wearing her Audrey Hepburn, *Breakfast at Tiffany's*, shades in class. Not that they didn't complement in a weird way her checked pants, but this was the height of stupidity. Even in the glare of the overhead lights, anything that obscured your vision in a room filled with knives and bone-crushing equipment was equivalent to putting a sign on your back with the words, Hurt Me!

Icing a cake with such a deft hand I'd have sworn that she'd been doing it a lifetime, her spatula barely kissed the buttercream as she smoothed it over the sponge with enough buttercream to cover the cake completely, but not smother it. Normally, this takes hours of practice, cake after cake after cake to get the rhythm right. She probably could have done it blindfolded. And considering how dark were the lens of these glasses, she probably was.

I leaned over her and said into her ear, "Coolie, please take off the glasses. Not in the kitchen." If I'd been my usual self I might have said something along the lines of sacrificing fashion for her art, but since every word took an inordinate amount of energy, I left it at the warning.

When we were just about to break for lunch, I saw Coolie, still sporting the sunglasses, pushing a rack of completed cakes toward the walk-in. What the hell? When she'd put finished rolling the rack into the walk-in, I cornered her when she came out.

"Hey, I said no sunglasses. It's dangerous. Off," I ordered. The last thing I needed was for my favorite student breaking a leg because she tripped over a milk crate at her feet.

She lowered her chin. All I could see was the top of her paper chef's toque shaking no.

"Coolie," I snapped and pointed at my eyes.

Lifting her head, her body went rigid and then shuddered. With an impossibly long and elegant finger, the nail of which had been gnawed down to the nail bed, she slid the glasses down her nose to reveal a black eye. Someone had clocked her good; her left eye was almost swollen shut, the bruising and swelling looked fresh. Tears shimmered in the corner of her eyes before she shoved the glasses back up. Her mouth puckered and then quivered as she strained to keep from breaking down.

Students were pushing by us, arms full of crates of milk or struggling with filled stock pots, eager to get things put away before breaking for lunch. By not moving we were in danger of being trampled. I grabbed her by the arm and led her out of the kitchen into the dining room. We had a couple of minutes before the students started pouring in for lunch. I sat her down at a table. Huddling in her chair, her slim shoulders hunched forward in a painful U, she began fumbling with the salt and pepper shakers. She wouldn't look at me, her chin resting on her chest, her eyes obscured by the glasses. She said nothing, leaving it up to me to begin.

"Did your boyfriend do this?"

"No," she mumbled. "Don't have a boyfriend."

"Another student?" I tried not to sound too horrified.

A shake of the head.

"Someone I know?"

Another shake of the head.

"Mary," a low female voice called to me across the dining room. Marilyn Cantucci.

"Dean Benson would like to see you in his office." Twenty years of smoking had roughened her voice to a perpetual growl. Why does that sound sexy on Lauren Bacall, but on anyone else you wonder if they have a cancer specialist on speed dial? She flicked a quick glance Coolie's way, dismissive and patronizing.

I acknowledged her request with a curt nod, not trusting myself to comment just yet. I hid my dislike with a brief glance across the dining room.

Memo to self, the one repeated on a daily basis: do not make enemies lightly. Save your scorn for the assholes who really matter.

"I'm with a student, Marilyn. I'll be there in a minute."

Her eyes narrowed to slits, as if assaulted by a plume of cigarette smoke. "I suggest you end your conference immediately. Dean Benson would like to see you. Now." She pitched her voice even lower.

Coolie was nothing if not bright. Standing up, she pushed the glasses more firmly onto her face and said in my direction before scooting off, "Um, have something in the oven."

Marilyn winged a nasty little victory smile my way. "I see you're free." She turned around and marched away, the heels of her spectator pumps grinding sharp little points into the pile of the carpet.

I debated putting on a clean jacket; I had a smear of chocolate buttercream down the front of my jacket. As I walked to the elevator, I flipped one side to the other side (this is why chefs wear double breasted jackets) and turned my apron to the clean side. If you didn't look too closely, I appeared more or less professional. If Benson needed to see me right away, I'd better not chance the five minutes it'd take to get clean clothes from the locker room.

Marilyn hadn't bothered to hold the elevator for me. Bitch. I took the stairs two at a time and arrived in Benson's office a little breathless. On the top floor of the building, the walls were covered in that cold, photo-shopped artwork that screams interior decorator, only relieved by requisite plate glass window framing a view of the water. Or it would have been if it hadn't been January. As it was, swirls of moving fog being buffeted by strong winds coming in through the Golden Gate beat against the glass. With Benson's exaggerated sense of his own importance, he'd furnished the room in Asian antiques. But as befitting a man whom I suspect licks his plates clean when in the privacy of his own home, there were too many antiques, a little too much gilt. It had the feel of a high-class Singapore brothel.

Seated at a table near the window was Benson, in his favorite suit of choice, navy pinstripes with a white shirt and red power tie, and an older gentleman I didn't know.

But I knew the type well. My uncle is the lawyer to the movers and shakers in San Francisco. I've attended a number of parties at his home, filled to the rafters with the likes of the gentleman in front of me. Power and privilege. It wasn't the clothes, although his suit made Benson's Hong Kong tailored job look cheap—no small feat—nor the tan in the dead of winter, suggesting Christmas holidays in either of the Palms, Springs or Beach. It was the whole package. The fit and trim body broadcasting that five-mile-a-day run; the suit that hugged perfectly the cut of his shoulders, the swell of his chest. Lightly graying temples and a shave so close and tight he wouldn't have raised the nap on velvet if he'd roughed his cheek against it. It all spoke of someone who knew when to push. How to push. A lifetime of figuratively snapping fingers and watching people jump to attention.

Benson was pouring wine into the two wine glasses resting on top of a tonsu. The wine stained their wine glasses, the incomparable ruby color unique to a bottle of Robert Mondavi 1976 Reserve Cabernet Sauvignon. The bouquet of the wine as it caressed the bottom of their glasses was so intense, so full, I smelled it from two feet away.

"Mary," Benson stood up and gestured to the man still sitting. "This is William Martin. An old family friend from Chicago and on the Board of Directors of the school."

In my haste, I hadn't washed my hands. Were they clean? Not wanting to appear rude, I held out my hand. "Nice to meet you, Mr. Martin. You'll enjoy that wine. I know that particular vintage well."

He half-stood and gave my hand the briefest shake possible. Did our palms even touch? It was like the mere touch of my hand would cause the garters holding up his eighty-dollar-a-pair socks to disintegrate, resulting in unsightly puddling around his ankles. I didn't even merit a hello.

"Pardon me for interrupting, Dean Benson. Marilyn told me you wished to see me."

Benson's eyes didn't meet mine, but stared at the blob of buttercream on the edge of my lapel. I cursed myself for not changing my jacket.

"Uh, yes, M…M…Mary. It's about one of your students."

I regarded the chair in front of me, then Benson. He had the grace to blush and then moved his eyes to a jade Buddha just behind me, refusing to make eye contact. Only a complete social troglodyte wouldn't have offered me a seat. Or someone with an agenda. And Benson had the nervous stutters and twitches of someone who knew that what was about to come down was going to be ugly.

"Oh, which one?" I asked, casually bringing up a thumb and forefinger to hide the stain.

"My daughter, Melissa." Martin spoke for the first time. His voice possessed the casual, classic American, easy-mannered, friendly, how's the golf game going, kind of bonhomie. I'd been given a short and succinct lesson on exactly how unreliable that manufactured friendliness could be when at a Christmas party one year at my uncle's house one of his business partners had asked in an identical manner, "Want to suck me off, young lady?" He could have been saying, "Shot an eighty at Spyglass yesterday, how'd you do?" It was that nonchalant.

Martin picked up his glass and swirled it around, letting the wine climb up the sides of the glass. Before taking a sip, he smiled. Not a nice smile, but one that had sized me in the one minute I'd been standing there and had determined that he didn't like me. His eyes roamed slowly over the not-so-clean jacket, the scuffed up kitchen clogs, the bags under my eyes. The ghost of a smirk appeared and then smoothed away as if I weren't even worthy of the effort it took to openly sneer at me. And to hammer home his dislike, he tasted the wine and pronounced, "Delicious, Bob. Don't let your wine sit there gathering dust."

Benson grabbed the wine and gave it a perfunctory sip. "Yes, wonderful, William. One of my favorite wines," he gushed. It could have been cat piss and Benson would have still been tripping over his Bruno Maglis in his effort to stroke Martin's ego.

"I don't have a Melissa in my class." I flicked my eyes from Martin's glass to his eyes and back again. I wanted him to know that I knew he disliked me and that whatever he wanted, he could kiss my ass. Benson was only a handmaiden in this exchange. It was down to Martin and me, and both of us knew it.

"You know her by a bizarre nickname. Coolie?" Martin leaned back in his chair in a casual motion and took another sip of his wine. Focusing intently on the smear of chocolate on the right front of my jacket, he curled into his chair with the ease of a man who smelled a fight was brewing and knew he was going to win. He twirled the stem of the wineglass in his well-manicured hands; his right hand sported two slightly split knuckles.

"Yes," I agreed. "Coolie's in my class."

I slouched a little and wrapped my arms around myself in a defensive posture, just to let him think I'd cave in, a couple of snaps of the fingers away from capitulating.

"I have a request. There's a space for her at my alma mater. She's exceptionally bright. Speak to her. Suggest she leave."

Another thing I'd learned about these types. They spoke in code, the passive quality of the verbs masking the true nature of the demand. Suggest really meant order. Persuade really meant demand. Request really meant, "Do what I want and no one will get hurt. Your bank loan won't come due. Your car won't be stolen. Your house won't go up in flames. Just a simple request."

"It would be better coming from you." He took another sip of his wine and smiled to let me know exactly how delicious it was.

The smile did it.

"I understand she's of age—"

"—she's little more than a child—"

"—and has the funds to do what she wants—"

"—her mother is a fool—"

"—she was born to hold a spatula in her hand—"

"—I won't have my daughter be a goddamned cook!" he shouted, all his cards now on the table.

"And I won't have my students being beaten up. How did it feel to smash your fist into that beautiful face, Martin?"

Benson gasped. I turned to him. He'd spent most of this heated exchange downing his wine and was quickly filling up his glass with a shaking hand when my comment about Martin hitting Coolie stopped him mid-pour. Not bothering to look where he was putting it, he banged the wine bottle down on the table and shrank into his chair with that horrified air of someone who'd found himself too close to a flame and knew he was going to get burned.

"Dean, she's got it." Benson knew what I meant. That pipeline, that *groove*, that ESP about food all great chefs have. I didn't have it. I looked on colleagues who did and envied them. Not that they didn't work just as hard, but they had an intuitive sense of what worked, what didn't. I earned that knowledge through reading cookbooks, trial and error, watching other chefs, inhaling every bit, and working my ass off. My punishing drive and love for food masqueraded as greatness, but it was, literally, pie in the sky. Coolie? I knew.

"You know me. I'm not bullshitting you. She's the sort of alumni who will make this school famous one day." Benson squeaked something, not a word really. Trapped between wanting the glory for the school and acquiescing to Martin's demands, unable or unwilling to choose sides, his eyes danced frantically back and forth between me and Martin.

I turned back to face Martin. We locked eyes. I had a momentary internal shudder when I realized his eyes were the same color green as mine. "Such a gift shouldn't be thrown away."

Martin abandoned his false bonhomie. Sitting stiff and straight in his chair, he re-buttoned his jacket and cinched tighter the knot of his tie with a short, sharp jerk. In the corporate world, this is tantamount to shoving a clip in your 9mm Glock and aiming for the head.

His eyes never leaving my face, he growled out of the side of his mouth at Benson, "Fire her, Bob. Then tell Melissa to clean out her locker. She's through here." The gloves were most definitely off.

Well, time to peel off a few gloves of my own. Normally I don't throw my uncle's name around, more to protect my own reputation as a flaming liberal, but clearly the big guns were in order. I turned and faced Martin. Eye to eye.

"Dean Benson, if either of these actions were to happen, I'd have to call my lawyer." I grinned. "You remember my uncle, don't you, Bob? Dominique Porcella?" My uncle's name rolled out of my mouth in slow, honeyed tones. Flicking a quick glance at Benson, the wrenching paper-white rictus contorting his face was proof positive he *hadn't* forgotten.

My uncle was a silent member of that clique of older men who actually run this country; the CEOs, the members of the boards of corporations who wielded the real power, politicians be damned. Judging by all that Florida tan draining away, only to be replaced by the ugly flush of pure fury, William Martin knew exactly who he was.

"Just so we understand each other, I want you to know he's been retained by your daughter." A little lie, but what the hell. "He's drafting up a restraining order as we speak." Okay, a couple of lies. I swung around and faced Benson. "I suggest you rethink any thoughts you've entertained about bouncing her *or* me out of here. You want the weight of Winston, White, Howe and Porcella on your back, keep pushing on me."

"This isn't over," Martin threatened, menace punctuating every word. He coiled his fists, the shoulders of his suit jacket straining as he reared his arms back, his chair scraping against the hardwood floor from the force of his rage.

I faced him, fighting the urge to droop my shoulders, the adrenaline that had been carrying me through this exchange suddenly deserting me. "No," I stated. "I don't imagine it is. Call my lawyer."

Chapter Twenty-one

It was only eleven o'clock. Clutching the banister with one hand, I slowly wound my way down the staircase to the basement. Although I'd won the first battle of the culinary equivalent of the Hundred Year's War, I knew my threats needed teeth to them. Verbal bravado meant nothing to a man like Martin. The students would be back in the kitchen by now, but I had to make my phone call.

Standing on a bench with my head and ear pressed against the glass in an attempt to get a signal, I called my aunt.

"Aunt Mary, it's Baby Mary," I announced.

It's a very bad idea to name your child after living relatives. If you choose to give honor by naming your child after them, please make sure that they are dead as doornails, or you will be subjecting your child to embarrassing nicknames and monikers that will, trust me on this one, torture them for the rest of their born days.

I was named after my aunt. My exceptionally hale and hearty aunt, who will, no doubt, outlive me. To differentiate me from my aunt, my uncle started to call me Baby Mary. It stuck. Granted, at the age of four, it made sense. Less sense, but not that annoying, at age eight. By sixteen, it was supremely mortifying. The nadir was at my wedding, my uncle mock-admonishing Jim to take care of his beloved niece, Baby Mary. Fortunately, fully one-fourth of the guests were homicide cops, because it stopped me from stabbing my uncle with the broken end of a champagne flute.

But now, at thirty-five, I'd given up. I likened it to those people who get tattoos as teenagers and six decades later will still have sex kitten inked onto a wrinkly shoulder; of course, by then it will look like "**s e x   k i t t e n ,**" relegating you to wearing turtlenecks for your entire retirement. Short of going into a witness protection program and changing my name, I would be Baby Mary with certain members of my family until the day I died.

"Mary!" My aunt sounded very pleased.

In another century, while her liege was off fighting Infidels and squandering the family fortune on ill-conceived crusades, my aunt would have paid the tithes, planted the fields, fed the serfs, and had her children fluent in four languages by the time they were six. Like some secular abbess, albeit with five children and a husband who was one of the most powerful men in the United States, she was the right-hand "man" of the bishop of San Francisco, a fund-raiser extraordinaire, and the behind-the-scenes liaison between the mayor and the church—in old Irish Catholic cities like Boston and San Francisco, the church is still tremendously powerful. Graced with faith bone-marrow deep, my aunt's and uncle's greatest joy was seeing their eldest son, my cousin Joe, join the priesthood. To give a son to God; there was no greater blessing in their eyes. The rest of the family, with the exception of Joe, naturally, saw this as an act of madness, although all of us grudgingly admitted that Joe was supremely happy as a priest.

My lack of faith irritated my uncle and distressed my aunt. As I grew older, I conceded that their horror for my mortal soul was a sign of love, not knee-jerk nagging. Now, I acknowledged the spirit in which it was given and sloughed off good naturedly the constant arm-twisting about returning to the church. A sort of détente had been reached. At some point in our conversation, my aunt would whisper in my ear that she'd lit a candle for me that morning, and several times a year my uncle asked me wasn't it time to stop this rebellious nonsense and return to the church? I'd kiss my aunt for her prayers and tell my uncle, "Apparently not."

After missing half the family gossip due to big trucks roaring by and blocking my signal, I got down to why I called. "Is Uncle Dom in town?"

"Yes, he is. The new bishop is coming over for lunch. He should be home any...Ah, there he is. Would you like to talk with him?"

A loaded question at best. My father's abysmal lack of parenting skills prompted Uncle Dom to micromanage my life in as many annoying and completely overbearing ways possible. That he did this to no one else in the family, not my sister, nor his own children, seemed not to matter. The rest of the family accepted this as our "special" dynamic. Like it was an honor to lock horns with Dom Porcella on a thrice-yearly basis. I mean, there are five-star generals that go out of their way to avoid him in the hallways of the Pentagon, and I was supposed to accept this officious, irritating, nosy, and pushy interference into my affairs with grace and aplomb—two things I'm short on at the best of times?

My choice of profession met with complete scorn: "A cook? With your mind? I hope you're joking." My choice of husband: "Him? You'll be bored in five years." My first house: "Are you mad? In the Sunset? Fog three hundred days a year. You'll be itching to re-pack all your boxes no sooner than you unpack them." The fact that he was right two out of the three irritated me all the more.

"Baby Mary. How is teaching?"

The job at École was a step up in his eyes. At least I was out of the kitchen. Sort of. Despite growing up in a large Italian family where attendance at meals was nearly as sacrosanct as attending mass on Sunday, he'd never appreciated the physical and emotional satisfaction I gleaned from cooking. Why the food at his mother's table tasted so delicious was because it was served with love and not just a little kitchen savvy. That I'd parlayed that into a career seemed completely inexplicable to him.

"Okay," I lied, leaving out the bit where I thought Allison had been murdered and someone who had access to the changing rooms was attacking lockers with a crowbar. "Um…," I stammered. Now that I had him on the line, I didn't really knowing what I was going to ask for.

"The bishop will be here in ten minutes," he reminded me.

"Do you know a man named William Martin? Out of Chicago. High-class attorney. Has money based on his manner and tan. He has an Aspen, Palm Beach, or Palm Springs over Christmas kind of tan." I paused. "Expensive suit. Two thousand minimum."

I'm a total fashion victim as far as what I put on my back is concerned. Inexplicably, despite the fact I buy my underwear at drugstores, I can nail the cost of an outfit within fifty bucks. This is probably more a tribute to the issues of *GQ* I'm forced to read while waiting in dental offices than any real innate ability, but I must say being a fashion idiot savant has come in handy, earning me many a dinner invitation and a goodly portion of my Christmas checks from Uncle Dom. I once told him that a potential business client was skimping on the make of his suits; therefore, any deals should be scrutinized. The man went bankrupt three months later.

Silence. Goddamned trucks. Stupid cell phone.

"Uncle Dom? You there? Am I losing you?" I leaned as far as I could toward the street. "He knows you." Again, I left out minor details. Like Martin went apoplectic at the mention of Uncle Dom's name.

"I am here. Wait, Baby Mary. I need to take this in the study." A hand covered the mouthpiece, but I could still hear him call to my aunt, "Mary, do not disturb me." I heard the click, click, click of his handmade brogues—he and Prince Charles have the same shoemaker—then the sounds of a door being shut and the squeak of his study chair as he sat down. "Now. This, this Martin. How do you know him?"

Only the family can hear this, but when Uncle Dom is upset he doesn't yell, he doesn't threaten; he sounds Italian. The vowels become more pronounced, lengthen and round out; the cadence of his sentences begin to rise and fall, to sing a little. Although he grew up in San Francisco, he was first generation, and I imagine it's a throw-back to his childhood and the loud, angry arguments between his parents. When upset, the clipped baritone he'd spent a lifetime cultivating, a voice meant to be listened to and obeyed, doesn't become eclipsed, but the singsong *patois* of his youth creeps in. Most people miss it. But with his family, when you hear his sentences start to sing, it's time to start sweating bullets.

"I have a student. Her father, Martin, wants her to quit the school. He threatened me with termination if I didn't ask her to leave. He's on the Board of Directors."

Silence again. I stood on my tippy toes to keep the signal.

"Uncle Dom, you there?"

"Mary, I am here. You must stay away from this man. This student—"

"Coolie—"

"You cannot involve yourself with this girl. Martin's daughter. This is not negotiable." He had used that same dismissive and abrupt tone with me when he'd reamed me seven ways to Sunday when I told him I'd abandoned college for cooking school. Discussion closed. Well, it might work for MBAs who are a little wet behind the ears, but not on me.

"I need a restraining order. To keep him away from her," I insisted.

Silence. Then….

"A restraining order against a man like Martin?" he scoffed. "You will not involve yourself with this girl," he repeated, pausing ever so slightly between each word. Like there were periods between each one.

I lost it.

"This is not going to turn into one of our power struggles, Uncle Dom." I tried not to yell, but, goddamn it, I was done with being the niece who forever was treated like she was six. Who didn't even rate an adult name. "He struck her. She's got a black eye covering half her face. If you're not going to help me, fine." My legs finally gave out, and I crumpled into a heap on the bench. "There are twenty million lawyers in this town. I should have no trouble finding one to get me a simple restraining order." I snapped my phone shut, not even caring if he'd heard the last line or not.

Why has every man in my life failed me? From my father to my husband to my uncle...My watch began to beep signaling the hour. Curt the maitre'd, with menus tucked underneath his arm, would be showing the first patrons their seats. I tucked my phone in my back pocket and shuffled to the elevator. It was time for lunch.

Chapter Twenty-two

I found Coolie secreted in the corner of the student's locker room, sitting on the floor with her back against the wall, arms wrapped around her knees, sunglasses firmly in place.

"Does he know where you live?"

She nodded. We both knew who "he" was.

I handed over my car keys, house key, and address, lied about the restraining order (I'd take care of it in the morning), and told her that we'd make a trip over to her place sometime tomorrow to pick-up her clothes. She'd stay with me until we could find her a new apartment. That got another nod and a quiver of her bottom lip. Once I saw her step into the garage, I went back to the kitchen to finish up lunch service, and then it was another seven hours of teaching until I could finally call it a day. It was probably a blessing that I'd given Coolie my car because I was so tired by the end of the night that I wouldn't trust myself to drive; I took a cab home.

"Is this it, young miss?"

The cab driver's sing-song accent, a reminder of his birth in some horribly impoverished Caribbean island, woke me up. I had fallen asleep before we'd even hit the bridge.

It looked like my neighborhood. Yeah, the trikes of the triplets next door littering the sidewalk, the twinkle of Mrs. Harmon's Christmas lights (she confessed to me once that they'd been up for ten years now because she was too lazy to take them down), and, oh, my uncle's Town Car, parked right in front of my house.

"Yeah." Even though the meter said forty-two seventy-five, I handed him my sixty bucks and told him, "Keep the rest." I doubt I could have handled change my hands were shaking so much. Merely because I was exhausted, I told myself.

One doesn't hang-up on my uncle. Not that I regretted it. But I was also not in any physical or mental shape to butt heads with him after a mere eight hours sleep in the past thirty-six hours. I walked up to the car. The driver's side window slid silently into its sleeve.

"Evening, Luciano. My uncle?"

He pointed to my house. I had never heard Luciano speak in the twenty years he'd worked for my uncle. The house was completely dark except for the kitchen.

I let myself. Might as well get this over with.

My uncle and Coolie were sitting at my kitchen table, a pot of tea in front of them. Little wisps of steam rose from newly filled coffee mugs. Coolie still had her sunglasses on; her head was bowed.

Uncle Dom said quietly, "Good evening, Mary. We shall talk. But first, you should go to bed, Melissa. You've had a long day. My driver, Luciano, will pick you up tomorrow at 9:00 a.m. and take you to your apartment to get your clothes. I think you can miss one day of school. Yes?" I suppose that was said for my benefit. I nodded. "You will come back here?"

She looked at me for confirmation. At my "Sure, sounds good," she hoisted herself up from her chair and held out her hand. "Thanks so much, Mr. Porcella."

"Uncle Dom," he insisted and didn't shake her hand so much as grab her hand in both of his and squeeze.

"Uncle Dom," she repeated, with a trace of her natural charm.

"Second bedroom on the right," I called after her. "I'm pretty sure the sheets are clean. Towels in the hall closet."

"Thanks, Chef Mary. Don't know what I'd do without you." Her teeth worried her bottom lip, as if she were trying not to cry.

"Bed," Uncle Dom reminded her and with another nod she was out of the room.

"Anything left in the pot?" I yawned, trying to forestall our confrontation.

"Sit, Baby Mary, you look exhausted." Uncle Dom fetched me a coffee mug and then filled it with herb tea. Based on the aroma, I guessed peppermint. Not that it mattered, I was so tired I could have had injected espresso I.V. and still be asleep as soon as my head hit the pillow. He sat down at my table with an ease suggesting he'd lived here for twenty years.

He's like that, a person who physically dominates any situation, despite being only five feet five inches tall. I towered over him. One of those shrimpy Italian men whose physical limitations lead people to underestimate him—always a fatal mistake—it was years before I realized he uses that to his advantage. He actually likes it when people underestimate him because it gives him an immediate edge. The thought of his butting heads with Martin, who could have been a Ralph Lauren model for the older man, was amusing. No contest. Uncle Dom would wipe the floor with him.

We sat there for a couple of minutes in silence. I blew on my tea, coughed, fiddled with the salt and pepper shakers, noticed my tablecloth needed changing, coughed again, sipped my tea, crossed and recrossed my legs, determined not to be the first one to talk.

"She's a lovely child."

I nodded.

"Martin is an idiot."

I took a sip of tea.

"Your aunt will adore her."

I nodded again.

"You were right and I was wrong."

Dear God. The sky was falling.

He reached into his jacket and pulled out a folded piece of paper, "The restraining order," he grimaced, and laid it on the table. "Melissa will stay here." It wasn't a question.

I raised my eyebrows.

"I have spoken to Jim," he paused, "and others in the police department. Your neighborhood will have extra patrols."

Which in Uncle Dom-speak I took to mean that my house was now going to be staked out. That woke me up.

"Do you really think that is…"

"You have no idea who you're dealing with, Mary. None. I trusted you on Melissa's situation. You must trust me on this. This is beyond whatever…" he paused, "…remaining unpleasantness between you and Jim. I will not remind you that I told you repeatedly that marrying him was a mistake…—gee, despite my nearly terminal case of exhaustion, it sounded like another reminder to me—"…but that is done, and you must move on. It's a blessing you didn't get married in the church."

I began to giggle. As if I was ever going to be married in the church. The candles would melt, the stained glass would break, the hand of God would smite me down…A look stopped me mid-chortle.

"Martin and I aren't on the best of terms, but I will call him in the morning. And make things perfectly clear. To bed, Baby Mary," he admonished.

I shoved back my chair and had braced myself on the table to haul myself up, but then stopped. A healthy dose of being so exhausted my defenses were kaput, combined with burning curiosity of "why me," so I asked.

"Why do I always feel I'm failing you, Uncle Dom? You don't do it to anyone else in the family. Not like me."

He covered my hand and gave it a tiny squeeze.

"You always underestimate yourself. I…" he paused, to pick his words carefully. "You take the easy way. Always. You cook because you are good at it. You married Jim because he loved you."

"I loved him," I protested and pulled my hand away.

"Perhaps," he admitted. "But you let him go so easily. The fact is that he didn't know how to fight for you. He let you bully him. He lost respect for you and himself. What sort of relationship is that?"

"I don't know," I admitted and groaned. "I only know it hurt like hell, and it still hurts."

Was it was more the life we'd mapped out that I had lost, not Jim himself? I honestly didn't know how to separate Jim from that scenario. We were going to have the kids. We were going to have stints on the PTA. Christmas Eves were going to be spent assembling tricycles and bikes. We were going to spend a third of our lives picking-up six metric tons of Legos off the floor and debate whether Barbies were politically correct. It wasn't like I had a million men auditioning for the starring role that he played in that fantasy reel. No one was storming my front door for the chance to date me. We're not even talking about a measly coffee here, and my tryst with Marc in the back of his van demonstrated I couldn't even orchestrate a pity fuck with any success.

My therapist had suggested that my resulting depression after the divorce wasn't about losing Jim so much as my general issues with abandonment. The headache that dogged me for three days after that therapy session told me that perhaps there might a grain or ton of truth in that suggestion. But I wasn't remotely ready to face that issue any time this century.

"You are tired. Mary. Go to bed. I will let myself out. You think I'm over-bearing and preemptory, but it's the only way I know to fight for you." He squeezed my hand hard. "Otherwise, you would ignore me like you do most other people. And do not sneer. You know it's true."

I squeezed his hand back, too tired to either agree or refute him.

"To bed," he chided me.

I kissed his forehead, and as I staggered down the hallway to my bedroom, the lights behind me were doused, and I heard the click of the front door before I fell into bed. Just before I went under I murmured a "thank-you" into my pillow, grateful. Grateful that as over-bearing and irritating as he was, he'd listened to me. Grateful that he had trusted me enough to come here and humble himself, admitting to me he was wrong. And finally, oh God, so grateful that at least one man in my life hadn't abandoned me.

That cup of tea saved my bacon. Without my bladder screaming in six different languages for relief at eight that morning, I'd have probably slept through breakfast *and* lunch. As I tried to scrape off a few sheets of a new roll of toilet paper with non-existent nails, something began nagging at me. *Goddamn, what was it?* I muttered to myself as I stumbled back into bed, bringing the covers up over my head, as if the dark would shut down my brain.

Shit! The jewelers. Today was the day Allison was supposed to pick up her wedding ring! I scrambled out of bed, dragging half the covers with me, took a two-minute cold shower to wake me up, and gave my teeth a frantic brush. Running into my bedroom and leaping over the obstacle course of heaped bedclothes on the floor, I made a beeline for my dresser and I tried to get dressed. Clearly, a lesson in futility.

Laundry hadn't been a top priority lately. Okay, laundry is never a top priority with me; I'm one of those people who will buy cheap underwear and socks if only to put off running the washing machine for yet another day—and I was down to the dregs. The clothes you wear when you have no choice. The sort of clothes that demand you slap on a pair of oversized, dark sunglasses because you don't want people to recognize you.

I shimmied into my last pair of clean jeans, the pair I'd bought in an emergency when I was late to an important meeting, and, because I was nervous about this meeting, I had spilled coffee all over my lap. Not wanting to look like I was in denial about an incontinence problem, I'd sprinted into an Old Navy and had grabbed the first pair of jeans I saw in my size. Little did I realize these were low-rise jeans, exposing a three-inch strip of my underwear peeking out over the top of the waistline. Thirty dollars wasted. Or nearly, because these pants were the last defense against wearing the seersucker plaid pedal pushers my mother had bought me last Christmas in an attempt to convince me to join them on a cruise they were planning. "And look, you've got a start on your wardrobe!" And, oh, shit, no clean underwear again, and the only shirt left in my dresser drawer was a joke tee-shirt from a former classmate that said, "Chefs do it with whips."

Memo to self: next therapy session discuss near psychotic hatred of doing laundry because you also hate going commando.

That jeweler wasn't going to give me the time of day dressed like this. Was I going to have to resort to an actual dress? No! Commando and dresses do not co-exist in my world. A quick rummage through my drawers confirmed that no nylons were to be had, and it was January so bare legs were out, even ignoring the commando factor.

Time for the big gun.

I unwrapped from its plastic a hellishly expensive tailored jacket my uncle had bought me several years ago. So classic that it never went out of style, so beautiful that I was afraid to wear it because if I ruined it I'd never own anything so perfectly made ever again. It was the sort of garment hand-stitched by ancient nuns who believed that every pass of the needle was a step closer to God. The sort of jacket that screamed gigantic fraud, but if you're going to cop to being a fraud, at least do it in cashmere.

Naturally, the tee-shirt was too short and didn't meet the rise of the pants, so I *had* to button the jacket. Which, considering what the shirt said was a given anyway. Topped with the jacket, I didn't look too bad. Perhaps the jeweler would take me for the eccentric, wayward daughter of some long-suffering rich family. Someone who had money, but who wore inappropriate clothes just to tick her parents off.

"Coolie," I shouted on my way out the door. "Wake up! Luciano will be here in under an hour." I didn't wait for reply but sprinted to my car. Breakfast would be a quick trip to the drive-in coffee place where you ordered the latte because you needed the milk to cut the flavor of lousy coffee, with the added bonus of helping to wash down an over-priced, dry muffin. The people who make money are the people who capitalize on other people's incompetence or laziness. Welcome to yet another breakfast with me driving over the bridge, eating hunched over the wheel of the car, trying not to spill coffee or get crumbs on my clothes.

Chapter Twenty-three

North Beach is dying.

Fifteen years ago, Chinatown began its slow but inevitable march across Broadway. In its heyday, Broadway wasn't only the strip club Mecca of the West Coast, it was also the impregnable divide between Chinatown and North Beach. In my childhood, you'd walked Grant shielding your eyes from the doomed crabs swimming in cramped aquariums, then crossed Broadway plugging your ears to muffle the shouts of the strip club barkers trying to lure tourists in with the jaunty patter, and a few steps up Columbus and you'd immediately see rolls of salami hanging from shop fronts instead of duck carcasses.

Now, there are as many Chinese-run businesses in North Beach as there are Italian-run ones. Italian shopkeepers who had worked like dogs to put their children through school were gone, and their children had become investment bankers and doctors; they weren't interested in selling ravioli or working an espresso machine. Combined with the ever-escalating price of real estate, family-owned businesses are falling to the wayside, if not to the Asian shopkeepers, then to chains like Starbucks. Even the U.S. Restaurant has closed its doors.

Not bothering to search for a parking space, I went straight to the garage on Vallejo.

The jeweler's was just off Washington Square. The sidewalk in front was still damp from a hosing down, the windows filled with traditional wedding bands and watches. I imagined it might survive another three years before closing its doors. Couples bought their wedding bands at Tiffany's these days, oversized rocks being the order of the day. The simple and restrained gold rings in these windows would have little appeal to a generation who measured the strength of their commitment to each other by the number of carats, the more the better.

As I opened the door, a little jangle announced my presence. Flocked wallpaper, the height of chic in 1963, graced the walls. Glass and mahogany cabinets formed a small U that made up the whole shop. I amended my prognosis. It would close by the end of the year, no doubt to be replaced by an upscale ice-cream place.

A small, well-dressed, older man appeared from behind a curtained alcove. He would have done hand-springs if I could have played the Uncle Dom card. But I couldn't exactly do that since Plan A meant lying through my teeth in order to find out the identity of Allison's lover. The faint smell of starch preceded him. I immediately envisioned his wife starching and ironing to perfection seven white shirts every week. Topped with a red tie, a white button-down shirt complimented a black pinstriped suit, a white carnation in the lapel. He probably had worn the same outfit for the last forty years. Probably doubled for selling wedding rings and attending funerals. Although for funerals he'd switch the jaunty red tie for a somber blue one.

A quick up and down of my attire left him with a puzzled crunch to his forehead. He brought a hand over his bald spot, as if polishing his head were going to provide inspiration. Decades of selling jewelry had, no doubt, given him a preternatural ability to guess the balance of his client's bank accounts down to within a five-dollar estimate solely based on their wardrobe. The jeans, tee-shirt, red Converse high-tops without socks, and fifteen-dollar haircut relegated me to constant overdraft, a bankruptcy imminent; however, the cashmere jacket screamed constant funds, hence the confusion.

A heavy-lidded blink of his eye and a sonorous, "Madam?"

"Good morning. I'm here on behalf of Allison Warner."

"Yes?"

He wasn't even giving me a tiny opening. Damn. I brushed a hand over the lapel of my jacket to draw his attention *away* from the cheap silver hoops in my ears.

"On behalf of her parents," I lied. "I worked with her." *That* wasn't a lie.

"Oh?"

"At the cooking school. École? We had gone to school together and we were friends and…were…" I started to falter, followed by a completely spontaneous spilling of tears.

I hadn't realized he was that close to ending our exchange until the rigid cast of his shoulders fell dramatically. He whipped out a handkerchief and handed it to me.

He bowed his head. "A great loss."

I nodded and dabbed at my eyes. "A friend…" My voice trailed off. I was thoroughly ashamed of myself and was frantically thinking of a way to exit gracefully, because once again, in an effort to prove how smart I was, I'd conveniently forgotten that there was a real person in all this drama: Allison. Who should have been standing here instead of me, trying on her wedding band for that final fit.

"Loretta," he called into the back. "A cup of coffee."

I waved a hand in weak protest.

"No, I have to go. I'll just…" God, how could I get out of here? I began mumbling some nonsense about leaving. I was roundly ignored. Before I knew it, I was hustled into the back, beyond the curtain, and pushed rather forcefully into a chair. A steaming cup of coffee with a small plain biscotti nestled on the saucer was placed before me.

"Drink," he commanded in a severe tone so like my uncle I suspected they might be fifth cousins once removed. I knew when I was beaten. I drank the coffee black and nibbled on the cookie. I could hear the rhythmic hiss and steam of an iron in the next room. We sat there for several minutes in silence. There were no other customers, and I had the grim feeling that I was possibly the first and last customer of the day. And I wasn't even a customer.

"Mr. ?"

"Garibaldi," he finished for me.

"Mr. Garibaldi. I think I've made a mistake coming here. I don't know if Allison's parents knew she was getting married, and I thought that I..." I didn't finish the sentence because I couldn't say, "Hey, I'm playing Nancy Drew and came in here prepared to tell you any number of bald-faced lies because I want to know who Allison's boyfriend was."

"That explains it," he nodded thoughtfully.

"Explains it?" I asked, the slightly evil side of me, the one whose middle name is curious, taking over the show once again.

He waved a hand in the direction of the shop. "When you've been in business as long as I have, you know the types. The young couple who return six months later trying to resell you the set because they are already getting a divorce. The older couple who are desperate to keep their marriage together and think that purchasing new rings will get them another ten years. The ones truly in love, these are my favorites, whose hands shake as they try on their rings. I've seen them all." He paused. "Then there's your friend and you." This was said with the tip of a half-eaten biscotti pointed in my direction. He popped the rest in his mouth and chased it with a mouthful of coffee.

I managed a weak smile.

"Me?"

"That jacket isn't really you. You wear it as if it itches. I suspect it was a Christmas present." He looked at my feet and pointed at my red Converse. "Those are you." He continued, politely ignoring my blush. "She was a very beautiful woman."

"Yes," I agreed. "You read about her..." I let the word "death" hover in the air.

"Quite sad. Her ring was very unusual. She was one of those very much in love. I remember her coming in to the shop, her hands, rough and red from the day's baking. She didn't want any of the standard rings. She wanted an heirloom ring, an antique from Italy. I carry a small number. Most people think they are too gaudy, too Italian, but that is what she wanted. She was quite insistent. Her fiancé was Italian."

Unfortunately, I had just taken a sip of coffee and found myself coughing to stifle what was definitely a choke of dismay.

"You know him?" Mr. Garibaldi asked sharply.

"Um, vaguely," I said, thinking I was going to rip Antonello's head off the next time I saw him.

"I never met him. Which is why she stuck in my mind. I have been in business thirty-nine years and always meet the fiancé."

I stared at him. "He never came in?"

"Not once. How well do you know this man? Is he the type of man to let a woman pick out her own wedding ring?"

I thought about all the help that Antonello had given me over the years: first as a mentor, then invaluable career advice, then the friendly shoulder to cry on when Jim left me. Was he that type of man?

"I don't know him well at all," I confessed.

⟨⟩⟨⟩⟨⟩

I left the shop with a raging headache, wearing a pair of gold filigree hoops that Mr. Garibaldi assured me brought out the green in my eyes. A guilt purchase, yes, but when I saw them nestled against the black velvet, the delicate intertwining of the hair-thin gold strands, I thought again of Allison's lingerie and how I'd systematically denied my femininity, from the white cotton of my underwear to the serviceable, cheap haircut. I put them on before I left the shop. A definite, if expensive, step in the right direction.

I knew this sort of headache. It would prove impervious to any milligram combo of Motrin I could safety inflict on my stomach lining. It was a stress headache, and the only way to stop it in its tracks was to shove Antonello up against a wall and scream at him until I was hoarse.

I zigzagged my way through town to the school, cursing city planners and traffic engineers and plate tectonics for creating a city that was all hills, one-way streets, and timed lights. I was in even a worst mood when I arrived at the school than when I left the jewelers, not a mean feat, only to be greeted with a scene that was becoming all too familiar; students milling around in the dining room with coffee cups and cheeks wet from crying.

Before I could open my mouth, Antonello grabbed my arm.

"Mary, oh my God, Mary! Where have you been?" This segued into rapid-fire Italian, of which I understood nothing, and gigantic hand motions, of which I had to step back to avoid being whacked in the head.

"Stop! What's the matter?"

"She never showed. The morning pastry chef. The Japanese one. Benson's been calling you all morning."

I dragged him into a now empty kitchen.

"She's Chinese," I snapped at him.

"Where were you, Cara?"

"In North Beach, you bastard. At the jewelers?" I checked my cell. Dead. Of course. "Don't look so innocent. *Cara*," I mocked. At his look of confusion, I growled at him, "Stop it, Antonello. Just stop it. I—"

Someone grabbed my arm, digging fingers into my bicep with such force that I flinched. I whirled around to protest until I saw who it was and the look on his face. It was Marc. "She's dead, Mary. Shelley's dead!"

Chapter Twenty-four

Why is it when you're going through something like this it seems to take forever? Every word you utter, every swipe of your hand through your hair, every roil of your stomach, even batting your eyelids, takes so much goddamned effort and time, and yet when you look back you can't pinpoint anything; it's a blur.

My inevitable confrontation with Antonello was postponed.

As if it were humanly possible to stand in that dining room and be oblivious to the clusters of people guzzling coffee, smoking cigarettes, and crying into their aprons, several people came up to me demanding, "Did you hear?" Shelley had been killed in her apartment. When she hadn't shown up for work, Benson had called the cops and they had sent over a squad car. During one of these ghoulish exchanges, out of the corner of my eye I saw Marc being politely escorted out of the dining room by two uniforms. At which point, O'Connor hooked an arm through mine and more or less dragged me to the oven room to give me the quick run down.

Given the temperature in the apartment and the lividity marks, the coroner estimated that Shelley had been strangled sometime late Sunday night, possibly early Monday morning. The television show CSI not withstanding, time of death isn't that easy to pinpoint; no coroner wants to go on record for the exact time of death and then get his or her ass handed to them in a sling when it gets to court. But given that it was winter, plus an analysis of the contents of her stomach and the cartons of take-out in the refrigerator (The Slanted Door would later confirm that she'd picked up her order and was very much alive at 7:45 Sunday evening), the coroner would commit to a twelve-hour window between ten Sunday night and ten Monday morning.

Being her boyfriend immediately made Marc the prime suspect. On top of that, everyone in their apartment building had heard them screaming their heads off at each other for nearly two hours, punctuated by lots of swearing and door slamming, and culminating in Shelley dumping Marc's clothes in the hallway.

Under normal circumstances, Marc looked mighty good for it.

But Marc had a really nice alibi. Me. From nine o'clock on, Marc and I were shattering public indecency laws in the back of his van in the school's parking garage. (Security tapes would corroborate our stories, explaining the security guard's broad leer when I drove in today). And the two hours before that, we'd been eating dinner. And drinking. And dancing. And fantasizing about committing those indecent acts.

"They're taking a statement from that over-sexed spatula king down at the headquarters, but I need to hear it from you first so I know if this is related to, you know," O'Connor looked over his shoulder, "why I'm here. At the school. Anyway, you can vouch for him from what time to what time?"

For two people who rarely blush, both our faces were flaming. Which was six hundred different kinds of ridiculous, since neither of us were sweet sixteen, but that didn't seem to make a damn bit of difference.

I was standing with my back against the wall. "You think this is related to…" I waved a hand in the air. "You know, why you're…"—cough, cough— "…here?"

He didn't answer for a second. Then, "I don't know. Seems likely, but damned if I know how."

Turning away so that I didn't have to see his face, I mumbled, "Seven that night until about six," and then began arranging a jumble of oven mitts into neat little piles to avoid looking at him.

"Six in the morning?" In an equally pathetic attempt to avoid looking at me, O'Connor began opening and closing the doors of the deck ovens, as if checking for a forgotten sheetpan of cookies.

"You, um, saw us. The elevator, remember?" The piles weren't completely even. I moved one mitt from pile A to pile C.

"Give it to me." O'Connor had finished checking all the decks and started all over again, because I had a monopoly on the oven mitts, and short of whipping out a screwdriver and disassembling the entire oven, there wasn't any other possible distraction. "Blow by blow."

I tried not to wince at that.

"We had dinner; that took a couple of hours. Then we—"

"It took you guys two hours to have dinner? What in the—?" He slammed one of the doors with a wee bit too much force.

I messed up the three neat little piles I'd made and then threw the mitts on top of the deck oven.

"Goddamn it, O'Connor. We ate dinner, we sipped champagne, we danced. We fed each other raspberries dipped in melted chocolate. Then around ten—I'm kind of fuzzy here about the time because I was nice and toasted by that point, but let me assure you, he wasn't out of my sight for a second—we managed to stagger our way to his van, in the garage, and then we fucked like rabbits for several hours until we fell asleep around four. You saw us at six. In the elevator. Then we showered and got ready for class. He wouldn't have had time, at any point, to kill her, because he was either flirting with me or fucking me. Got it? I refuse to be embarrassed about this. Do you hear me?"

I knew I sounded strident and, all protests to the contrary, embarrassed, but hell. I wrapped my arms around myself as if to physically brace myself because I half expected him to snap back, "It would be hard not to as you're shouting," but he said nothing. He just shared my shame.

"You need a ride down to headquarters?"

I shook my head.

"I'll let them know you're coming. Give them a head's up about his alibi. He's not going to do anything stupid and lie to protect your honor, is he?"

I bit back a bitter chuckle, because that's exactly what O'Connor would have done, but I doubt that Marc was that chivalrous. It probably would never occur to him.

"Don't worry. I imagine he'll give a hickey by hickey account of the whole evening."

"Mary, Christ…"

At that I left the room.

Like I said, a blur. Coolie appeared out of nowhere and insisted that she drive me to headquarters. It wasn't until the drive home that I remembered that she wasn't even to suppose to *be* at school, but clearing out her apartment; I'd ask her about it later.

It is a measure of how insane the last six months of my life have been that being interrogated in a murder case was now ho-hum. Been there, done that. Yeah, I know the coffee machine is in the basement and that it really sucks.

I managed to keep a few shreds of dignity, brazening it out with the interrogator, giving Marc his written-in-stone alibi with a minimum of detail. But I knew. By midnight, the only people who didn't know that Jim's ex-wife had bonked a guy ten years her junior in the back of a VW van would either be dead or on vacation. A phone call from Jim was inevitable, and if I thought my embarrassment with O'Connor was extreme, discussing my Sunday night high jinks with Jim would be the Olympics of mortification. I'd rather stick a fork in my eye. My only hope was that his embarrassment was so great that he'd just leave a message.

Although questioned separately, Marc and I finished up our statements at the same time. We shuffled down the hall together toward the exit, mute, Marc sniffing every other step. Coolie took one look at Marc, and suddenly I found myself with *two* houseguests. Coolie herded us into the car, drove us home, and slung a slim arm around Marc's shoulders, steering him into her room the second we crossed the threshold. Which was a good thing, because he'd been on a crying jag since the entrance to the bridge, and I was on the verge of beating him into silence with a handful of maps when we pulled into my driveway. Even I knew that this was beyond the pale—the guy's girlfriend had just been murdered—but it was an indication of how close I was to losing it.

I was exhausted and wired and felt like total shit, a charming combination, so I did what every red-blooded chef would do. I began to cook.

Luciano must have done some food shopping because my refrigerator was full. I could do something with this. Yeah. Several bottles of wine, fresh pasta, basil, spinach, and feta; a baguette and two baskets of organic cherry toms sat on my countertop. It was too early in the year for any decent local fruit, but a bag of Courtlands screamed baked apples.

As I knew it would, the smell of baking raisins, sugar, cinnamon, and apples somewhat restored my equilibrium. I had no intention of getting fancy here. What we all needed were some greens, a good hot meal, and something sweet. I washed the spinach, sliced some red onion, crumpled the feta, and tossed it all in a tart basalmic vinaigrette. Once the apples were done, I brought water to a boil, chopped basil, sliced the toms in half, threw the fettucine in the hot water for a couple of minutes, drained it, and then tossed it all in olive oil, with lots of salt and cracked pepper. The carbs would do us good.

The door to the guestroom was open. The two of them were lying on the bed, Marc's head resting on Coolie's lap. She was stroking his forehead and singing him nursery rhymes in French. His eyes were closed. He didn't look any less miserable, but at least he'd stopped crying.

"Dinner's on the table. No arguments. We all need some food. Come on, it's getting cold," I ordered with something close to my usual spunk.

I turned to go back to the kitchen and heard the squeak of bedsprings behind me.

I was pretty generous with the wine, pouring glass after glass of an Italian Pinot Grigio—thank you, again, Uncle Dom.

We ate in silence.

Marc sort of pushed at his food, but managed to get a few bites in to sop up all the wine he was guzzling. Coolie, as is always the case with these thin girls, ate every single frigging morsel. I didn't say anything until we'd finished dessert.

"Marc, I didn't tell them at headquarters about your thing with Étienne because it's your business. But if you didn't, I'm going to rip you a new one."

The guilty flush on his face told me all I needed to know.

Chapter Twenty-five

"Do I call the police, or do you decide to grow a pair and dial the number yourself? The phone in the living room on the end table will give you some privacy."

I knew I sounded unbearably snotty and, in a horrifying way, overbearingly maternal, but I was feeling a tad cranky. An enormous amount of the greatness that I'd gleaned from a decent meal and a couple of glasses of fine wine had been destroyed by Marc's immaturity and stupidity.

Coolie's mother might be bat-shit insane and her father might be a suited-up thug, but they had inculcated some manners in her. Picking up immediately on the irritated tone in my voice, she pushed her chair back as a prelude to leaving the room.

Before she could stand, I motioned with my hand to have her to sit back down. "Don't bother. Marc's getting up. He's going to be on the phone for some time."

"Don't think so. None of their business," he drawled, sounding all Texan and cocky, obviously trying to brazen it out with me. Who in the hell did he think he was dealing with?

"I think differently," I shot back. At Coolie's raised eyebrows, I said, "Seems he left out some details that the police might be interested in."

"None of their business," he repeated, but this time with a decided pout in his voice. I wanted to smack him.

"That's not for you to decide. This is now bigger than you and your father." I pointed out. I knew I sounded somewhat cryptic, but I was trying to preserve a modicum of his privacy.

Marc didn't react to that, but began staring at the tablecloth, absentmindedly twirling the wine in his glass.

All right, Marc, if you want to play it that way. I grabbed his wine glass and placed it out of his reach.

"Have you given any thought to the idea that maybe it wasn't Shelley they were looking for?"

His head snapped up, his eyes wide.

"That maybe your stirring up the shit to fuel your vendetta against Étienne made you really disliked?"

He shook his head in a panicked "No."

"That maybe other things are going on at the school that you don't know about and your snooping—"

With a tortured groan, he pushed back away from the table and ran out of the room. He had gotten up with such force, his chair clattered to the floor.

After a few seconds we could hear the low murmur of his voice interspersed with the occasional agitated "I'm sorry," as he made his mea culpas to S.F.P.D.

"I know about his father," Coolie confessed. She got up, righted the chair, and began clearing our plates. Where's a videocam when you need it? Here was Coolie in her Audrey Hepburn shades, clothed in Urban Outfitters chic, loading up my dishwasher. "Marc asked me about my black eye. I told him about my father laying into me because I wouldn't leave École. Then he told me about Chef Étienne being his father, and acting like Marc was something that crawled out from under a rock. Kind of funny, huh? He wishes he had a father and I wish I didn't. Do you think—"

"Coolie," I began and then stopped, not knowing how much to reveal. First of all, what I knew (Allison's fight with Marilyn, Allison's secret engagement to Antonello, and Marc's stupid attempts to get his father fired by digging up stuff with which to blackmail Benson) didn't add up to murder. Oh sure, a lot of people might get fired should any of this come to light, but

I couldn't see any connections between Marc, Étienne, Benson, and Allison. Somehow, Allison figured into this, otherwise why destroy her locker? My caustic remarks to Marc aside, could Shelley's murder have been some random burglary gone bad? Regardless, I couldn't exactly admit that S.F.P.D. had an undercover cop masquerading as a student. For reasons as yet unknown. To me. I stifled an internal grumble.

"Well," Coolie shrugged her shoulders before loading the last fork into the dishwasher. "If my father is on the Board of Directors, then it stands to reason that the school is most definitely a Mafia front, and I—dishwashing liquid?"

Mid-choke, I pointed to the cupboard under the sink.

"—for one, would immediately assume that Chef Shelley was murdered because of something that Marc had uncovered. I imagine his," she paused, filled the reservoir, shut the door, and pushed the start button, "*curiosity* about the school, on any level, wouldn't have been appreciated. They were probably looking for him, found her, and then for some reason had to kill her."

I stopped breathing. Just for a second. As my wine glass was empty, I made a grab for Marc's and finished it in one enormous gulp.

"Probably money laundering." She began to wipe down the counter. "At the school, I mean. Since my father does not do small time, the money they are funneling through the school must be phenomenal. Sort of what he's good at. He's certainly put his Harvard MBA to good use, hasn't he?" She squeezed out the sponge and threw it against the backsplash; it fell into the sink. She frowned. "Small wonder that I have no desire to follow in his footsteps, but then again, I take after my mother's side of the family. We might be crazy, but we are rather honest. Mainlining, hanging ourselves, raging alcoholism, jumping off of buildings? Anything that is remotely self-destructive and we're all over it. Consorting with Mafiosi, however…Chef Mary, what's wrong?"

I was utterly speechless during this monologue. An uncommon state for me, but the nonchalance of her voice juxtaposed to the what she was actually saying—tossing off that her father is a henchman for the mob and by the way, where's the soap? How do you respond to that? At something of a loss, I gave myself a couple of more seconds to get it together by pouring us both another glass of wine.

"First of all, it's just Mary. Bag the 'chef' stuff unless we're at school. And secondly, are you saying that the school is a front for…" I made indiscriminate hand gestures with my free hand. The other one had a death grip on the wine bottle.

"Most definitely. If my father's on the Board," her mouth turned down in another, deeper frown and she took a swig of wine. Holding up her wine glass, she beamed. "This really is a nice wine, isn't it? I should buy a case."

I suppose if you'd been brought up by that sort of father, the reality that he was a mobbed-up lackey for a bunch of Tony Soprano types wouldn't be jaw-dropping. Talk about that walking in someone else's shoes shit. My litany of complaints regarding my brilliant, completely dysfunctional father seemed ridiculous in comparison. In addition to his abysmal parenting skills, his most glaring sins were a penchant for Cuban cigars and nightly tête-à-têtes with a bottle of twenty-one year old Glenfiddich Grand Reserve single malt scotch whiskey; self-destructive, but not sinister. Given a choice of fathers, I'd choose self-destructive jerk over immoral troll any day.

"Why did you come to the school, then, if you knew he had some association with it?"

"I didn't know," she admitted. "He's got fingers in a lot of disgusting and illegal pies. I never thought he'd be associated with a cooking school. And certainly not École. That's why I came to the west coast, trying to avoid any schools in the Midwest or the eastern seaboard. His traditional criminal stomping grounds. I doubt he has ties in Europe, but I wanted to stay close in case Mom had a breakdown. Which she always does. Have break-downs. But…" She threw her hands up.

"Maybe you could apprentice somewhere overseas. Hey, why were you at school? I thought you were going to clear out your apartment."

"I did. That reminds me; I'd better get my suitcase out of the trunk. They moved everything else to your uncle's house. It wasn't much. Lots of cooking equipment and an ancient piano that belonged to my great great-Aunt Marjorie. She was one of Zelda Fitzgerald's pals in Montgomery. She didn't live very long. Jumped out the window of her room at the Peabody Hotel the day she turned thirty-six. Left a suicide note saying that she'd discovered her first gray hair and that it was going to be nothing but down hill from there. Sad." She held up her wine glass. "I'm definitely buying a case of this. It complemented the tomatoes just perfectly. It's not sweet enough for the dessert, though," she added, pursing her mouth in frustration.

"I'll lodge a complaint with Uncle Dom," I deadpanned. I'd given up on commenting on anything but the last sentence, suffering from a mild case of mental whiplash as she ping-ponged her way from clearing out her apartment to Uncle Dom's house to her piano to her aunt to Zelda Fitzgerald back to her aunt to the gray hair to the suicide to our dinner and finally to the wine. I practically needed a passport.

I guess if you've got mob lawyers on one side and constant suicides on the other, it doesn't do to give it much thought, because the future is pretty damn bleak with those genetics staring you in the face. Aside from my father's chronic misery and that aunt on my mother's side who stopped speaking at the age of ten, the people in my family tended to live to be a ripe old age and were staggeringly with it. All that robust mental health was a blessing, really, since we went gray early. I couldn't help running a hand through my Clairol-ed locks.

"Uh, Coolie, do you mind if I, uh, pass on this information to someone I know. Someone in law enforcement?"

"Be my guest." She began dusting off imaginary crumbs from the tablecloth. "Maybe the only way to get Dad off my back is to have him do time in one of those country club prisons. I thought I was safe from him here, but guess not."

I had to lean forward to hear her, the breezy chatter gone out the window.

"He scares you, doesn't he?"

She nodded.

"I'll see what Uncle Dom can do, okay?"

That got a small smile and a nod.

My limited experience with Uncle Dom's well-heeled associates made it doubtful in my mind that Coolie's father would spend any time behind bars, but he could incur some pretty frightful legal bills and enough headache to keep him so busy he wouldn't have the time to jet across the country to smack his daughter around. And something told me that the law firm of Etc., etc., etc., & Porcella would be quite willing to offer their services to the U.S. Attorney's office pro bono, if it meant hosing Robert Martin for every cent he was worth.

Marc was going to be on the phone for some time, so I excused myself, holed up in my bedroom, and called O'Connor on my cell.

"Yeah, we know about Martin."

I swallowed a huff of frustration; thanks for telling me, asshole.

"You know?"

"Why do you think I'm at the school?"

"Oh, because you're on stress leave, perhaps?" I laid on the scorn with a very wide spatula.

"Look, Mary, for the record, I'm not allowed to discuss this case."

Sigh.

"How about you tell me a bedtime story about if you were going to be undercover, why you'd be at the school. Complete speculation, of course," I wheedled.

Four beats and then he sing-songed, "Once upon a time, S.F.P.D. got a tip that money was being laundered at a magical castle where they cooked a lot of food. The Captain might be pressured by the U.S. Attorney General's office to turn it over to them, but being the Captain, he'd hold on to the case as long as possible. The A.G.'s office might be keeping this under wraps, because if the I.R.S. hears about it, then they will take it over.

And nobody wants that because the I.R.S. are dicks. In this story. Normally, they are really sweet and if Jesus Christ were alive today, he'd be an I.R.S. agent. If an Irish cop named O'Connor had heard a princess was going to teach at this castle, he would have offered to go undercover because, well, because. And if this princess had an ex-prince, he might also apply some pressure and call in a few favors. The big bad A.G.'s office would refuse to issue a subpoena for the castle's records unless these undercover types could find probable cause. But everyone's under the gun, because if the F.B.I. finds out about this, they will pull rank with AG because they would smell RICO material and the Feebs don't share. In fairy tales. In real life, they are absolute peaches. Meanwhile, nothing gets done because of these fucking turf wars. Everyone on the Board of Directors of this castle would have ties to some mob boss in some part of the kingdom, but they would all have a great cover. Someone an awful lot like Martin would be smart and cover all the bases by marrying princesses with big bank accounts and having fancy degrees like he does. If they didn't graduate from Prince School, they would make sure they looked real American and apple pie. Theoretically, of course. Own crap like baseball teams. Like Benson's father. All would look real legitimate. If this were real. Which it is not. And they lived happily ever after The end." He coughed.

"Benson's father?"

"If those kinds of princes need lawyers, they would need a lawyer like Martin."

I mulled over that for a second and things started to fall into place. It wasn't some no-name company that bailed Benson out. The pharmaceutical company couldn't make it work with Benson at the helm, and finally Benson had no choice but to beg his father for help. Being a lapdog to bottomfeeders like Martin was the price Benson paid for keeping his dream alive and kicking.

"So, in this fairy tale you wouldn't have access to the castle's records."

"No. We'd have only one more week before the AG pulls the plug."

"And you wouldn't *legally* have access to their records because of this turf war."

"No. Allegedly."

"But what if in later chapters someone who worked there, someone who was, say, fooling around on the castle's computers playing solitaire, just happened to find something in the castle's database that pointed to some weird financial stuff, like the evil Chancellor was printing money in the basement, would that be enough to make the judge reconsider? I mean, wouldn't that make an interesting chapter?"

He didn't say anything for a long time. I could practically see the mental ping pong. The frustration of having gotten nowhere all these weeks; the bodies piling up, and he didn't have a frigging thing. Except me. Who had a legitimate reason to be at the school after hours.

"Don't," he whispered.

Rather than lie or argue, I hung up.

Chapter Twenty-six

I can text message on my cell phone. I can log on. I can bring up email. I can even write email—a necessity when my sister moved out of state. I can, occasionally, open attachments. I can play solitaire *and* hearts. Go me. This is, however, the sum total of my technological savvy, and, as sad as that is, hard won. I acknowledge how pathetic it is. Which is why I cook. One of the last bastions of those of us whose ancestors were the original Luddites, I knew that I'd be wearing an apron and wielding a whip for the rest of my life when I saw FedEx drivers operating hand-held computers.

Machines and I do not get along. Unless it whips butter, bakes cakes, or melts chocolate, I don't want to have anything to do with it. I am one of those people who are beloved by auto mechanics; they rub their hands in glee when they see me coming. It's like some sort of invisible tattoo is emblazoned on my forehead that says Mechanical Idiot. They can say to me, "Your left blinker doesn't work? That will be $2000, please," and although I'll have a vague idea that's patently ridiculous and it's probably nothing more than a burnt-out bulb, chances are I will nod numbly and write the check. Because although my idiocy is obvious, I hate to admit I'm clueless, and it's less embarrassing to write the check than admit I don't know jack shit about cars.

To sum it up: machines + Mary = unmitigated disaster.

This begs the obvious question. How am I going to search the school's computers when I can barely log on? I needed someone who knew food, could hack into a computer, and didn't mind doing something nefarious. And since I am, in general, surrounded by chefs, people who seem as technology challenged as I am (because if you didn't have to, why would you work in an industry where you are not paid well and consider it a miracle if you get bennies), the pool for potential cohorts in crime was non-existent. Add the this-will-entail-committing-a-felony factor, and I came up with nada.

Except one name.

Not going there. No way.

I flipped through every phone number listed in my cell phone. Twice.

Then I unearthed an old address book and poured through that.

Came up with no one else.

Shit. Shit. Shit.

I opened my cell phone again. Reality was staring me in the face. There was only one person who fit the profile." Needs frigging must. Swallowing my pride, I dialed.

"Hey, Thom, it's Mary Ryan," I said in response to his coy "Hello." I questioned the wisdom of his answering the telephone as if trolling for a hook-up, but then again, I'm not exactly fending off the men with both hands, so I refrained from commenting on it. Plus, I needed him, so it wouldn't be very smart of me to offend him right off the bat.

"I don't know a Mary Ryan," he drawled. "The Mary Ryan I *used* to know, the one who was Amos' friend, is dead as far as I am concerned. Would that she were dead to Amos, because then I wouldn't have to listen to him bitch about what a—"

"This isn't about Amos—" I interjected.

"As far as I am concerned, if it's not about Amos, then this conversation is over."

Amos Savage is Thom's boyfriend and my ex-best friend. We met right after I'd graduated from École. He is the son of a

Baptist minister who interpreted his son's homosexuality as a sign he was Satan's minion. After being bodily thrown off the front porch of the family home, Amos kissed his mother good-bye and booked a ticket on the first Greyhound out of town.

Like most gay men of a certain age I've cooked with, he's HIV positive. Gobbling a truckload of pills everyday, he keeps chugging along, his T-cell count holding its own. Like most bullies, I cave when someone calls me on my bullshit, and he does this pretty well. Three days into working together, he said to me after some caffeine-fueled diatribe on my part, "You have that hissy fit all by your lonesome. Just be quiet about it. We got a shitload of work still to do, and I want to get home sometime before midnight. Hush."

I hushed.

We'd leap-frogged from pastry chef job to pastry chef job together as I slowly worked my way up, each kitchen being a little more prestigious than the last until we found ourselves cooking at the late American Fare, which was named one of the premier restaurants in the United States only three months after the opening.

"Look, I need your help." I tried to keep my voice even and non-confrontational. "I don't need you to lecture me on what a shitty friend I'm being."

So much for non-confrontational.

That got a pause, then, "*My* help. Surely, I heard you wrong, sugar. You couldn't possibly want to pollute your soul by consorting with me of all people."

I didn't know what to say to that because it was true.

"He's forgiven me, Mary, why can't you? It was stupid and skanky, and I'm sorry I did it. I don't really care if you absolve me of my sins or not. But why are you punishing him for staying with me?"

That was also true.

"I...."

"Look, I make him happy." His voice, low and somber, had temporarily lost its characteristic bitchiness. "We have a lot in common. We both work in the food industry, we both like boys, and we both have religious nuts for fathers. God knows how it works, but it does. So, honey, can you get off your high moral horse and cut him *and* me some slack?"

When a member of the pastry staff at American Fare was murdered, it started a domino effect of events, which ended up with Amos revealing his relationship with Thom, who was the controller of American Fare. Who was now currently paying fines to the tune of $200,000 for manufacturing illegal green cards and selling them out of the restaurant so that he could afford five-hundred-dollar dress shirts. Funding his penchant for expensive clothes on the backs of illegals was pretty damning in my eyes. Once his nasty little sideline had come to light, my dislike had morphed into hatred. Hence my issues with Amos having a relationship with Thom. It didn't elevate Thom in my eyes, it debased Amos.

"How could you sell those cards?" I blurted out.

"The only person who is more ambitious than me is you. It was stupid, and I did it because I thought I had to dress the part. I was getting paid some nice money but not enough. Those S.F. society matrons? They wouldn't have given me the time of day if I'd turned up in a tie I'd bought at Nordstrom Rack. You know what it costs to live in this town. I'm sorry. I've said it at least twice in this conversation and am in debt for the rest of my life. Can we move on, for Christ's sake?"

I backed up and started over.

"I need someone who knows food *and* can hack into a computer. I can do the food part but not the computer end of it."

"You need someone who knows food and can hack into a computer," he repeated. "You're full of surprises! Let me get this straight. You can't stand the thought that I sold fake green cards on the black market, but you have no trouble asking me to break into someone's computer system?"

Putting it that way made me feel like a total troll. Thom and I were now neck and neck in the immoral Olympics. Oh sure, I could do some pretty mental acrobatics justifying that this illegal act was in search of the truth about Allison's murder, whereas his illegal acts were for nothing more than a tawdry desire to clothe himself in Ralph Lauren's latest, but at least he hadn't colluded with anyone else. No matter what way you sliced it, if we got caught, he was at serious risk for prison time.

"Forget it. I'm going to hang up now, and we'll both pretend that this little conversation never—"

"Why do you want me to do this?"

"One chef who worked at École has been killed outright, and another chef has also died. She was a pretty good friend. I think she was murdered, but I can't prove it. I need to hide someone in the school and hack into the system after hours."

Silence.

I thought of Allison, all of that beauty and talent now gone. I remembered the jagged twist of metal that used to be the door to her locker. My pride and common sense took a hike.

"I'm groveling here, Thom. Gro. Vel. Ing."

More silence and then, "Pity I'm not in the room because groveling is a *very* good look on you, honey. I suggest you hone those groveling skills, because that's exactly what you're going to do with Amos when this is done," he hissed. "On your hands and knees if necessary. You've really hurt him, you heartless bitch, and while you can hate my ass as much you like, I do *not* appreciate you hurting him. Why he cares is beyond me, but he does. So I do your dirty work for you, then you get over here and beg for his forgiveness. And I want to hear every word."

Chapter Twenty-seven

No sooner had I hung up my cell phone, than it rang again. Benson called to say, first of all, did I know my home phone was out of order—he'd gotten a busy signal for the last two hours—and second, the school will be open for business on Wednesday, and I was on double shifts until they hired someone to replace Allison, which probably wouldn't be until the beginning of the next semester—as in April. But being a seasoned pro, two months of double shifts would be nothing! Oh yes. Nothing. Great. Greatness even. And did I know anyone who was looking for work because we needed to cover Shelley's classes as well.

My back seized up in anticipation.

Memo to self: stock up on support pantyhose.

When I heard the thud of the newspaper hitting the porch at 5:30 a.m., I sprinted to the front door. Over a double espresso, I poured over the San Francisco Chronicle searching for some mention of Shelley's murder, but didn't come up with a single paragraph. Benson must have called in a ton of favors to squelch that news.

It was a pretty silent drive into the City. I doubt any of us got more than three hours of sleep. I'd snagged the shower first and managed to rustle up a thermos so that we could keep refilling our coffee mugs as we crossed the bridge. Marc rode shotgun and was placed in charge of the coffee. Coolie sat in the back, her iPod cranked up so loud I could hear the tinny feedback of the music leaking out through her head phones. Aside from the occasional request for more coffee, followed by her mug appearing over Marc's shoulder, she didn't say anything, nor did Marc. Apparently Marc was pissed off at me for outing him about his father and was indulging in a good old-fashioned pout by not speaking to me. He'd shuffled in the kitchen around six, his eyes at half mast, still sleepy despite his shower. I'd pointed to the fresh pot of coffee and said, "Help yourself." That got nothing more than a grunt of thanks.

Bite me, Marc.

The homicide inspector hadn't been too pleased with Marc for withholding information (like that was *my* fault), and had had him on the phone for several hours the previous evening. Plus, he had to go down to headquarters after his shift today so they could grill him again. I couldn't muster up any sympathy for him, because, hello, murder investigation? But apparently Coolie had that covered. I'd thrown an extra pillow and a couple of blankets on the couch, and they were left untouched when I got up that morning. I could hear them talking most of the night, the soft tones of their voices leeching through the lathe and plaster from the room next door.

It had been a long time since I'd had someone next to me, someone to talk to in the dark of night. I couldn't hear what they were saying, just the low rumble of Marc's voice, occasionally punctuated by a higher-pitched cadence. It was hard to imagine what an East Coast blueblood and a Texas redneck had in common besides being the children of assholes.

Both of them were young, so youth, I guess.

Cooking.

What they had listed on their iPods.

Hearing the high and low of their voices though the walls reassured me that his momentary fascination with me was as fleeting as my momentary fascination with him. Not that I thought Marc and Coolie were doing anything but confiding in each other. Marc's passion for Shelley had never been in question. Although when you're young you feel so much, yet you heal so much faster. I was beginning to think I'd never escape the failure of my marriage. It was like a scab that kept breaking open. I'd nurture it, do all the right things, then move wrong, and it would tear open again.

They were probably talking about their fathers. Benign neglect—something I could relate to—or not-so-benign neglect versus control masquerading as love. A part of me wanted to climb in bed with them and snuggle under the covers, regaling both of them with my childhood horror stories. I had a shitty father, too! Can I play with you guys?

And if the conversation had shifted to doomed love affairs, hey, I can compete on that score as well! I had one foot on the floor, giving serious thought to joining them under the pretence of asking if they were okay, when I heard Marc crying and then corresponding murmurs. Whether it was crying for Shelley or his father, it didn't matter; I doubted I was needed or wanted. The fact that I needed and wanted didn't mean a thing.

Which sucked.

Though I'd rather give myself a lobotomy with a clam knife than let Marc touch me again, at the very least I wanted a shoulder to cry on at two in the morning—or not cry—but have the frigging option.

Memo to self: time to hit www.Match.com.

When we reached the school, the three of us parted at the elevator, each to our respective locker rooms. Me: "Uh, I'm working double shifts for a while, so, uh, can't give you guys a lift home," with the tacit tagline that I *had* to work double shifts because Shelley wasn't alive to help me cover *Allison's* shift, not to mention her own. Marc mumbled through his exhaustion, "No problem. My van's still here. From yesterday. So..." To which Coolie replied, "I'm going down with him to headquarters after class. We'll wait up for you."

I guess my place was chef central until Uncle Dom got her an apartment.

"Don't bother. By ten tonight, I'll be virtually comatose with exhaustion. I'll spend the night with my aunt and uncle," I lied.

The thought of spending the night in a closet and being cheated yet again of a decent night's sleep caused me to suppress a scream of frustration and turn toward the locker room. Ignoring her insistent, "We'll have a nightcap together," I shuffled off to the chef's locker room to change into chef's whites for class.

No sooner did the doors to the elevator open than Antonello grabbed my arm and pulled me aside, waited for everyone else to exit, then pushed me back into the elevator, and punched the button for the basement. He didn't even bother to wait for the doors to close before he started screaming at me in Italian. I started screaming back at him in English, neither of us stopping until we had reached his car. He opened the door, and with a flick of his wrist he bade me get inside and sit. When I didn't move, he shoved me into the front seat of his Lancia with a look that said if I moved a muscle he would kill me, got in the driver's side, and locked the doors for good measure.

"We have class," I reminded at him.

"Yes, that is true. Now why are you so furious with me?"

"As if..." I sputtered.

Even in the tiny confines of the Lancia he managed to throw his hands up in frustration.

"Couldn't you have least gone to the jewelers with her to pick out the ring? I don't think that was too much to ask."

His face went smooth, lost all expression.

"What do you know about her ring?"

"Dum dum de dum," I hummed. I never knew that you could hum belligerently. You learn something every day.

"Then you know it would have been most inappropriate for me to go with her to the jewelers."

I stared at him.

"Cara?" he questioned.

"Never call me that again. Never!" I hissed. "How could you? She trusted you. She bought all this lingerie for you and you inscribed cookbooks to her and she loved you so much and you treated her like total shit. And your wife and..."

By this time I was blubbering into my hands. The visuals of that apartment frozen in time did me in. The carefully folded peignoirs, scented with Chanel No. 5; the cookbooks sorted first according to type (general all purpose, Italian, dessert), then alphabetized, the plethora of kitchen gadgets, the overblown flowers on the upholstery, the cool, sexy satin in the bedroom.

"How…how could you?" I repeated through my tears.

There was silence for several seconds, then a string of Italian at the top of his lungs.

"Translation please. I don't speak perfect asshole," I spat out.

He gripped the steering wheel, the knuckles of both hands gleaming white from the furious hold he had on the leather.

"How could *you?*" he repeated back to me. "How could *you* think I would…with Allison? She was like a daughter to me. Both of us. We…what is *wrong* with you, Mary?"

I had my first fissure of doubt, but with my usual bull-in-the-china-shop style, I didn't let that stop me from digging my own grave.

"You know about the wedding ring," I accused.

He let go of the steering wheel, ran his fingers through his hair, and threw his head back against the headrest. Closing his eyes as if exhausted, he said slowly, as if every word were an effort, "What do you think?" he said slowly. "She told me. She did not tell me who. Although I can guess. *Bastardo*," he murmured under this breath, and he hit the steering wheel. Hard. "It was not me. How you could believe—"

"The cookbooks. In her kitchen, they are inscribed to her," I protested. "They all say 'To Cara.'"

"And this, this is the brush you, you…" Whenever he is upset his English goes. He brought his head forward, turned to me and opened his eyes. Waiting. And like a thousand times before, I supplied him with the right word.

"Tar? Tar you with the same brush?"

"Yes, tar me with. Is it my handwriting?" he demanded.

What had that handwriting looked like? I'd probably killed most of those brain cells after downing all those martinis at Foghorns, but what I remembered was a sort of a scrawl.

He pulled a pen out of his chef jacket pocket, grabbed my wrist, shoved up the cuff of my jacket, and wrote "Cara," on the inside of my forearm.

It was nothing like the writing in the cookbooks. Like all Europeans, his writing was delicate, with lots of curlicues on the edges. Almost feminine. The writing in those cookbooks had been spikey and determined, the serif of the "r" particularly brutal.

"There. Is it the same?" he demanded.

I shook my head and raised my head to meet his eyes, which were so cold with disgust that I knew he never *would* call me "Cara" again. I had broken the faith irreparably.

"Her funeral is Friday afternoon," he said. "You will be working. I will send your condolences to her parents. So there are no more misunderstanding between us: I did not give her those cookbooks; I was not her fiancé. Lock the door before you leave. I don't want CD player stolen." Then he got out of the car, slammed the door, and headed to the elevator.

I pulled down my sleeve in a futile effort to hide my shame.

Chapter Twenty-eight

We'd left my house with no time to spare, so those few minutes spent in the garage destroying my friendship with Antonello meant I was late getting to class. The worried pinch on the students' faces told me that I looked about two seconds away from a nervous breakdown. Even though Coolie was still wearing the sunglasses, I could tell she was concerned and confused. She kept looking at me with her head cocked to the side and mouthing my name whenever I caught her eye, as if to ask if I was alright. I'd been exhausted and cranky that morning, but not upset. She hadn't been in the elevator when Antonello commandeered it and me; however, enough students had, so that by the mid-morning break the whole school would know about our argument.

By tacit agreement, I abandoned my usual place next to Antonello at the chef's table and sat next to Marc. It was a subdued meal. Someone had thoughtfully removed the extra chair, but we all knew Shelley wasn't *there* and *why*. Marc ate three bites, then got up from the table without saying a word. I didn't manage to eat much more, before mumbling something about preparing for the evening class and fleeing the dining room.

Which I needed to do, but I needed to call Thom first.

"I've made you a reservation tonight under the name Tom Brown."

I couldn't think of anywhere private I could call, so I ended up calling him from my car. The slim hope that the cameras had not caught Marc and me staggering toward his van in drunken lust the other night was dashed at the parking attendant asking me for a date when I walked by the parking kiosk. And if I wasn't exactly sure what he meant by date, he repeated himself and then grabbed his crotch. I flipped him off and then hunkered down in the front seat of my car to call Thom. With the phone in one hand, I fished under the seats with the other, trying to find the flashlight I had in my car for emergencies. Aha!

"Once you hung up, I realized that I might be able to do this from home, thereby saving my paroled ass in the process. Is the school networked?"

"I don't know."

"You can't see me, but I'm giving you several looks laden with scorn."

"I don't ask you to make a meringue, so don't diss me because I'm computer stupid."

"Our entire interaction over the last two years has been characterized by mutual scorn. I really see no reason to stop now. Why spoil a good thing? What's your email address at the school?"

"Maryryan@ecole.com."

I could hear the faint clicking of computer keys.

"I'm in the system. For your information, yes, you are networked. Don't you check your email at home?"

"I can check my email from home?"

"Hopeless, you are utterly hopeless. Yes, you can, and you have thirty new emails. What's the name of the controller?"

"Uh? Brian something."

"That's very helpful. Don't quit your day job." A couple of minutes of silence, then, "Is that Brian Williamson, Brian Dresslar, Brian Hampton, or Brian Keeley?"

"Brian Williamson. What are you—"

"Quiet," he demanded. I cooled my heels for a couple of minutes, hearing over the phone line the clicks as his fingers moved fast and furious. Gee, my hands looked dry and, yuck, old.

"You basically only have permission to access your email and the files available to the public. You are a no-one in the hierarchy."

"In computer moron, please."

"I can't hack into the system from a remote location, i.e., my living room. I might be able to do it from there. Which means, in short, good thing I'm free this evening. Did you include the aitch in 'Thom'?"

"We are about to commit several felonies and your primary worry is whether you have an aitch in your alias? You know, you might want to see someone about your aitch complex."

"I might have expected that sort of reaction from you. Do you even wear matching socks? What's on tonight's menu?" he asked.

God give me patience.

"Green eggs and ham. It doesn't matter what's on the menu. You just need to show up, and study the menu and the wine list. I want you to get a handle on what our food costs might be. The lunch menu isn't much different. A little less posh. Lollygag over your meal, and then I stash you somewhere until the place closes down."

"Won't it look odd that I'm dining by myself?"

Good point. I turned on the flashlight and prayed, prayed that it didn't need new batteries…Score! I turned it off. I'd smuggle it upstairs, hidden under my apron.

"Tell the waiter that you're a wine buyer and that you're checking out what we've got stocked in the cellar. Hint that you can undercut whatever we're currently paying. You'll probably get a few nice glasses of wine out it. There's a janitor's closet around the corner from the elevator. If I can, I'll get rid of as much of the janitorial stuff as I can. Duck in there. We need to wait until the janitors finish up with the dishes and then mop the floors. Sometime around eleven, I'm guessing. I'll come get you when the coast is clear."

"I think it's high time to cut out the goody two shoes act. You think like a criminal."

"I'll tell that to my ex-husband. The cop. I got you a table in the second seating so spin out your meal. Try to be the last one to leave the dining room so that I can make sure the classroom is shut down."

"Yes, Bonnie," he smirked.

"Shut-up, Clyde."

The day was endless. The only bright spot was that O'Connor didn't show up for class. People were on edge, snapping at each other and barely managing to be civil. Curt barked at the student waiters to such an extent that several of them threatened to walk out. At some point I snuck down to my locker to grab some Motrin from my purse to muffle the exhaustion headache drumbeat. While gulping them down dry, I heard through a closed door Marc and Étienne screaming at each other in French. Marc's laconic southern drawl sounded bizarre wrapped around the precise and delicate cadence of the French, but it sounded like he was giving tit for tat well enough.

The students dealt with all this tension among the staff by making unbelievably stupid mistakes. Like overturning an entire rack of cakes in the walk-in. Like a senior cutting herself so badly while deboning a salmon that someone had to take her to St. Francis for stitches. But she had company because another student slipped in the walk-in (the floor was wet and slippery from cleaning up all those smashed cakes), and from the angle of his hand and the instant swelling, most likely he'd broken his wrist. Another kid to the ER. It was a miracle we had enough dessert to serve. It was too late to whip up more cakes, so we tried to compensate for this disaster by having several different ice cream sundaes on the menu that day. Which considering it was the end of January, didn't have much appeal.

I managed to take a small cat nap in the afternoon on the flour sacks in that dead hour between when the morning classes ended and the evening classes began. If I was going to play Bonnie to Thom's Clyde, I'd better steal as much sleep as possible. Of course, we know what happened to them.

My cell phone kept beeping, alerting me that I'd missed a call, but whenever I went to check it, the display said restricted number. It could have been anyone, but I suspected it was O'Connor, so I turned it off all together. I wasn't in any emotional shape to lock horns with him so I didn't call him back. If he wanted to talk to me, he knew where I worked.

Despite the lack of sleep, by nine that night I was so hyped I was zipping around the classroom as if possessed. The students kept their distance, obviously wondering if I was going to snap and start stabbing people. In between bouts of barking out mania-fueled instructions, I kept making excuses to go to the bathroom so that I could see how far along Thom was in his meal, and how quickly the dining room was emptying out. The students probably put down my irrational behavior to a fever due to a raging bladder infection. Wednesday nights weren't exactly hopping, and my initial guess that the second seating would probably wrap up around ten seemed pretty accurate.

On one manufactured trip to the john, I had managed to scrawl a sign and slipped it underneath my chef's jacket. After ascertaining that no one could see me, I detoured to the janitor's closet. There was nothing I could do about the vacuum cleaner stashed there, but I grabbed the bucket and mop used to wipe down the foyer in the morning. At least we'd have somewhere to sit. I wheeled them down to the locker room—if anyone asked me later what I'd been doing, I'd growl that the toilets had overflowed yet again—stashed them in one of the stalls, made a quick prayer to the Nancy Drew gods that no one would need the extra mop that night, attached my Out of Order sign on the stall door, and then collapsed on the bench outside the john, hyperventilating for five minutes from stress.

Thom had taken my advice and lied through his teeth about being a wine buyer. By the end of his meal the table was covered in wine glasses. I saw him sipping a glass that was dead-on the color of one of the most expensive sauternes on the wine list.

Right about the time when I suspected my blood pressure was hovering around two hundred and forty from sheer anxiety, a four-top of extremely drunk older women finally heaved themselves up from their table and staggered out of the room. He was the last. I couldn't very well slip into the dining room unnoticed, but I pulled one of the student waiters aside and told him to tell Thom that Chef Mary sends her regards. I stood just inside the glassed-in wall that housed the main kitchen. Thom caught my eye and raised his sauterne to me in salute. I made a quick look around, didn't see anyone looking, and made a cutting motion across my throat. He could interpret that any way he liked.

By the time I'd returned to the pastry kitchen, the students had rolled their knives up into their knife rolls, ready to call it a night. I sent them on their merry way, made a beeline for the public restroom, changed into an all black cat burglar outfit that I'd stashed in my desk, hung up my chef's jacket and pants on a hook in the stall, (I'd get them in the morning), and sat in the public john to wait for an hour.

As I discovered last fall, once you start actually thinking about breaking the law, it's shocking how easy it is. At the morning coffee break, I'd scoped out all the hallways, elevators, and classrooms for cameras. There were surveillance cameras in the lobby, elevators, the hallway to the garage, and the garage itself, but no where else. As in *not* in the offices and *not* in the stairwells. Which seemed pretty shabby security to me, and I'd write an anonymous letter to that fact once this was all over.

Computers? You are so our bitch.

Of course that meant spending the night in a janitorial closet, unfortunately. But no matter which way I cut it, there was no way that I could get out of the building without the security cameras capturing us on tape. I'd have to smuggle him out in the morning when all the students were in the elevator. He could escape out the lobby relatively unnoticed in the hustle and bustle of arriving students. I'd flip my uniform over to the clean side and put on the previous day's chef's uniform, no one the wiser.

All that mania was bound to burn itself out, and sure enough, after thirty minutes of cooling my heels while I sat on a commode, I started to fall asleep. Setting the alarm on my cell phone for vibrate thirty minutes hence, I leaned against the wall of bathroom stall to catch some zees. The janitors should have finished mopping the floors and have punched out by then.

Memo to self: falling sleeping on a toilet is one of the most stupid ideas in the world.

When my cell phone started tickling my hand, I woke up with a jerk. As is often the case with short naps, I felt a hundred times worse than before. My body was one gigantic ache. And I had a new and improved headache to go with all those muscle aches. I stumbled out of the stall, hitting my forehead against the edge of a sink. The flashlight, which had been resting on my lap, clattered to the floor. Biting back a groan, I fell to my knees, cursing silently, as I felt along the floor for the flashlight with one hand, pressing the burgeoning knot on my forehead with the other. I found it and turned it on. Light.

I straightened up and reached for the doorknob. Before easing the door open, I turned off the flashlight. Poking my head out, I tilted my head in the direction of the dish room. Silence. The hallways were dim, just the emergency lights on, casting shadows right and left. I didn't want to waste the batteries on my flashlight, so I made my way cautiously down the hallway to the janitor's closet, listening for footfalls. I didn't think I'd have the nerve to go through this all again and sent another prayer to the Nancy Drew gods that Thom had managed to get to the closet unseen.

I opened the door slowly. And was greeted by the sounds of snoring and the sweet overwhelming smell of sauterne.

Closing the door behind me, I eased into the closet and accidentally stepped on Thom's hand. He woke with a squeal and pushed at my leg. Simultaneously, I brought my foot off of his hand and tried to find another foothold that didn't have a hand underneath it (although the closet wasn't really big enough for one person, never mind two), started to fall over (because I couldn't see and I was on one foot), reached for something to hold on to, and wiped out a bunch of cleaning supplies in the process. Which fell on Thom's head. Which caused him to squeal again. At which point I yelled at him to shut up.

At least we knew that no one was in the school, because short of a ticker tape parade and a herd of elephants, we'd done a pretty decent job of broadcasting that we were hiding in that closet.

"You've ruined a fifty-dollar manicure with those hooves of yours and probably broken my—"

"Shhhhhssssh!" I hissed. "I'm going to break every bone in your body if you don't shut up."

I counted to one hundred, put my ear to the door, listened, didn't hear anything, counted to one hundred again, and still didn't hear anything. Then and only then did I turn on my flashlight.

With a motion to keep his lips zipped, I pointed at the bottles of industrial cleaners and solvents. He began handing them to me one by one. Once we'd finished putting them back on the shelves, I whispered, "Move."

"Can't," he whispered back. "It's not exactly Buckingham Palace in here. You're going to have to scooch up against me if you want to sit down. Don't worry; I'm a perfect case of arrested development. I thought girls had cooties in the third grade and nothing in the subsequent twenty-five years has changed my mind. Here." He offered his hand.

I hesitated for only a moment before grabbing hold. I then twisted myself a dozen different ways trying to find a way to sit down without knocking his teeth out.

Once I'd nestled against him, I asked him in a whisper, "Does Amos know you're doing this?"

"Are you out of your mind?" he whispered back. "I'd sooner tell him than kiss you. Which is not so much a reflection on you, you clean up adequately, not quite an act of God, but close. It's that female thing you have going on. He'd kill me if he knew I was jeopardizing my parole. Which is the point in this conversation when you get down on your metaphorical knees and thank me for my stupidity. That's how much it means to me to have you two make up. I hear him mention your name one more time and I'm going to hang myself. Talking in whispers is exhausting. How long do you plan to make us sit here in Hotel du Dustmop?" he complained in a soft murmur.

"Just another few minutes. Enough to sober you up. How much wine did you actually go through?" I chastised in an equally soft voice. "You've been burping sauterne in your sleep."

"I haven't had that much," he protested. "Besides, General Patton, wasn't it you who ordered me to pretend to be a wine buyer. That waiter was practically force feeding me booze."

"Poor you. I noticed that you sent for all the really expensive stuff."

"I did?" he mocked. "It's a decent wine list but nothing to brag to *Wine Spectator* about. Plebian in a fashionable sort of way. All the trendy vineyards you expect to see, with a healthy stocking of the big wineries that will be familiar to tourists. No real surprises. Who buys the wine?"

I shrugged against him.

"Curt, the maitre d' I think. I've been keeping my head down, keeping a low profile."

That got a snort of derision.

"Where's Mary Ryan and what have you done with her?"

"Shut up. There's been all this political shit going down. I won't bore you with the details. So, yeah, low profile. All I care about is stocking the shelves with Valrhona chocolate and butter with a decent fat percentage. Did you study the menu?"

"I want to know who handles your PR, honey, because they do a bang-up job promoting the dining room. I've wanted to eat here for years based on the buzz, but the verdict? Schizophrenic. I didn't know if I was at eating in 1965 Paris or 1995 Mission Street or 2007 Bangkok. It's like people playing pick up sticks with knives. You throw it all up in the air and hope someone doesn't get stabbed or lose an eye. Were you the brain child behind some of the gems on that stunning dessert menu? The black pepper ice cream with chives sundae?"

"You worked with me for two years. Give me a break. I'd sooner bite off a toe than serve that shit. The chef who was killed. That was her style. Pushing the boundaries between savory and sweet." I tried not to sound condescending out of respect.

"I might hate you, but your desserts were universally delicious. You know what you're doing."

I didn't know how to respond to that without sounding extremely snide. I was aching to reply, "Gee, Thom, I wish I could say the same about your green card scam; but those pesky immigration officials just had to put a crimp in your criminal empire," but figured that was a one-way ticket to losing my computer hacker.

I left it at, "The feeling's mutual." Which I'd hoped was ambiguous.

Apparently not ambiguous enough because he said into my ear, "Bitch," but there was a laugh behind his voice.

We sat there for a few more minutes until he started to snore in my ear, and I realized that if we didn't get started, it would be seven a.m. before we knew it. Sober enough or not, we had to move it.

"Thom," I said in a forceful whisper and shook him awake.

Chapter Twenty-nine

To avoid the cameras in the elevators, we used the stairs instead: the flashlight was a godsend as the emergency lights didn't seem to be activated here. Another item to add to my anonymous letter to building maintenance detailing major deficiencies.

"Do you have *any* idea what I'm supposed to be looking for?" Thom asked as we made our way up the stairs.

I whipped around, shined the flashlight in my face, glared at him, and brought a cautionary finger up to my mouth.

He stuck his tongue out at me, but didn't say another word until we'd reached in the school's offices. I shut the door behind us and turned off the flashlight.

"You are the worst burglar! Why not start screaming out our names and social security numbers so when they book us for breaking and entering, the paperwork will go that much faster and we can get to our cells in record time."

"I might be a piss poor burglar, but I happen to know a lot about computers, so I suggest that the next one hundred sentences you utter sing nothing but my praises."

Point.

I counted to five.

Memo to self: the next time you need a partner in crime…

What am I saying?

Memo to self: there will not *be* a next time, so the issue of a partner in crime and their particular skills set will *not* be an issue.

"Um, right. Money laundering, but we don't know how."

He snorted. "*That's* helpful. Needle in a fucking haystack."

"It's the best I've got."

Even though his face was in shadow, I could *hear* him rolling his eyes.

"Where does the controller sit?"

I turned on the flashlight again, and pointed it in the direction of cauliflower guy's door. I had a moment of panic that he locked his door at night. While television makes the credit card/lock thing look easy, I bet it's *not*. But luck was with us. The door was shut but not locked.

The glow from the screensaver bathed the room and the two of us in that peculiar artificial computer light, like a strobe light without the strobe.

Well, Thom may fail big time as a burglar but as a computer hacker, he knew his stuff. The second he sat down in front of the computer his posture gentled and the partial sneer he usually had on his face disappeared. I probably looked the same way standing in front of a mixer. That feeling that you knew this world, that there weren't any secrets; in fact, you *owned* this world. Thom pulled a couple of disks out of his pocket and shoved them in the machine, and a black screen with a bunch of white type appeared.

"What are you doing?" Not that I would understand a single word of what he was saying, but I needed some buzz words from him to assure me *he* knew what he was saying.

"Keylogging," he muttered.

"And that would be?" I prompted.

"Tells you what key sequences you've typed in. Lucky for us, you can download this stuff off the Internet."

Another reason *not* to do my banking by computer.

The computer blinked a couple of times. More black screen, white type shit.

"Bingo, we are cooking with gas," he muttered under his breath.

"Where are the fields and blue sky? The Windows screen. That looks scary. Like the type is yelling at you." When I see anything other than the Windows default on my screen I start hyperventilating and have to blow into a paperbag.

"That, my technology-challenged kitten, is DOS. No, I'm not going to explain it to you because you wouldn't understand it anyway, and I don't want to waste my time. The field will come up in a second…Yes!" A few more clicks and the classic Windows field appeared in all its glory. My pulse, which had raced to stroke-inducing heights after dumping all those cleaning supplies on Thom's head, slowed just a tad, putting my pending aneurism on hold. "See? All the lovely directories lined up in a row. What sort of software is this beotch using?"

"It's a guy."

"Of all people, you are the last person I need to be giving gay slang lessons to, Ms. Fag Hag of 2006," he huffed. He turned back to the screen, clicked some more, and then turned to me with a really evil grin. "It's the same software I used at American Fare. Honey, this will be a piece of cake."

"You are enjoying this far too much."

"Quiet you. Park that hetero ass of yours in a chair and sit back for a bit." After that, he began scrolling through directories and files, murmuring phrases like, "No you don't," and "That was stupid of you," and "Come *on*," as if he and the controller were playing some sort of game. Then he got silent and his shoulders stiffened.

"Thom?"

"Shhh, just a minute."

There was more scrolling but he'd ditched the obnoxious patter. The suspense was killing me. I began kicking the desk legs.

"Stop that or I'm going to stab you with a pen. Per day. How many seatings?" he demanded in a flat voice, his eyes never leaving the screen.

"Three total. Lunch, then the two at dinner. You had the last seating," I responded, puzzled.

"Five days a week?"

"Yeah. What—"

"So simple and so sweet. Who ever devised this is a genius, betting that the I.R.S. flunky who reviews their returns wouldn't know a soup spoon from a teaspoon, and they were right."

"Stop heaping praise on your fellow criminals and start explaining what's so freaking brilliant about this?"

But Thom wasn't listening; he began rifting on the set-up, the pros and cons, continuously scrolling through files, bringing up other folders. "Controller is definitely in on it, but receiving? Debatable. Accountants? Also debatable. This could all just be paper. All of it. Wouldn't necessarily have to…hmmm, must have taken quite some time to set up the credit card thing. I *knew* it. Legit bank accounts. At least three months before recycling the numbers, then—"

"Tell me," I demanded and thumped him on the shoulder.

"Ow, you awful woman, that hurt," he complained, rubbing his shoulder. "I'm guessing a hundred tables in that dining room?"

"Ninety."

"You have three seatings total per day, right? Hazard a guess on the average tab, keeping in mind that lunch won't bring in as much revenue as dinner."

I thought about the cost of lunch versus dinner, wine, how some people drink like fish, other's don't drink at all or have only one glass; lunch probably comes in at around sixty per head, dinner probably eighty per head, but then the dinner crowd tends to drink up…

"Eighty-five bucks per head?"

"Based on the tables surrounding me and the hollow legs of *those* hags, I'd up that to ninety on average. Look at the deposits. You do the math."

He brought up a screen that showed the daily totals, then the weekly totals, and finally the monthly totals. Math and I are mortal enemies; adding and subtracting is about as complicated as I want to get, and here Thom was asking me to do division! But even I could tell that the numbers didn't add up.

We were making way too much money on any given day, even supposing that people were ordering magnums of Cristal.

"Someone's inflating the number of lunches and dinners sold?"

"Yes, that's exactly it. Fake restaurant tabs. This is so diabolical. I'm truly impressed. Don't quote me," he held up a hand, then smirked, "yet, but I think they're doubling their turnovers. Two seatings at lunch and four at dinner. Which is legitimate for any other restaurant but not this school. Even at my most conservative estimates, they're funneling over $300,000 per month through this place, but I bet it's probably more like half a million. A quick glance at the VISA receipts? A lot of the credit card patrons are ordering the most expensive wine on the menu. And if tonight's menu is any indication, they are using actual menus. In fact, the only thing they're faking are the customers."

This would be so easy to do. It would take some organization, but once you had the credit cards set up, it would be a piece of cake.

"Do you think they rotate the cards?"

"I know they rotate the cards," he said with a self-satisfied air. "Keylogging. A hacker's best friend. He connected with the bank this morning, allowing me access to his password. I brought up all the credit card action for the last six months, chose a name, and started searching. The same name and account appeared twice."

"But what about food costs? You have all this revenue, I mean tons of it. It wasn't that long ago that this place was bleeding money. The board of directors would have to know that this school couldn't possibly generate that sort of income."

Unless the entire board is corrupt.

Thom frowned, the glow from the screen highlighting the grooves on either side of his mouth.

"The food cost is problematic, I agree. There are two ways this could play. One, they are manufacturing receipts so that the revenue isn't out of whack with the costs. Anyone with a scanner and Photoshop could produce fake receipts. Or your suppliers could be part of the scam. All that would need to satisfy your average I.R.S. flunky is that your revenues are in line with your expenses."

He clicked some more, brought up a bunch of invoices, and then began crowing, "I'm a genius. I'm brilliant." Poking a finger at the screen, he said with not a little reverence, "Look see. You're paying twice the going rate for strawberries, at least thirty percent more for your dairy; and the liquor? The more I think about it, the more I'm convinced that a good chunk of your suppliers are in on this because the checks to them would have to correspond with the invoices. Your garden-variety I.R.S. agent would compare invoices to checks, expenses to revenues, and if it jived, then there'd be no reason for an audit. This is very big, Mary. This isn't little ole me using Photoshop to crank out a bunch of green cards. We are talking organization and lots of it. Let me burn a CD of these files. This is very, very clever. Lots of balls to juggle, but it's all out in the open, nothing to hide from the I.R.S. This guy sends in the school's returns electronically. No one actually comes to the restaurant or the office. It's really very smooth. I'm impressed. It's perfect on paper. Here's a CD with the financial history for the last six months. If the hard drive gets wiped, you're covered. Someone needs to move money from business to business to business, and this school has become the outlet for the credit card end of it. I'd be curious if all these credit cards were issued from the same bank. So much crime, so little time."

I didn't have any pockets, so I put it in the hood of sweatshirt.

"Thom, these people are looking to spend the rest of their lives in federal prison. You avoided rubbing elbows with them by the skin of your teeth." I reminded him.

He began shutting down the system, closing tabs, and covering his tracks. "I know that. But once you start thinking like a criminal, it's astonishing how easy it is. And don't tell me differently. Your shoulders have that rigid set to them, which means you're going to get all moral on me. You orchestrated this break-in like a pro. Let me delete all this history and then we're done. Where'd you put the mops and things? Let's put them back and then hit the trail." He logged out.

"Uh, no, we can't. Security cameras are going to pick us up the minute we leave."

He turned slowly to face me.

"Mary, are we spending the night in that closet? Did you deliberately forget to mention that little fact?"

"Hmmmm." I scratched one shoulder.

"Did you also plan what I was going to say to Amos when he wakes up and thinks that I'm a cheating little whore because I didn't come home tonight?"

"Thought that was part of the apology package."

"And when he finds out that you jeopardized my parole? A tidbit I had no intention of telling him?"

I'd never gotten that far, frankly.

"Are you guys living together? I didn't know." Which made me feel six hundred kinds of guilty because in another time I'd have known that about Amos.

"Since I am working at that hellhole for children as part of my community service, for minimum wage, I might add, and Amos hasn't worked since *American Fare*, we decided to pool resources. Plus, believe it or not, we care for each other. As in a relationship."

I ducked my head, not knowing what else to say. Back to the drawing board. I needed to get us out of here.

"Do you think you could stand to kiss me?" I said in all seriousness.

His eyes enlarged to the size of dinner plates; he stared at me in abject horror.

"K…k…k…k…kiss you?" he stuttered.

I nodded.

"Surely you're joking?"

"I'm not exactly doing cartwheels at the thought of it, but yes. Kiss me."

"The answer is no. Absolutely not. I don't do women. Please don't take this personally, but the thought is making me ill." He did a full-body shiver and then wrapped his arms around himself. "Girl lips were never part of the equation. No, no, and a thousand times, no."

"The only way to get you out of here without the cameras seeing your face is if we make like sluts. If you wear my chef's jacket it will cover up *your* jacket so there's no way for anyone to identify you from earlier tonight. We'll take the service elevator down to the garage, sucking face the entire time. The second the elevator doors open, I'll put my hands on your cheeks, which I'm hoping will conceal most of your face. You back me up again the wall so that the camera only sees the back of you. Don't angle your face when we kiss, that way, hopefully, my face will hide most of yours. We need to keep this up all the way to my car. Then we shove you down into the front seat, and I drive you home."

He folded his arms around himself even tighter.

"Please, Thom?" I begged. It was now one a.m., and I had to be back here in less than six hours.

"Are you sure there are cameras in the garage?"

I thought of the leer on the guard's face earlier today.

"Dead sure," I said with emphasis and hoped he didn't notice my blush.

"You'll probably be fired for this. They will think you're seducing a student. Holding romantic trysts after hours on school property."

I nodded. "I thought of that already. But I really can't see any other way out of here."

"For me?" Which sounded snide, but he didn't have his usual sneer pasted on.

"Yeah, actually," I admitted. "I owe you one, you know that."

We stood there for several minutes; at an impasse.

"Let's get a knife from the dishroom. We are abandoning Operation Infecting Thom with Girl Cooties and now adopting Operation Tablecloths."

‹›‹›‹›

"This is ridiculous. I can't see a thing."

"Not my idea, remember? Line your eyes up. Ow! That's the third time you've stepped on my heel."

"You didn't cut the slits evenly. My eyes are actually level with each other. And while you were at it, a hole for my mouth would have been appreciated. So that I can breathe. Perhaps I'm being unreasonable."

"Suck it up! I'm not the one with the irrational hatred of 'girl lips.'"

We were stumbling down the staircase to the garage, tablecloths over our heads to conceal our identities. Feeling an increasing anxiety that we were pushing our luck every minute we were in the school, we'd done nothing more than hack slits into the tablecloths with a butter knife. Unfortunately we hadn't hacked enough, and in order to walk and see, we had to prop open a slit with one hand, while our other hand gripped the handrail. Which basically made us half blind and unsteady on our feet.

The tension between us dropped exponentially when we reached the door to the garage. Of course, the minute we came into view by the garage cameras and then sidled into my car, I was busted, but at least Thom would get out of the school, with no one the wiser as to his identity.

"My car is at the far corner of garage near the guard kiosk."

"That was smart. What part of 'clean getaway' didn't you understand?"

"FYI. I'm assigned that space. It's that Subaru wagon—"

"As opposed to all the *other* Subaru wagons in this garage? Trust you to have a boring car."

"A boring car that runs." I clicked on my remote control. "Your side is open."

We'd made it. I could navigate the exit with this stupid tablecloth over my head, drive to Amos'…

The gate to the garage began to roll back and the garage filled with light. From headlights.

"Duck!" I yelled.

Chapter Thirty

I made to grab the door handle, but my hand got caught in the folds of the tablecloth. I began to panic, which escalated into a crushing claustrophobia as I fought with the tablecloth to get my hands and head free. Finally, I grabbed one end and wrenched the blasted thing off my head.

"Chef Mary?"

"Mary?"

Coolie and Marc stood there in front of Marc's van, their bodies shadowed in the harsh light from the headlamps. But there was no mistaking that Audrey Hepburn silhouette, nor that Texas drawl.

There was no rational way to explain why I was fighting a tablecloth at one thirty in the morning in the school's garage without sounding like a total lunatic.

So I did the next best thing. I turned the tables on them.

"What are you guys doing here? It's after one a.m." I snapped.

"I was worried. You weren't answering your cell," Coolie replied. "You were so weird today." I couldn't argue with that. "So I called your uncle's house to see if you were okay and you weren't there. We came to the school thinking that maybe you were still here; that something had happened. Like maybe you'd gotten into another fight with my father…" Her voice trailed off.

Her concern was well founded, but hell. Why is it that I want people to care about me, but when they do, it's always irritating? I groaned out loud. My plans to get Thom home safe and sound with no one the wiser just collapsed. Perhaps I could say I was working late and then crashing at Amos' place. But that would mean actually crashing at Amos' place, because something told me that there was no way I was getting out of this garage without an escort home. If Thom hadn't been hiding on the garage floor next to my car, I would have called it a night and just gone back up stairs. I was going to be on the phone for the next five hours lying to various relatives, ex-husbands, and angry Irish cops about why I was still at work. Because dollar to donuts, Uncle Dom would have called my mother who would have called Jim who would have called O'Connor. Why O'Connor wasn't here already was a complete mystery.

The thought had just formed in my head when the gate, which had clanged shut earlier after they had pulled in, opened again.

We all turned and watched the dark shadow of a long Town Car pull into the garage behind Marc's van. Five men got out. The gate closed. Not O'Connor then, but the next best thing.

Uncle Dom. Thank God. I couldn't distinguish him among the other men because the glare from all those headlights reduced them to nothing but silhouettes, but we could all go home now and get some sleep. I'd have them follow me over to Amos' house and...

"Melissa, come here," ordered a voice.

"No, Daddy," Coolie shouted back; she walked toward me and found my hand and held it tight.

Stupid me. Not Uncle Dom's. Because he wouldn't have had the remote to open the garage But Robert Martin's men? Yeah, especially since one of them was Dean Benson.

‹ › ‹ › ‹ ›

They frog marched us to the service elevator, which, conveniently, was big enough hold three hostages, three goons, Martin, and Benson. Martin pressed the button to the production kitchen. Even as we stood huddled together in that elevator, I still had this utter sense of *what the fuck?* because they didn't know about Thom breaking into the computer, but the sense this was a scene from a TV movie titled Dead Chefs Walking was overwhelming. There was a part to this puzzle that was missing.

Marc wasn't stupid, and once Coolie had made her stand, he raced over to her side and grabbed her hand. We obeyed Martin's demand, "All three of you, in the elevator," and when the doors opened into the production kitchen, we instinctively headed toward the far right wall, as far away from the elevator as possible. We moved as a tight-knit group, carrying along the person who stumbled, never letting go of each other's hands. I didn't look up, terrified of making eye contact with the goons. All I saw of them was their shoes; even their laces looked menacing.

Coolie was our only salvation. Martin might rough her up, but I doubted he'd seriously hurt her, and I suppose her rationale was that he wouldn't hurt us if he had to hurt her to do it. Which seemed a pretty damn accurate rationale up to this point. We weren't dead yet. If we could stick to her for just a few more minutes, then hopefully Thom would call the police in time before Marc and I ended up in the bay riddled with bullet holes.

Perhaps I was over-dramatizing these events. Benson and Martin stood huddled in the opposite corner of the kitchen whispering to each other. Maybe this would be another heated verbal exchange between Martin and me, with Benson reprising his role as a total coward and Martin making threats and then I'd would pull the Uncle Dom card again and then…Maybe not. Because at some hidden signal from Martin, I heard the rustle of fabric and raised my eyes enough to see that the three goons pulled out three guns. I knew guns (you couldn't be married to a cop and not know far more about guns that you ever wanted to know), and those Glocks with modified barrels could blow a hole in your shoulder the size of a large apple. One artery blasted away at a minimum.

Why wait until now? Of course. The cameras in the garage. I suppose there were several plausible stories that Benson could have told to explain the events down in the garage. He'd caught us stealing food or wine. That would work. Training guns on members of your staff and a student, whose father happened to be on the board? It would be much harder to come up with a plausible lie.

Martin and Benson kept talking, although now I got the sense that they were now arguing. Martin's voice remained low. I still couldn't hear what he was saying, but I didn't imagine it boded well for either Marc or me, because Benson kept repeating in agitated voice to Martin's quiet murmurs, "No, not here!" Which I interpreted as, "Yes, somewhere else."

At the sight of the guns, I couldn't help it. I began shaking from sheer terror. Coolie squeezed my hand in comfort, her hand cool and dry. I heard the tiniest of whimpers as Marc began to lose it. Come on, Thom. There was no way to interpret that scene in the garage with Martin and his thugs hustling us into the elevator as anything but threatening. Would he have the smarts to demand to speak to O'Connor or even call Jim? But that wouldn't do us any good. For the first time in my life I cursed not changing my name when I got married because Thom wouldn't know that our last names were different and how in the hell were we going to get out of this alive?

Martin broke away from Benson's grip on his forearm.

"I heard you, Bob," he growled and made his across the kitchen over to where we stood clutching each other.

"Lapin, that wasn't very smart of you."

Marc didn't answer, the whimpering got louder.

"Shaking Benson down. Stupid."

"What?" The words were out of my mouth before I could stop myself.

"Yes. It seems Bob is quite the lady's man," Martin sneered. Benson blushed. "Courting both the pastry chef *and* the office manager. And it seems that Lapin figured this out and demanded that Benson fire his father or Benson's peccadilloes would become public." At that Marc gasped. "Yes, we know. Your father. When you began making threats against Benson, we bugged your apartment." He paused and then sneered at me. "And your car. Quite the little sex kitten, aren't you, Ms. Ryan?"

They'd heard us rolling around having sex on Marc's clean laundry. I wasn't going to give Martin any satisfaction. I refused to blush and just stared back at him.

"That other chef. She really *didn't* know what you were up to, did she? And then we lost sight of you, but you were at Mary Ryan's house." He turned to me. "You interfering bitch." He raised his hand, just slightly, and for a moment I thought he was going to hit me. Turning back to Marc he ordered, "Now tell us the full story and what you've told the police, so that we can let you go home."

I stifled a snort because you don't pull guns on people and then let them go home. Did he think we were fools?

The missing part of the puzzle. This wasn't about me. It was about Marc. He'd lied to me. He *had* found out about Benson and Allison, Benson and Marilyn. He'd already put his blackmail plans in motion. I turned to glare at him. Tears were streaming down his face. Shelley. She hadn't known anything and they must have gone overboard in trying to find out what Marc knew.

At some point, I might appreciate the irony. Like maybe in sixty years. Because it wasn't Benson's love life that had brought us all here. They were afraid that Marc had uncovered the money laundering scheme. They could beat him to death and he wouldn't have a clue what they wanted. It would be a repeat of Shelley. It was cold comfort to think that once they'd do the post-mortem on me, they'd find the goods with which to convict Martin et al. Unless Martin stripped me.

I needed time. By now, Thom should have gotten through to someone, or O'Connor should be here to see what in the hell I was up to. O'Connor loved nothing more that reading me the riot act. If he had to drive in from the Sunset, he'd probably be double-parking right now and making his way up the stairs. Benson was the weak link. The son who couldn't make it on his own, whose father had had to bail him out. Whose father owned a baseball team and the school and used Bob's dream to launder his mob money. Just a couple of minutes should do it.

Turning away from Martin, I said in a slow voice, "She loved you, Bob. Do you know I went to the jewelry store where she bought her wedding ring? I saw it. It was a beautiful ring. Allison must have adored it. I put it on my own finger," I lied. Benson paled and he began to twist his signet ring around and around. "I've been to her apartment. I saw her checkbook. She'd paid for your honeymoon. I saw all those cookbooks you'd given her over the years, inscribed to her." His face crumpled in on itself. I was getting to him, gaining us a few more seconds. O'Connor, dammit, where are you? "Her bedroom—"

"Shut up," Martin ordered. "Melissa, let go of their hands. You need to go home. Your mother is quite ill and needs you. She's asking for you. You know how only you can soothe her when she's like this."

That part was probably a lie, but when he'd turned to her and spoken, he'd said it in a pleading voice, as any other father might. She didn't let go of my hand, but her body language stiffened for the first time. Coolie's weak link? Her mother.

"When?" she whispered.

"Last week. I have a plane waiting at the airport. Come, darling."

She shook her head.

"Please, sweetie," he said quietly and calmly.

"You won't hurt them." I could barely hear her, but Martin didn't strain forward to catch her mumble.

"No, of course not. In fact, Benson is considering filing charges against Lapin, but perhaps we can come to some understanding once we talk to him. If you like, they can go with us to the airport, so you can see that they are alright, and then we'll continue this discussion in the car."

Yeah, right. Discussion first, torture second, pushing us in the path of an incoming 747 third. Or something that made it look like a murder-suicide pact so that Marc and I were both taken care of. The garage's video camera of Marc and me the other night would play right into their hands. Then tonight's video of me sneaking someone down the stairs. Whatever was going to happen, Marc and I would be going there together.

It all happened so fast.

Marc must have put two and two together, realizing that he had nothing more to tell them, but that they had a hidden agenda that he knew nothing about. Those terrified whimpering noises he'd been making non-stop for the last ten minutes exploded into complete panic. He began screaming, "NO! NO!"

I watched in horror as the thug closest to me pistol-whipped Marc across the jaw. Coolie's grip on my hand broke, and the two of them went tumbling to the ground. As Marc and Coolie fell, everyone's attention shifted to them. The thug turned to me. I instinctively raised a hand to shield my face, when he pushed his sunglasses up onto his head. It was Brad the blacksmith. We locked eyes. He looked behind me at the wall next to my head. Where the fire alarm was mounted. He mouthed, "Now." I reached and pulled the red lever.

Gallons of fire-retardant foam began spewing from pipes in the ceiling, blinding all of us. Over the whoosh of foam, I heard the roar of guns and Martin shouting, "Melissa!" and Coolie shouting, "Daddy!" and someone screaming my name. I dragged an arm over my eyes to wipe my eyes free from foam. O'Connor came barreling across the room from the open elevator. I moved toward him, slipping on the foam. I remember falling. I remember pain. Then nothing.

Chapter Thirty-one

Brad the blacksmith was undercover as well. In our last conversation O'Connor kept saying "we." I'd assumed that was an all-purpose we, as in S.F.P.D. No, it meant him and Brad, who seemed to be doing double duty as undercover cop and cooking student by day, undercover cop and mobbed up enforcer by night.

Brad disappeared after that night, so a lot of what went down that night remains speculation. I can only assume that somehow Brad tipped off people that some sort of showdown was in the works. The roar of guns was caused by Swat team guys. Stakeout cops alerted headquarters that Coolie and Marc had left the house. Martin and goons knew that Marc's van was in the garage because of the homing device. Martin must have been pretty nonplussed to see Coolie there with Marc. Me? Along for the ride. Swat team then broke into the school and were waiting for the opportune moment. I suspected someone was miked to Brad, but I'll never know.

Bullets flew *everywhere*. Benson didn't make it. Neither did the two goons. Martin caught a bullet in the thigh throwing himself in front of Coolie. Coolie stayed with him in the hospital until they could load him on a plane. Then they went home for a while. The last time I heard from her, Martin was marshalling legal power for the case against him, and Coolie was leaving for France to join Marc.

I wish I could say that Étienne and Marc had reached some sort of understanding, but the news from Coolie was that Marc's recent brush with near death had done nothing to awaken any latent paternal feeling on Étienne's part. Étienne had never wanted anything to do with Marc, and that Marc was nearly a victim of a mob hit did nothing to change that.

That pain was my head hitting the tile with such force that I ended up with a severe concussion. They kept me in the hospital for a few days until the swelling subsided. O'Connor would visit me very late at night and hold my hand for an hour or two. I'd pretend to be asleep. He'd pretend I was asleep. The ER techs who'd undressed me had probably seen it all and didn't question why I had a CD hidden in the hood of my sweatshirt, they just included it in the plastic bag with the rest of my clothes. It wasn't until the third night in the hospital that I remembered the CD. I had it in my hand when O'Connor arrived. He removed it and then whispered in my ear, "Macushla," and left. Robert Martin's legal problems were just about to get a whole hell of a lot worse.

The severity of my concussion had forestalled most of the lectures from various family members. My mother stocked my freezer with soup, lasagna, and stew. Uncle Dom offered to pay my mortgage for the next few months until I got on my feet. I politely declined. I was on disability for a minimum of three months, the payments of which would cover my mortgage and nothing else. It didn't matter. I was done here. I didn't belong with all the young parents and the tricycles and the slides and the minivans. As soon as I could, I was going to put the house on the market. I wanted to get out while I could still break even. Every week, bold headlines in the real estate section of the *Chron* announced the reversal of the real estate market in the Bay Area. Houses in Albany were still at a premium because of the school district, but it was only a matter of time before the general slump affected that market as well.

A week after the showdown with Martin, although still shaky and headachey, I donned my darkest sunglasses, tanked up on eight hundred milligrams of Motrin, and crossed the bridge. The school was now closed (and the students shunted off to other cooking schools); its future uncertain. My gate card was still good in the garage. Hurdle one accomplished. I stopped at my locker, poured everything into a large plastic bag. If anyone questioned me, I was there to clean out my locker.

I took the elevator to the third floor, got out, and tried the door to the office. When it didn't open, I took a quick look around to see if anyone was around. At the all clear, I took a hammer from my purse (which had been wrapped a towel), and smashed the glass. I waited. No one came running.

Making my way to Marilyn's desk, I opened the top right-hand desk drawer and there it was. I took out the pair of tongs I had in my purse and put the bottle in a plastic bag.

My head was beginning to pound. I had about another two hours before I'd be whimpering and completely debilitated. I had to move fast.

I drove to North Beach and double parked. With the head-ache came the nausea, and I couldn't manage more than a brief walk; it was worth risking a ticket.

At the sound of the door jingle, Mr. Garibaldi came into the front, wiping the tiniest bit of cookie from the side of his mouth. I imagined him and his wife sharing this daily ritual: a mid-morning cup of coffee and a couple of biscotti. I envied him.

"Mr. Garibaldi, I'd like to buy Allison Warner's ring."

"I thought you'd be back," he said. "Some day, Ms. Ryan, you will wear this ring." He opened the box and put it on the counter.

It was very Allison, extremely feminine and delicate. Three rubies set in a row, nestled in a bed of intertwining gold filigree. Not the sort of ring you could wear while cooking. Which meant that I'd never wear it if I was going to continue cooking. If ever there was a life-changing moment, putting that ring on my finger was it.

Allison's fingers were bigger than mine, and the ring wobbled on my ring finger, but fit my third finger quite nicely. "I can't wait any more. I'm going to wear it out of door," I replied and handed him my credit card.

The headache and nausea only increased as I made my way back over the bridge. Every time I hit even a minor bump in the road, I winced, but I had one more stop to make.

I rang Bridie's doorbell. She opened the door immediately. There was one ancient suitcase just to the left of the door. She didn't look surprised to see me.

"I'd offer you some tea, but I'm off to visit my grandchildren in Arizona. The taxi should be here any moment."

A wave of nausea overwhelmed me, and I grabbed the frame of the door. "Bridie, could you let me in Allison's apartment?"

Her face got that same scrunch of concern that my mother's face got when I was ill or depressed.

"You don't look so hot, sweetheart. Why don't you come in—"

"No, I just need to return something I borrowed from Allison. Her parents will want me to. Then I'm going to go home and go to bed. I promise."

She let me in only after I had agreed to come over for tea in three weeks when she'd returned to town.

Allison's apartment was exactly as O'Connor and I had left it. Her parents obviously couldn't bring themselves to empty it out just yet. I removed Allison's bottle of diet pills from her purse and replaced it with Marilyn's bottle of diet pills that I'd stolen from her desk. Her stash of pills that had her fingerprints all over it.

After they'd discharged me from the hospital, I'd gone to my mother's for a couple of days at her insistence. I was sitting at the kitchen table having a cup of tea, debating whether or not to go back to bed, when my mother came home from a trip to the drug store, laden down with Dove ice cream bars, microwave popcorn, and bottles of root beer. Comfort food. I went to help her put the groceries away when my hand wrapped around a bottle of what I thought was pills. It wasn't. It was a bottle of VitaLife.

"Mom?" I squeaked and held it up for her to see.

"Oh, the clerk at the store told me she dropped fifteen pounds on it. I thought I'd try it."

I looked at the back of the bottle and, yep, there on the warning label was the admonition to not take this supplement if you were allergic to shellfish.

Pouring the contents down the sink, I flicked the switch to garbage disposal. It didn't take an Einstein to figure out what had happened.

It had nothing to do with the money laundering and everything to do with jealousy. Given Allison's stupid obsession with her weight, Marilyn Cantucci only had to smooth a slim hand over a slender hip, leave the diet supplement in plain sight on her desk, and Allison would tumble. Given that Marilyn smoked at least two packs a day, I had serious doubts that Marilyn's slender frame has anything to do with those stupid diet supplements and everything to do with smoking two of her meals.

Allison's allergy to shellfish was well known. I can't imagine that Marilyn didn't know. They had worked together for years, eaten countless meals together. It had to have come up. At three pills a day, given Allison's severe allergy, it was only a matter of time before the iodines built up in her system, causing anaphylactic shock. I'd let the jury decide whether it was deliberate or not. The leeching off of the warning label told me it was, but that was my opinion.

I suspected that Benson had told Marilyn to take a hike and the pills probably appeared in Allison's mail disguised as a promotional gimmick. But with the warning label missing.

I'd like to think that Bob Benson had every intention of marrying Allison. His grief seemed genuine. If they didn't nail Marilyn on the murder charges, knowing what I knew about the school operating as a front of mob money, it probably wouldn't take too much digging to discover that she was complicit.

Eventually, the murder charges went nowhere, but email trails between her and Benson, Senior, supplied the feds with more than enough evidence to charge her under the RICO statute. She's using the same law firm as William Martin.

Bridie stopped me on my way down the front steps. She had her suitcase in one hand, the wedding ring quilt slung over her other arm.

"I finished it yesterday. For you," she insisted and pushed it into my arms.

I shook my head.

"Friendship can also be characterized as a ring," she reminded me. "Love comes in many shapes and forms. There's my taxi. Tea. Three weeks from today at 3:00. Don't be late."

She hauled her suitcase down the steps, ignoring the outstretched hand of the taxi driver. "No, young man, I don't want any help. Open the trunk, if you please. Do not play the radio on the way to the airport or you won't get a tip."

The taxi tore away from the curb, the order for radio silence obviously rankling. Something told me that guy wasn't going to get a tip. Period.

I made it home without being sick on the front seat of my car, more or less passing out on the couch for three hours. When I woke up, the headache lingered, a sign I'd overdone it, but I still had some phone calls to make.

I got the hardest one out of the way first.

I called O'Connor's cell.

"Hey, it's me. I just wanted to say that you might want to check out the contents of Allison's purse. Um, you might want to fingerprint the stuff in there."

That was met with silence.

"Okay, I need to go now, my head is killing—"

"Moira's going to have another baby."

I swallowed.

"That's great," I forced myself to say. "You love children."

"A girl. We had an ultrasound today."

His voice went all soft and scratchy, like he'd swallowed a bunch of rocks. He had always wanted a girl. Oh, he loved his sons. He was never too tired to throw a ball or read a bedtime story. But he'd look with envy at those with tiny daughters. At precinct picnics, at some point you'd find him in a discreet corner of the picnic grounds, playing Barbie dolls. He'd never leave Moira now. Ever. He already loved that little girl more than he would ever love me. I could hear it in his voice. The joy, the wonder, the goodbye.

I sat there clutching the phone in my hand, unable to say anything, not even my own goodbye, when I heard victory whoops in the background. Exactly like the ones I'd heard in that threatening phone call.

"What's that noise?" I demanded.

"Oh, the boys' video game. Every time they kill someone it makes that high-pitched noise."

We'd both underestimated Moira. Not that I would tell O'Connor, because it didn't matter anymore. A well-placed threat was entirely in her rights.

"Congratulate Moira for me. Goodbye." I hung up.

Before I could think too much about this, I called Amos and got his answering machine. I left a rambling message apologizing for being a first-class jerk and inviting him and Thom to dinner on Saturday. I'd give him a more polished apology when I saw them. Once again proving that he was a much better person and begging the question why I deserved such a friend, Amos had sent me a dozen roses while I was in the hospital. I wasn't sure how much Thom had told him about breaking into the school, so I'd have to play it by ear. I should have gone back to bed, but I needed to do one more thing.

I turned on my computer, logged on, and typed in www.match.com.

To receive a free catalog of Poisoned Pen Press titles, please contact us in one of the following ways:

Phone: 1-800-421-3976
Facsimile: 1-480-949-1707
Email: info@poisonedpenpress.com
Website: www.poisonedpenpress.com

Poisoned Pen Press
6962 E. First Ave. Ste. 103
Scottsdale, AZ 85251

CPSIA information can be obtained at www.ICGtesting.com
Printed in the USA
LVOW05s1539110913

352006LV00002B/394/P